# OPERATION
# DOWNFALL

# OPERATION DOWNFALL

## Daniel McNeet

A Novel

**intrepid**

**PUBLISHING COMPANY**

SANTA YNEZ, CALIFORNIA

OPERATION DOWNFALL. Copyright © 2010 by Daniel McNeet

For information regarding subsidiary rights contact:
Intrepid Publishing Company
P.O. Box 575
Santa Ynez, California 93460-575

www.IntrepidPublishingCompany.com
books@intrepidpublishingcompany.com


ISBN 978-0-9846886-0-9

PRINTED IN THE UNITED STATES OF AMERICA
FIRST EDITION • OCTOBER 2011
10 9 8 7 6 5 4 3 2 1

*To the love of my life, my beautiful wife, who is supportive of my writing career.*
*She is my second reader and my honest critic.*


To the authors whom made a difference and did not stand by waiting for someone else.
This novel was inspired by the intrepidity of:
Naomi Wolf who wrote "The End of America Letter of Warning to a Young Patriot",
Frank Rich's "The Greatest Story Ever Sold",
"Hubris" by Michael Isikoff and David Corn,
Thomas E. Ricks' "Fiasco"
and Justin A. Frank's, M.D. "Bush On the Couch".

No man is above the law and no man is below it: nor do we ask any
man's permission when we ask him to obey it.
— President Theodore Roosevelt


I am primarily concerned with the lack of moral sense in man and his
constant verification of my concern.
— Daniel McNeet

Adolph Hitler ordered Polish men removed from one of Germany's concentration camps. He had them dressed in Polish-military uniforms, murdered, placed on German soil at a radio station on 1 September 1939 and publicized this as the Polish invasion of Germany. He used the incident as the excuse to invade Poland, which was the start of World War II.

Of course, this could not possibly happen again — not until the president of the United States and his colleagues, the cabal, conspired to do so.

# OPERATION
# DOWNFALL

# 1

## 2:02 A.M.  Bel Air, West Los Angeles, California

She booted her laptop in the basement four stories below her room on the top floor, opened the vault program, connected to the vault's computer, activated her decryption software and deactivated the alarm. Then the combination to the keypad which was located on the left of the vault door was decrypted, because entering the combination onto the keypad activated the retinal-eye identification system and the cameras outside and inside the vault would record the activity. Thus neither was activated and her entry and exit wouldn't be recorded. She removed her driving gloves from her jacket pocket, opened the well-balanced door with ease, and the recessed overhead-fluorescent lights in the ceiling went on.

The vault was ten-feet high and wide by twenty-feet deep, and had been made of super-strength concrete and hardened with steel fibers and reinforcing bars to withstand thirty thousand pounds per square inch of pressure. Only the door was visible and its concrete of the same quality was encased in stainless steel to provide an aesthetic finish.

She walked inside and placed her empty hard-cased luggage on the rectangular table in the middle of the vault and opened it. A large metal drawer labeled DVD & VHS was opened with her key. She selected the ones she wanted and placed them into her luggage. Then the metal file cabinet was unlocked, opened and selected manila folders were placed into it and the cabinet relocked. Finally, she took her key, opened the cash locker's stainless-steel door and removed the metal box. She emptied the box and filled the remaining space in her luggage with sixty bundles of one hundred Benjys each held together with currency straps. The bundles were stacked neatly, and then the empty metal box was returned and the door locked. The cash locker was sad because all of her old friends were gone, but the DVDs, VHSs and folders enjoyed their inheritance.

She took the Victorinox luggage from the vault, closed the door, locked it with her laptop and checked it to make sure she had not left any tracks of penetration. Then reset the alarm with her laptop and closed the screen. She stood in her jeans,

Pendleton shirt, sheepskin jacket, tennis shoes and ball cap, with no logo, for a few moments and listened. Her wrist watch read two twenty. Right on time. She picked up the Victorinox again with her right hand, because the wheels made too much noise when it rolled across the hard floor, laptop in her left and bag over her right shoulder. The elevator would make too much noise, so she walked up the stairs with calm and silence, her two essential close friends who were part of her needed persona and arrived at the massive foyer and stopped. She raised the screen on her laptop, deactivated the estate's perimeter alarm, and the five of them went quietly through the massive front doors, still close friends.

She and her companions went to the garage and used her garage door opener, went to her Ford Escape, opened the rear cargo door and placed her hard case next to a duffel bag filled with clothes and some personal belongings; then placed her laptop on the passenger seat with the screen facing her. The Escape with the close friends inside traveled down the half-mile long driveway from the house, stopped before the massive-double wrought iron gates that matched the height of the estate's surrounding granite walls of twelve feet and allowed the electric gates to open. After driving through, she stopped, reactivated the perimeter alarm with her laptop, made sure her penetration was not detectable, turned it off and placed it in her briefcase which was on the floor in front of the passenger's seat. It was next to her new constant companion and close personal friend, Mr. Glock 21, who had .45-caliber persuasive skills and had had rhinoplasty, a sound suppressor attached to his muzzle. *All is well that begins well.*

Lillian McGraw smiled with satisfaction as she drove north to Mulholland Drive, then turned right, passed Beverly Glen, Coldwater Canyon, Benedict Canyon and Laurel Canyon and headed to Multiview Drive. She turned left and went down to the house of a friend who was out of town. The view from the living room and the observation deck overlooked the kaleidoscope of lights that shimmered in the San Fernando Valley and Universal Studios.

*Now it's my turn.*

# 2

*What you see is an illusion; it is what your opponent wants you to see.*

## 5:00 P.M.  Raymond's Bar, Downtown Los Angeles

*I'm sittin' in this big city neighborhood bar where I do my drinkin' and eatin'. Tonight I'm havin' the gourmet special — cut franks, burned in spots at my request, and barbecued beans served in a bowl. For dessert it's the usual three fingers of I.W. Harper inna Baccarat ol' fashion tumbler. The place's empty, so I'm able ta engage in fine dinin' with some peace and quiet fer a change.*

*Soon the place'll be filled; it's a cop's bar. Former and present day cops, spooks, black baggers, Special Forces, CIA operatives and SOFs, or Soldiers of Fortune, abound. The former spooks and CIA field agents are lookin' ta get back inta the great game. Jus' 'bout finished with my beans and franks and gettin' ready ta have my dessert — the three fingers.*

*The bar's been in this tall-office building maybe, fifty, sixty years. I've only been officin' here fer 'bout ten. It's called Raymond's Bar. It's always been Raymond's no matter who owned it. Somethin' 'bout the goodwill of the name; another joke, because it sure ain't location, location, location. It's changed hands more times than the life of a one dollar bill in abused circulation before being sacrificed ta the goddess of fire.*

*The bartender, the guy who owns it, ain't Raymond, his name's Greg, Greg Emerson. He's a former Special Forces guy. That's why all those military types come in. They like 'im and so do I. He bought the place 'bout two years ago. Smells like 'em all, stale beer. Long bar on one side with stools in front of it, and the ubiquitous bartender behind it. Across from it there are twelve hard wooden booths with a table that's perpendicular to the wall. They're in line one behind the other against the wall. The lightin's amber after dark so it'll be more complementary ta the ladies who visit. I always call 'em ladies until I find out otherwise.*

*Yu've ta pass the juke in the back in order ta get ta the restrooms. I put a buck in the juke. Now, I'm listenin' ta one of my favorites, "I Only Have Eyes For You" on a Jackie Gleason album, For Lovers Only. I'm just a romantic, I guess. "I'll Be Seeing You" is one of my favorites, and it'll play soon. Greg put the album on the juke fer me when I asked.*

*The hard wooden booths put in here in the 1920s have seats which are only good fer people with a lot of fat on their tush called steatopygia, but that ain't me so I don't sit too long. I use a cushion instead under my skinny ass. If I didn't, I'd have very short office hours, a shortage of clients, which'd generate a shortage of money and which'd generate a shortage of a good disposition. Sittin' on the cushion allows me ta look down on my clients, impressive and intimidatin' too. The high-straight backs of the booths also operate as ineffective partitions so the customers can't see or hear one another in the other booths, another of life's little illusions.*

The front door opened with its usual squeak and this guy walked in. A real Charlie Brown Shoes. He looked around and went to the bartender. They had a brief, the bartender fingered me, and he came to my booth and sat down opposite me as if he he'd been invited with an engraved invitation hand-delivered by a chauffeur in livery.

"You, O'Leary, the lawyer?" He asked in a tough no-nonsense attitude, which could only be described as: I don't want ta waste my time with ya because yu're a member of the lower classes, and I've better things to do. He had beady-shifty eyes and talked fast like a huckster on a television infomerical whose motor's revving at ten thousand RPMs.

"Who's askin' and wadaya want?" She asked in the vernacular of the neighborhood. "If it has anythin' ta do with aggravation or causin' me indigestion durin' the consumption of my gourmet meal, the answer's no. If yu've found my boyfriend who walked out on me today there's no reward, keep 'im."

"I'm Jones," said the one without manners, as if he was a one-word celebrity known worldwide.

"Of course, ya are."

The only thing she knew for sure: In this neighborhood bar, she just ate her franks and beans, was about ready to have her dessert and her name was O'Leary, Mariah O'Leary and a lawyer.

"I'd tell ya how many people've told me their names were Jones and they weren't, but I can't count that high. Ya wanta try again, Mr. Well Mannered. Sit down and make yurself comfortable. Ya came from a poor family whom couldn't afford manners or consideration for others? Wanta drink?"

He nodded and pointed to her dessert.

She continued to stare into his eyes and didn't look away when she said, "Greg, one more I.W. for my guest. And put it and my dinner on his tab too until he ain't a Maybe."

"Well, Jones, what can I do fer ya this lovely evenin' in the big city of almost four million and the same number of stories to match?"

"If you're O'Leary, I understand you're honest."

"Ya're right, but I actually have three disabilities — two of which are poor as a result of being honest. Ya sound like one of those business consultants who charge big fees ta tell the owner of a company about his company things he already knows. Right?"

"I went by the flea-bag hotel where you live, if you can call it that," Jones said. "The city should put a red label on it and demolish it. I hate slumlords. I asked the clerk if you were in, and he said no. He told me you were in your office, if you can call it one, and gave me the name of this stinking dump."

"Was my secretary there?"

"You mean your boyfriend? The clerk said he moved out."

"Same thin'. Tough ta maintain a relationship in my business and in this part of town."

"Why's a sensual-gorgeous woman like you working in this part of town, living in a shithole and officing in a dump like this? You could make one of Archbishop Mahoney's pedophile priests switch his sexual orientation."

"I've asked myself the same question many times. And, I'm always surprised when the next guy comes along, falls in love with me, wants ta get married, take me away from all this, but ends up joinin' me in shared bliss at the Brighton in my luxurious suite. All I do is sit here, and it happens."

"The Brighton? It should be called Castle Gloom. Your suite's a one-room shithole. By the way, . . . ."

Mariah interrupted her new best friend, sweet talker and said with respect and credibility, "Yur 'shithole' is my castle; so don't give me no shit, Maybe. Because yu're just a Maybe. Ya know, maybe ya will and maybe ya won't hire me. And, if ya do, I'm not sure I want ya anyway."

"Do you sleep in your dress? It has more wrinkles than a Shar-Pei. I really like the artwork on the front; who's the artist — Food?"

She saw the fear in his eyes and smelled it too. The fear of failure and the anxiety she had seen hundreds of times. She realized at that moment she was in charge of this meeting, so she took command. He thought denigration would give him an upper hand. Another misguided. Probably flunked Psychology 101 too.

"I'd like ta get back ta my original question, Jones, and have ya cease and desist makin' compliments 'bout my custom one off of the latest Paris designer's fashion that came directly from the runway, adorns my body, my livin' conditions and my elegant office. 'Who's askin' and wadaya want?' Ya wanta try Jones on me again?

"And speakin' of compliments, Sweet Talker, yur dressed like a gangster right out of Runyon's *Guys and Dolls* with yur black suit, red shirt and kaleidoscope tie, Mr. Sharp Dresser. Or, yur passin' as a hip mortician, consoler or in competition against the black pimps in my 'hood. Do ya have a mirror at yur place, Blinky?" Jones blinked his eyes frequently. *He reminds me of Richard Nixon. Ya could always tell when he was gonna lie, which incidentally was almost every time he spoke, because he blinked constantly.*

Jones moved his right hand toward the inside of his suit coat on the left.

"Hold it, Jones. Don't move."

He froze.

"I office here almost every day in this booth. I meet a lotta guys named Jones. Some're good guys, some're bad guys and some're wiseguys. I've always been a poor judge of character, my third disability. So, I try ta limit my errors ta correctible ones. So, hear this: whatever yu're gonna bring out of yur inside coat pocket, bring it out with yur thumb and first finger visible very very slowly. Because if ya don't my friend under the table'll, aka my best friend, will paint this booth, walls, floor and splatter my designer dress with red. Also, yur cadaver'll not be received at the gross anatomy class at our local medical school, 'cause of a lack of body parts due ta the extensive damage ta yur torso caused by the low-velocity hollow point .45-caliber slug passin' through. The bartender'll really be angry with ya if ya make a mess in his bar 'cause he has ta clean it up, capisce?"

"I understand. You don't scare me, O'Leary, with your bluffs."

"I hate people who call me a liar. People who know me don't call me a liar 'cause they know I don't. There's only one thin' I hate, and that's fer some ill-mannered nickel-and-dime gutter hustler droppin' in without an appointment ta question my integrity. I'll tell ya what I'm willin' ta do, Big Mouth."

She continued to look into his eyes while her left hand reached into her shoulder bag that rested on the seat beside her left thigh. Mariah pulled out a roll of hundred dollar bills bound by a flexible band of ten five-carat D flawless marquise cut diamonds attached and placed the roll between the two of them on the table. "There's 'bout five grand there. I know *I* don't scare ya, but *my* friend's a frightenin' cold-sweat nightmare. Wadaya bet I've a friend pointed at yur gut, Big Mouth? Place yur bet or shut the fuck up and get the fuck out!"

Jones sat there for a few moments, continued to stare at O'Leary with his hand still inside his coat and said, "I'm taking my wallet out with the thumb and first finger as you asked." He tried to determine if she was bluffing, but couldn't. "I haven't got five, but I've two. So I bet two that you're a bluffer and a four-flusher." Jones took out his wallet with thumb and first finger and put it on the table between them next to her ten diamonds. He reached in and removed twenty Benjys and placed them on top of O'Leary's roll. "I'm all in. Let me see your hand."

"Look under the table."

Jones looked under the table while she grabbed all the money and put it into her shoulder bag.

Jones sat upright and Mariah said, "Never read any Damon Runyon I see. This guy's walkin' down Broadway. A guy comes up ta 'im and says, 'Wadaya bet I can make the one-eyed Jack jump outta this deck of cards and squirt Ginger Ale inta yur left ear?' So, the guy bets him a Benjy and sure enough his left ear filled with Ginger Ale. So, Sucker, what's yur name and wadaya want?"

A depressed Jones took his business card out of his wallet that was still on the table between them and threw it at her.

"So, in addition to being without manners and no consideration for others, with no class, yu're a loser and a sore one at that. So, yu're Tom Jones. Sing 'What's New Pussycat?' fer me, and I'll believe ya."

"I came to tell you a story you might be interested in."

"First, Jones, tell me why yu're bringin' me this chocolate cake as opposed ta a hundred other lawyers?"

"I told you, they tell me you're honest."

"Is that the ubiquitous they, the father, the son and the holy ghost of the delusionals who believe they're up in nonexistent heaven, or do they have a name? I told ya, that's one of my three disabilities. 'Facilitator' yur card says. Isn't that the latest corporate buzz word fer bagman or janitor. Ya a bag man, Jones, a lobbyist, and ya clean up other people's messes? Or, are ya in the messenger delivery business? Ya parked yur bicycle out front and locked it; I hope if ya did. Reminds me, when I was growin' up these men came around once a week ta pick up our garbage, all in one before separation. We called them garbage men. Now, they're sanitation engineers. Ya a sanitation engineer, Jones?"

"Something like that."

"So, Mr. Facilitator, facilitate. Who's they?"

"You a smart ass, O'Leary?"

"All depends on yur definition."

"My definition is a person who talks like you, acts like you and with your attitude."

"Hey, no one asked ya ta walk in here and sit down without an appointment, an invitation or manners. So, whut'reya gonna do fer me, and what's the Wiifm, Jones?"

"What's Wiifm?"

"What's In It Fer Me?"

Jones spoke for about thirty minutes telling her this story. Then, he asked, "So, what do you think? See any Wiifm in there?"

"'bout what?"

"About what I just told you. This friend of mine is trying to find a lost secretary. She walked out and has disappeared and can't be found anywhere."

"I know how he feels, mine jus' left me. I guess he got tired of livin' in a cheap hotel room with no future."

"My friend's low profile, inquired around, you were recommended, and I was asked to come see you. Want to help my friend?"

"Who's yur friend?"

"I've to leave it confidential."

"Then this meetin's over. See ya later, Jones. It has ta do with ethics, my friend, ethics; somethin' bag men, janitors and facilitators don't worry 'bout, know 'bout or wanta know 'bout. The bar association's ethics' committee, a collection of tight asses, demand that I've a contract fer services ta be rendered with my client, not the messenger fer the client. And, lookin' at ya, speakin' of sartorial splendor, ya look like ya jus' bought what yu're wearin' at the Goodwill store down the street. So, I'm gonna need ta meet yur 'friend' before I decide."

"It's just a lost secretary."

"Has yur 'friend' thought 'bout sendin' a sharp guy like ya to find her? One who gets taken fer two grand by a lady with a wrinkled-designer dress, with fine Impressionism artwork by 'Food' on the front of it, adorned attractively on a five-eight slim of hip frame, not in heels, with a fighting weight of one twenty, and who don't speak good English. Also a guy who's incidentally a shitty gambler, not Nathan Detroit and can't play liar's poker worth a shit. I wear these Silhouette rimless round eyeglasses so I can spot nickel-and-dime gutter hustlers like ya. So, wadaya ya think, Shamus, why don't ya find her?"

"What I do for my friend is none of your business, Smart Ass. All I'm trying to find out is do you want to help my friend find the secretary? And, then I'm going to leave."

"I need ta meet yur friend, then I'll decide if I wanta go forward, get paid a substantial retainer fee, sign my employment agreement, and that's the way it is. Otherwise, I wouldn't be interested. And yur friend has one too, a disability that is. He picked ya; a guy who didn't get the lawyer ya were sent ta get. Bein' a messenger boy's a damn tough job. Employers never understand why when they give an order ta a classless minion like ya it never gets done."

"Look, O'Leary, do you want the job or not?"

"Sure, I'd like the job. Any legal work? Ya know, maybe a prenuptial agreement after I find her? Anything like that?"

"No reason to be a wise ass, O'Leary. For a gorgeous woman like you who looks one step above homeless, you've got some mouth. Spend much time in the ICU of your favorite hospital?"

"No, I've a friend. Ya've met my friend as I recall. I realize the introduction fee was expensive, but then facilitators like ya can afford it. When ya've a friend like mine, nobody and I mean nobody fucks with me."

"I'll tell my friend you're interested and get back to you regarding the meet. What's your number?"

"Raymond's Bar. Greg's my receptionist. He'll put me on the horn if I'm here. If not, he'll take a message. The next time ya wanta see me, Jones, make an appointment."

Greg walked from behind the bar with a lighted cigarette dangling from the left side of his mouth, smoke getting in his left eye which caused him to blink and gave the check to Jones. He had a bar towel thrown over his left shoulder. The apron he wore was so dirty it reminded one of modern art, a lot of drippings on it. Not quite a Jackson Pollack, but close. It was actually a Greg. Jones told him he didn't have any money because she had fleeced him. Greg stood next to him, stared at him, and said he was going to call the cops if he didn't pay.

"Ya see my policy is, Jones, if a client hires me, pays me cash on the barrel head, I pay fer the dessert and the special of the day. If the potential, a Maybe, interrupts me when I'm engaged in fine dining, just talks, the Maybe pays the check."

So Jones reached into his pants pocket and paid the check, but stiffed Greg on the tip. Jones got up, didn't shake her hand, didn't kiss it goodbye or extend any amenities.

*What happened ta the good ol' days of civility?*

Mariah got up and put her tent sign on the table top, "Back in fifteen minutes." She started to walk to her 'shithole' to use the easement room.

# 3

Jones called and left the client's address and time of the appointment only with Greg, but no client name. Mariah had an appointment this afternoon.

She knew the neighborhood was expensive and called a friend at the Hall of Records, Tax Collector, and had him run a property check for name of owner and assessed evaluation. Mariah crossed-checked it with another friend at the title company, a match. One of her bankers, Harry Burstein at JP Morgan Chase, who owed her big time, got her the last three years' tax returns and a recent audited financial statement of the owner's worldwide holdings from his banker, Edvard Lavananski, at the International Investment Bank and Trade. How Harry got it from IIBT she did not know, did not want to know and did not care.

Mariah was surprised. The owner had a dollar and a half in his piggy bank. Jones never used the pronoun he or she, just friend. *Must watch those facilitators every step of the way; never assume anything.*

She put on a simple-black Chanel business suit, white blouse, jacket and skirt. If you have nice legs, show them. She wore black pumps with two-inch heels and a necklace of iridescent peacock and cobalt-blue Tahitian eleven millimeter pearls. They were AAA with a nacre thickness of 1.0 millimeter. She could have easily won the award for the best legs in Hollywood. The necessaries filled her black ostrich briefcase. Mariah looked in the 'shithole's' mirror and was impressed. Her red hair was having an affair with her neck and red complemented the beautiful green eyes.

She walked down the stairs to the clean lobby with old leather chairs in good condition from her luxuriously appointed and elegant furnished fifth-floor suite, because the elevator did not work again today. *One of these days . . .* Mariah walked out the front of "Castle Gloom" and hailed a cab. She didn't have a car and didn't like to drive.

About thirty minutes later, the cab pulled up in the front of the estate's twelve-foot high wrought iron gates in Bel Air. The driver got out, read the instructions on the gate speaker and pushed a button. Then he came back to the car and asked, "Hey, Buddy, what's yur name?"

"O'Leary."

He returned, had another episode with a voice, returned to the cab and just like Ali Baba and the Forty Thieves, Sesame opened, and they drove in.

They traveled past the gate house on the driveway and about half a mile-plus to the house. When they arrived at the main house, a man stood erect with his nose raised just above parallel to the pavement. He wore a butler's uniform, stood at attention and looked straight ahead. He walked to the right-rear door of the cab, opened it and said in an English public school accent, but did not look at her, "This way, Miss."

She told the cabbie to wait.

After they were in the foyer he said, "This way, Miss, to the library. Mr. Jonathan P. Kennington will be with you shortly."

Mariah found a comfortable chair in the library near the real fireplace, which burned real wood, put out real heat and sat. She looked about and saw the walls were covered floor to ceiling with books. Moveable ladders with wheels on the bottoms were attached to the bookcases by a rail at the top of the ladders. She had her back to the light that came through the leaded glass windows and would shine into the face of J.P. Kennington when he sat opposite her. The chairs sat on an Oriental rug that was bigger than the footprint of the Brighton Hotel. She awaited the arrival of the man who had granted this audience. He was Bill and Warren rich. She opened her briefcase and pulled out the book she currently read on her Kindle. It was appropriate for the circumstances: *Audacity of Greed: Free Markets, Corporate Thieves, and the Looting of America* by Tasini. After thirty minutes of enjoyable reading and the warmth of the fire, her favorite butler returned and announced with the skill of a herald, "Mr. Jonathan P. Kennington." She pressed menu on her Kindle, added a bookmark, held the switch at the top for four seconds and allowed the screen to go dark. Mariah closed the Kindle holder and replaced it into her briefcase.

She turned her head toward the tall library doors that opened in the middle and saw this tall, handsome and imposing older man of about sixty-five or so. He had well-groomed gray hair and impeccably dressed in a dark, blue three-piece lounge suit. She remained seated. He walked toward her, and she extended her right hand to shake his. He took her hand gently, bowed from the waist toward her, looked into her eyes with his not-gentle blue eyes and kissed her hand gently.

Immense wealth or the reputation of it, whether you had it or not, allowed the person to project command. It intimidated the insecure, social climbers and toadies. No matter how despicable the conduct of the past or present of the person, the fawners lined up to pretend admiration and respect. They received an imagined benefit from the aura. When they left the person's presence, they didn't take a shower and wash their hair. But they did tell whoever would stand still for one second that they knew J.P. and gave every boring detail of the occasion to impress. Yes to self-impress, self-enhance in their mind and tried to impress the listener with the shallow insignificance of the braggadocio.

J.P. sat in a chair that was at a forty-five degree angle to the fireplace and opposite her. "Thank you, for coming, Ms. O'Leary," he said with an accent not recognizable by her. He stared into her engaging green eyes. Her well-coiffed red hair framed a face envied by all women. "I can't believe you're the same person. Are you Mariah O'Leary the attorney?"

"Yes, I am. Why do you ask? Would you like to see my passport; I have it in my briefcase. Like a Boy Scout, I like to be prepared. These days one can never be sure when they're going to be braced by the Immigration and Naturalization Service."

"I am genuinely stunned by your presence. I can't recall this ever happening to me previously. Mr. Jones described you in a very uncomplimentary way. He said something about your sartorial splendor and taste were truant and came from the 'Salvation Army's Dumpster' if I recall correctly. I believe Mr. Jones may need to contact an optometrist, or I need to replace the incompetent forthwith. You're dressed impeccably, tailor-made? He said you were attractive. I believe he has a limited vocabulary and needs the optometrist for another reason. I find your beauty ineffable. I'm having difficulty believing you're forty."

"I see you made an inquiry before this meeting. I thank you for the compliments. I do the best I can with what I have. Not tailored-made, but Chanel. Regarding Mr. Jones, 'forthwith' is a good idea, Mr. Kennington. Remember, you only get what you pay for."

"Ah, your wisdom is so sage. Not only was he incompetent in not being able to hire you without my granting you an audience, but a poor judge of character. He also said you spoke like an 'illiterate' or was it 'a poorly educated' person? It was one of the two. He may need an audiologist, too. Do you know anything about me, Ms. O'Leary?"

"A little. Only kings and queens grant audiences. I know you're not a king, even though you may believe you are, so the question is: are you a queen?"

"Touché, Ms. O'Leary, touché. Took fencing did we?"

"Actually, Riposting 101 at Yale to compete with the pseudo machos and self-impressed without foundation for which there were an infinite number, unfortunately. A riposte now and then is a good way to lay the pitch. So, level you know. According to them who say they know, you have never been married, but adopted a little girl and named her Victoria Kennington. Supposedly, her parents were friends of yours and died shortly after she was born. No one knows for sure, but you are selling what you have in stock. No one has seen her for over thirty years and no photographs are readily available; a good idea, keeps the entrepreneurs at bay.

"You are active in charitable work internationally. You build schools for girls in poor countries where women are oppressed, because you and I believe it is the only way for their societies to progress out of the dark ages. You run a multinational corporation. Your grandfather founded the company. When he died, you worked with your father. He died about ten years ago under mysterious circumstances, and you prevented an autopsy. A will appeared mysteriously from an attorney he never used, but was an acquaintance of yours. In it, he left the company to you. At the time of his death it was worth about 15B. You have been the chairman and CEO for ten years and it's now worth, depending on the close of the market today, about seventy-two and a half billion take or leave a B. You own Kennington Oil, a major oil refining company, Kennington Industries, the largest defense contractor in the U.S., Kennington Commercial Bank and Trust, a large-bank holding company and Kennington Chemical and Pharmaceutical, the largest in the world. Your lender is IIBT.

"I saw in a footnote you had some off-ledger transactions. Offices in sixty-three countries. You, Mr. Buffett, Mr. Gates and Mr. Carlos Slim of Mexico are always racing to be the number one on the Forbes list. But Forbes never ranks you because you are smarter than the other three; pay whatever it takes to stay off the list, and do all you can to remain anonymous, no personal financial information provided, no photographs of you or Victoria. All the other information I have wouldn't be relevant for this discussion."

"May I see what you have to make sure it's accurate?" He asked in the form of a command, and extended his left hand toward her at the same time.

"Yes, of course." She leaned over the right armrest of her chair, picked up her briefcase, placed it on her lap, opened it so the top obstructed his view of the contents. She didn't want him to see her paperweight and constant companion inside resting on the top of a manila folder titled *J.P. Kennington Dossier,* took it out and handed it to him.

"Thank you." He opened it. Turned the pages, stopped and read sometimes, and after ten or so minutes he closed the folder and returned it to her.

"I think you're right, Ms. O'Leary. Regarding Mr. Jones, 'Forthwith *is* a good idea.' I'd say you're very good at what you do. Well informed. Very thorough, I'm impressed and not very often, I might add. I seem to be complimenting you endlessly. I do believe I'm under your spell. Well, down to business. I didn't realize I was so rich."

"Maybe you need a new bookkeeper, Mr. Kennington? If I didn't know better, I'd swear you were a member of the Sapera caste." Mariah uncrossed her long attractive legs and then re-crossed them, right over left. She was a natural beauty who did need makeup nor wore any.

"So, you believe I'm a sweet-talking snake charmer from India?"

"I do, and with an ego bigger than the multiverse. What are the off-ledger transactions?"

"Those are transactions that are off-ledger."

*I guess that answer is a euphemism for mind your own business. Reminds me of a Chinese expression regarding corruption: "If the water is too clear, the fish will have nothing to eat."*

"One of my secretaries disappeared about five days ago, and I'd like you to find her. Mr. Jones told me you'd decide after you talked to me, is this correct?"

"Why not use Forthwith Jones? Or, your regular security people for search and rescue? How about the Coast Guard or the mountaineers? After all, you are using the best are you not?"

"Yes. You *are* knowledgeable. I'm looking for discretion. Large organizations have too many curious employees who incidentally may decide to go into business for themselves, a terminal illness when they do if you know what I mean."

"Oh, yes, I know what you mean, entrepreneurs. Yes, extortion is risky and *more* deadly than cancer, and one dies almost instantaneously of holes disease without rights or rites. You don't even have time for a doctor to guess how you died. Or, what medical people erroneously call diagnosis to lead the gullible to believe they know what they're talking about. Right?"

"Right, very cogent."

"Discretion is good, that's me. I have a reputation for not talking in my sleep, either. Hiring me because you think I am going to take a fall for some Machiavellian plan you international players enjoy? So, Jones told you he found a loser who was one step above homeless and didn't speak English correctly to fit your criterion? If I decide to go forward, you will need to sign a fee agreement which sets forth my fees and describes the work you wish done and eliminates any sleepless nights on my part wondering what you really want to accomplish."

"Would it be alright with you if I signed an agreement that described your duties as a corporate attorney and consultant and not have any specificity?"

"No. Specificity is my best friend. Never have any trouble with him and handsome, too. Never lets me down."

"Oh, very well, specificity it is. Her name's Lillian McGraw. She's been with me for about five years as a confidential secretary and traveled with me wherever I went. Very efficient and very smart. Good employee. I've had my staff prepare a file to assist you. It contains all I know about her, résumé, the works. She left without giving notice. I was surprised. No reason or explanation. I'm concerned about her well-being. When you find her, bring her to me or give me the information, and I'll go to her. So, give me your fee schedule."

*This man is not a good liar. He has looked everywhere in his room except at me when he talks. He should change his name to I.M. Desperate.* "I do not kidnap. So, if she wants to come and needs a ride or airfare, I will bring her back. Otherwise, I will tell you where she is if that is all right with her. If it isn't, I will not tell you where she is, assuming I know at the time we talk."

She looked into his eyes with her sincere Sarah look and said, "My retainer fee is five hundred thousand, payable on signing of my agreement."

"You must be kidding."

"Now it is seven hundred and fifty thousand. You must not impugn my integrity. You just called me a liar, and your conduct is unacceptable to me."

"All I said was: 'You must be kidding.' "

"Kidding is a euphemism for lying. A well-educated person like you knows that."

"Alright, five hundred thousand it is."

"No, alright seven hundred and fifty thousand it is or find another attorney." *He wants me specifically, or he wouldn't have sent Forthwith Jones, but why? He's about as hard to read as the comic section of the Times.*

"I get five hundred an hour plus expenses, billed weekly. It is my specificity corporate-client rate. No refunds of any monies paid under any circumstances. If you do not pay by wire transfer immediately to my account when my weekly bill is sent to you by e-mail, I stop working and all funds paid to me are forfeit."

"You're not trying to take advantage of a nice older gentleman like me are you?"

"If I saw a nice older gentleman, I would not take advantage."

"Any questions, Ms. O'Leary?"

"Did she take anything else from you other than her person? Anything else missing? Computers, computer data, money, personal property of yours or of one of your companies?"

"No."

"Have you done an inventory of what you would call your confidential papers and other property?"

"Yes, and there's nothing missing."

"You are very fortunate to have found such an honest and loyal employee." *I should make an appointment with this guy so he could tell me the truth for a change. Maybe a little time at Guantanamo with some enhanced interrogation might give him an epiphany.*

"Just one. There is no mention of marital status. A lot of background but no marriages listed. Is this correct, you have not been married?"

"That's correct."

"And just the one adopted child, Victoria?"

"Yes."

*When he said it, why did I think he just lied to me again? Boy he is on a roll. It is because I believe he did just lie to me again, still. Not unusual. Clients lie to their attorneys all the time to their detriment. Then when something bad happens as a result of the lie, they get bit hard on the ass, really hurts and need a shot to prevent Tetanus. He also lied when he said "I did not realize I was so rich." And what did he leave out, a lie by omission, about his desperation to find the 'confidential secretary'?* "You'll need to sign this agreement and the copy; then, I'll sign both and leave you a copy. There is a need for a retainer check upon signing, seven hundred and fifty thousand dollars, and one thousand for the two hours I have spent for you so far."

He picked up the telephone and told the listener to issue her a check for the retainer fee, one thousand in cash and bring it down immediately.

They signed the two documents while they waited for the money god's messenger. She gave him a copy and placed a copy in her briefcase.

"I do have another question. Who recommended me?"

"I don't recall at this moment. I talk to so many people. But the recommendation was accurate. You're as represented."

*This is a very good four in the afternoon bullshit missile.* "Is it high tea time, Mr. Kennington? I love high tea."

"We don't serve high tea."

At that moment, Mr. Tom Jones, also known as, aka, Forthwith Jones, came in with an envelope. I said to him, "I'm still waiting for you to sing 'What's New, Pussycat?' for me, Tom." He gave it to J.P. He opened it, checked it and handed it to Mariah.

As Tom was leaving, she said, "Forthwith, see you later."

J.P. handed her Lillian McGraw's dossier. She opened it. First thing on page one, a photograph of an absolutely gorgeous woman of about twenty-five. A real winner. She looked through the file and said, "I don't see any birth certificate, the listing of mom and dad or their address. I want this information, too. When can I have it all?"

"I believe you have all I have, Ms. O'Leary."

"You did not vet her any deeper than what is here for a position as sensitive as 'confidential secretary' if that's what she was?" *Why do I believe he just lied to me again?* "If I have any further questions about Ms. McGraw that's not in here may I call you?"

"Yes, only me."

"I see you have surveillance cameras. I would like to see the video recordings of the comings and goings on the day she disappeared. Also, before I leave, I would like to see her room."

"What room are you talking about?"

"You know, where she slept, kept her clothes and personal property. You know, where she was living."

"What makes you think she stayed here?"

"Because you do not want me to see it, and incidentally, there's no address in here for her." *Good excuse, even though it isn't the reason. Well, well, so she did live here. Interesting. Good guess, Mariah. Just logic. Caught another liar at work and play. How can you not love Sherlock Holmes?*

"I'll arrange that for you. Good day to you, Ms. O'Leary," he said dismissively, with the same arrogance of a king, or was it a queen. "And, thank you again for coming. Please post me any time you've progress. My card and private number are in the envelope. Humphrey will show you out."

"I'd like to see her room now, before you sanitize it, meaning now."

"Not convenient today, Ms. O'Leary."

He disappeared smartly and then came Humphrey, Mariah's favorite butler. He walked perfectly erect, eyes straight ahead, nose slightly elevated in front of her at an unhurried pace which would lead one to believe he believed he was immortal. She walked three paces behind her guide so she would not get lost. She felt like an old-Asian or Muslim wife. A little oppression went a long way, reminded her of slavery.

J.P. met Jones in the foyer after O'Leary left. "Jones, you told me she spoke poor English and used poor grammar. You said she was a slob and had food stains on her clothes. You said her dress was wrinkled and unkempt and something about the 'Salvation Army and a Dumpster.' The woman who showed up here today isn't the woman you spoke to obviously. Her English was perfect and her grammar correct. Her suit was very expensive and her shoes were Ferragamo and highly polished. She was well-groomed and with a manicure. She had impeccable manners. You told me she was dumb and that's the reason you chose her. But this woman isn't dumb; quite the opposite. I sure hope I haven't made a mistake based on your suggestion, Mr. Jones. She may be an attorney from the ghetto — but dumb, I don't think so. You said you found the right lawyer for the job. I have my doubts. I could see the wheels turning in her head as we talked. I don't know what you have done to me. I'm concerned about your competence. I'm concerned about my decision."

Jones was pleased that he was pleased because maybe, just maybe there would be a bonus.

"To make sure I don't have to suffer an inconvenience caused by your incompetence or stupidity, this is what I'm going to do. As far as this company, your employment is concerned, you're discharged, Jones, forthwith. I'll have security empty your desk and escort you from the premises. Make sure you give them your badge."

"Why?"

" 'Why?' It isn't a question you can ask, according to my contract with you. It states clearly you're an employee at will. And, you have no right to ask the reason. I'll tell you this: you need to get your eyes and hearing checked."

"I'll bet O'Leary had something to do with this, right?"

"From now on, you'll be working for me personally. You'll be paid your regular salary from one of my non-domestic companies. A messenger'll find you once a week and pay you in cash. If he doesn't find you, you'll not be paid. If anyone checks your employment here, it'll show you've been terminated. Now, this is what I want you to do." J.P. explained his new assignment.

"Thank you, Mr. Kennington, it'll be my pleasure. You can count on me." Security arrived and escorted Jones and his car to the gate and retrieved his security card and pass.

Mariah walked through the massive and impressive front door and walked toward the cab and her patient cabbie, who called her "Buddy."

What you see is just an illusion. It is what your enemy wants you to see. Why was she having thoughts she did not like? Reminded her of walking through the jungle. You put your right foot down and you fall into a hole that is filled with sharpened bamboo stakes with dung on the points. You talk about having a bad day.

To pay this kind of money to find a secretary and get her back, she did not think so. What does this Lillian know that J.P. does not want anyone else to know, including her? It must be nuclear. She considered what to do and her options. Find the girl, or more importantly, find out why J.P. really wanted to find her? What did he want to do with her when he got her? The answer to that question would produce the gold ring, because I believe he believes he has put me on a merry-go-round?

J.P. lied better than most, but he was still a liar. He probably believed he was believable, or it did not matter whether the listener believed him as long as he received what he paid for. Kings and queens believe they're above the law anyway. Getting the truth from these kinds of people was almost impossible. She decided she would try to defeat him if he didn't give her an honest first count.

She could perform a little oblique public service. Had he already killed Lillian or had it done? These types always had guys like Jones to do their killing, house painters. She knew why he hired her. He wanted her to do everything possible to find her and be unsuccessful. Then he could call the police feeling secure Lillian could not be found. What does Lillian know, what has she got that J.P. fears so much? Evidence?

She entered the back seat of the cab and the driver said, "Where to, Buddy?"

"Brighton Hotel. Do you always call ladies 'Buddy'?"

He looked into the rear mirror and into her eyes and answered, "Yes. I served with some damn good ladies who were soldiers in Afghanistan. They were my buddies. They watched my back and front, and I watched theirs. That's a buddy. Now, I call ladies Buddy, it's a name of respect I use like ma'am."

*Well, he is right about that.*

She opened the envelope, pulled out the check for seven hundred and fifty large, kissed it, counted the ten Benjys and thanked the money god. *Another good day's work.*

*Why do I believe there's a fire burning under the ashes?*

# 4

**Day 3   10:00 A.M.   The White House, the Oval Office**

"Thank you for seeing me, Mr. President."

"You're welcome, Mr. Jones, always glad to see you," he said without an accent. He had taken diction lessons and his entire Midwestern twang was almost gone.

"Thank you, Mr. President, for the compliment. Your friend and my employer asked me to see you pursuant to the agreement between the two of you so you can have deniability."

"Yes, thank you, he has always been considerate of me."

"He wants you to know that he has had an unexpected turn of events and needs to enlist your help. It appears there has been an episode of disloyalty in his organization by a trusted employee. It's a lady you know in every meaning of the word, L.M. It appears certain private materials have gone missing, and he believes L.M.'s in possession of them. She and the materials can't presently be found. He said you'd understand. If the wrong person were to come into possession of these materials during your re-election campaign this year, it'd be devastating to all concerned. 'Devastating to all concerned' were his exact words. He said you'd understand. I'm not privy to the materials or the information contained therein, but I'll tell you this: he's quite disturbed by the unexpected and unfortunate turn of events. I was to tell you the gravity politically in military terms was a 'nuclear implosion plus the fallout.' "

"What does he suggest?"

"Two things. One, during these uncertain times please don't have any communication with him under any circumstances. If he wishes to talk, I'll convey the information in this usual manner. Second, he'd like for you to use the vast resources of your office to find L.M. When you do, deliver her and the materials to him."

"You may tell him I'll get right on it. Anything else, Mr. Jones?"

"Yes. I've always had great respect for you as a result of the continuous compliments and praise my employer gives to me about you. I noticed while we have been talking you have been drinking coffee from a White House mug with the presidential seal. Would you have any objection to giving it to me as a gift?"

"No, considering the circumstances, it'd be my pleasure. It's empty now, here." The president handed the mug to Jones, and he placed it into his briefcase.

"I'll give you my cell number. If you need me for any reason or need to talk to my employer, please use it and not call any of the numbers you may have for him for your own protection. We both want you to be re-elected this November and for nothing but good things to happen to you." Tom handed him his card.

"Thank you, Mr. Jones. Give my best regards and thanks to your employer for protecting me." They shook hands across the top of the president's desk.

"One final thought, Mr. President. If it becomes necessary for you to resort to the final solution, and if no one else has provided results to correct this situation, you may call upon me. I've very discreet people who operate on a need-to-know basis and have exceptional skills in ferreting and magic. You'd be surprised how a good illusionist can make a person disappear without a trace."

"Thank you, again, Mr. Jones; I'll keep it in mind." *An interesting fellow, Tom Jones.*

A member of the president's Secret Service detail entered and escorted Tom Jones from the White House.

# 5

## Day 4  3:00 A.M.  A House on Multiview Drive, Los Angeles

Lillian McGraw had picked up Sean Harrison, the president's son, at the Los Angeles International Airport (LAX). He had eluded his Secret Service detail, had gone to the Ronald Reagan Washington National Airport and had flown on a commercial flight, also known as a flying contagious disease ward, to LAX. He had looked very military in his jeans, Belleville combat boots, blue Levi work shirt, sheepskin vest, mirrored aviator glasses and Special Forces ball cap.

They had been enjoying one another's company since their arrival. Sometimes they had even forgotten they were in hiding, who they were, their responsibilities, potential consequences and were just two young people in love. Hiking, reading and enjoying the outdoors and beautiful weather were standard fare every day. Sean enjoyed cooking and they enjoyed gourmet fare. She called the place "paradise on earth".

It was three in the morning when Lillian awoke in the king-sized bed in the dark master bedroom. She knew she couldn't sleep longer. She left Sean sleeping, closed the door, went to the guest room, took a shower and dressed so she wouldn't awaken him.

She had procrastinated long enough. She picked up the Victorinox and placed it on the dining table, opened it and removed the VHS tape from its sleeve titled "Kennington and Harrison, June 1987." She took the Harmony remote, turned on the sixty-inch television and placed the VHS into the player.

She sat on the sofa and watched the tape in its entirety, about fifteen minutes. It showed J.P. having sexual intercourse with Lillian McGraw Harrison, the president's wife, and her enjoyment. When they finished, he got up, dressed and stood over her smiling. She said, "Thank you, J.P. I've been trying to get pregnant by Robert. My gynecologist says I've a tipped uterus. He wants a child, but so far no luck. You made me pregnant before, so I thought we'd try it again. If I do get pregnant I see no reason to tell Robert, do you? Speaking of before, how's our daughter, Victoria?"

"I saw her about a year ago. She's still mentally ill and staying in the convent in Italy. She doesn't remember me or her past. Obviously wouldn't remember you. You went back to high school right after her birth in Paris and never did see her. I agree; there's no reason to tell Robert."

Lillian removed the VHS from the player and replaced it into the sleeve. She returned to her chair and stared at the tape. She then opened the manila folder labeled "Lillian McGraw Harrison." There was a birth certificate of Sean Harrison. The father was listed as Robert B. Harrison and the mother as Lillian McGraw Harrison. Mother's religion was Catholic. Father's religion was Southern Baptist. There was a Sean Harrison DNA Paternity report listing the father as Jonathan P. Kennington and Lillian McGraw Harrison as the mother. *Well, isn't this a sticky wicket.*

Lillian looked at the other documents. There was the birth certificate of Victoria Kennington. Born in Paris. Mother was Lillian McGraw, age 16. *She's now the president's wife. Another surprise:* Father: "Unknown." The Paternal DNA Report listed Jonathan P. Kennington as the father. *Now, I know why Mrs. Harrison said, "You made me pregnant before, so I thought we'd try it again." He made her pregnant when she was fifteen and again after she was married to Robert twenty-three years ago and had Sean.* She closed the folder and replaced it into the hard case.

She removed the folder titled "Lillian McGraw". She looked at her birth certificate. It listed the mother as Victoria Kennington and the father as "Unknown." She picked up the Paternal DNA Report. It listed the mother as Victoria Kennington and father as Jonathan P. Kennington. *Well, well, well, he do get around. I do believe I now understand and know from which fountain his power flows. Unless my genealogy is askew, I do believe Sean and I are half-brother and sister, and I'm the granddaughter of Lillian McGraw Harrison. Now, this is a problem. No legal marriage for us. The question is: When and how do I explain this to him if I do? My usual way I guess — with honesty when the moment presents itself.*

She opened the folder labeled "Personal" and read it. She could not believe what she read. It couldn't possibly be true. But there it was in black and white. There were two signatures at the bottom of the document. The first was Robert B. Harrison and the second was Jonathan P. Kennington.

Lillian waited for Sean to get up after she reviewed the files. After breakfast Lillian said, with a native California delivery, "I'd like to show you a couple of things." She then showed him the VHS of his mother having sexual relations with J.P.

As he watched the tape, he became more and more agitated. Finally, when the tape ended he yelled, "Kennington, I am going to kill you!" He walked about frenetically and without speaking. Finally, he sat on the ledge in front of the fireplace, leaned forward, put his head in his hands and started to weep. *I must think of a way to kill him as slowly and mercilessly as possible.* Time passed and neither spoke.

She watched him and was still undecided as to whether or not she had done the right thing. But she knew he wouldn't believe her if she just said they couldn't get married because they were too closely related. He would have wanted an explanation. And "Trust me" wasn't going to cut it. The tape and the Paternal DNA Report would be the substitute for a dictionary full of words. No words could erase a doubt. *Is ignorance bliss? I wonder.*

Lillian felt helpless as she watched her lover. She didn't know how to console him with words. No words could assuage his disenchantment. So, she said nothing, went to him, got on her knees in front of him, wrapped her arms around him and held him close. Lillian's compassion, empathy and the reality of their relationship would keep them bound for the remainder of their lives. The torrent of tears discolored her light blue work shirt. Quietude was the solace.

He put his chin on the top of her right shoulder, hugged her and his weeping turned to sobbing without control. When the sobbing stopped, the memory had engraved his mind forever. The hate wouldn't eliminate the sobbing; it would just make the tears boil. He released her. Held her at arms' length and said with eyes filled with tears, "I love you more than ever." He rose and went into their bedroom. He undressed and took a hot shower again. Afterward he spent time in the bathroom brushing his teeth, combing his hair and stood straight. He put on clean clothes and returned to her in a state of revitalization. He sat down next to her and asked, "Anything else?"

"Yes." Then she showed him his birth certificate and the Paternal DNA Report.

He read it. "I really do want to kill him," he said with calmness, the dialect and formality he had acquired while in boarding school in Massachusetts at Phillips Academy sometimes called Andover. He then went to Yale in Connecticut. Robert Harrison had been a graduate of Yale.

She gave him the file labeled "Personal." "Please read this."

Sean read the one-page document to himself. He sat in stunned silence. "I cannot believe my father would conspire with J.P. Kennington to commit treason and murder, but he had. This is his signature, there is no doubt."

"And it's J.P.'s too, there's no doubt."

"We need some serious help here. We need a messenger."

"Yes, we do. Doing J.P.'s a good idea, Sean, but instead of killing him we could deprive him of something he cherishes more than his life; money and power immediately come to mind. He worships money; deprive him of his and he'd have no power, except for the Harrison connection, and I know how to solve that problem, too. And, in his mind, he'd then be impotent and life wouldn't be worth living. And, with a little bit of luck, his depression might cause him to commit suicide. And, if it didn't, I know how to solve that problem, too. What do you think about not killing him, but just getting even? You know, retribution instead of revenge and engaging in thuggery. All J.P. wants to do is add another zero to his financial statement, be number one. What if we take advantage of his greed, and it causes his downfall?"

"I am in favor; what did you have in mind?"

She explained her plan.

"I like it. Let us do it."

"You realize we're half-brother and sister. We've the same father, but different mothers. I don't think we can legally get married. But I'm willing to continue our relationship if you like."

"I like. I love you very much."

"I feel the same way."

"Again, I believe your plan needs a messenger," he said, with enthusiasm. "A smart messenger or maybe a point woman. We need someone we can trust who cares about us. Your information and plan needs to be converted into a battle plan. My father talked frequently about this woman. He used to say, 'She was the only woman I ever knew who actually cared about people, and she was the brightest and most wonderful person he ever met.' I think he dated her when they were at Yale or she was at Yale and he was at Harvard Business School, I do not remember which. Evidently, she does pro bono work, charity work, in one of the poorest neighborhoods of Los Angeles, a ghetto. Maybe we should contact her and see how we can go about instituting your plan. What do you think?"

"I think it's worth a try. Until this is over, we're going to have to continue to be in hiding. I've bad feelings about people who do bad things to good people. I don't think we should make an appointment. I think we should go see her, maybe in disguise just in case. I'm afraid to use telephones or anything. Surprises will be our best defense for the future. We need a car to go to downtown Los Angeles. We can't use the Escape. We need to find a used car lot and buy one for cash. What's the lawyer's name?"

"Mariah O'Leary. My father respected her highly."

"How did you possibly remember her name?"

"Easy. Ever hear of the cow owned by Mr. Patrick and Catherine O'Leary and the Chicago fire of October 1871?"

"Sure, everybody knows the legend. We need a ride. I'm going to call a friend of mine nearby who'll come and pick us up and deliver us to the nearest used car lot. He'll get rid of the Escape. I see you went grocery shopping. We should be alright, and I've enough cash until I can get to my bank, change our identities and arrange for different credit cards if necessary," Lillian said.

"I used my credit card, because I was cash short."

She rose from her chair, looked into his eyes and stood tall and had head-turning beauty. Her light blue work shirt with a large discolored spot, Wrangler jeans which fit snugly over her slender body and cowboy boots, and said, "I told you not to. I've plenty of cash to accomplish our complete disappearances. All you have to do is ask and not take risks. You've just exposed us and interfered with my plans for disappearing. I'm in love with you Sean, but sometimes your immaturity, naiveté and unawareness are frustrating to me. You're not bullet-proof just because you're the president's son." Her gray eyes stared at him as she impressed him, but with love and protection. As she moved and talked, the natural-lighted room from the bright sun highlighted the shine of her long auburn hair as it danced on her shoulders. "I realize you don't know the seriousness of my situation or our circumstances, but you must do as I ask. J.P. has long arms and so has your father. They'll be searching for us quietly but with dedication, desperation and need. I assure you, they'll spare no expense. J.P.'s vulnerable and he knows it. Probably by now your father knows he's vulnerable, too. I don't want you to get caught up in what is my personal-temporary inconvenience and what could be permanent if found by the wrong person at the wrong time."

"My father will probably be ambivalent regarding my whereabouts, but mother and my grandmother will be distressed." His shock of dark brown hair was covered with a ball cap and the bill cast a shadow on his face caused by the skylight above. Seated, it was difficult to realize he was over six feet tall. His Levi-work shirt showed above the table top, but hid the jeans and tennis shoes below. Fresh-cut roses from the garden added a fragrance and beauty to the table and room.

"We'll probably be safe here until J.P. gets desperate, files a missing persons report with the police and puts my picture on CNN. Desperation is the mother and confusion is the father of poor judgment. He'll enlist the aid of your father to find me, clandestinely, of course. Your father knows we're together, so he'll try to find me using you as an excuse for his search I'm sure. I'm not sure whether J.P. knows we're together. Neither of them wants the devastating truth to ever be revealed. Not good for business, re-election campaigns, reputations, fund-raising for presidential libraries and could produce indictments and impeachment proceedings. Money and power are the only two things they have in common and will want to perpetuate no matter the consequences, cost or risk to others. The only thing a first-term president wants is a second term. The only thing J.P. wants is to add another zero, be first on the list of the richest, and he needs Robert's help to get there."

"What is the truth?" He had led a sheltered life. The only child of a wealthy family and knew nothing of the reality of everyday living. A little competition with sports here and there and socially with others at Andover and Yale. He had been surrounded by an entourage of sycophants whom he may or may not have recognized as such, because his father was the president during his four years at Yale.

Sean's rugged good looks, humor and athletic skills made him an attractive target for the ladies. The ladies were always trying to bag the only son of a Forbes 400. The aggressive and stiff competition always reminded one of the life and death struggles for the best gold claims along the South Fork American River in Coloma, California, at Sutter's Mill during the gold rush in 1849. The predatory mothers and fathers managed the campaigns of their daughters for their parents' social-climbing aspirations by buying the best pick, shovel, pan and ass. How does a man know if the troller loves him or his great expectations? Always difficult to determine who is and who isn't genuine. Should the candidates be subjected to extraordinary rendition, tortured by proxy in Syria or Egypt to determine their veracity before he commits to their wiles?

One had to admit his assets were a great trolling device to get laid a lot. As such, he was a harvester of the year-round crop of the apple orchard. Being a compassionate person, Sean was always willing to accept the apple when offered. After all, he was only trying to stay healthy by following the latest food pyramid advice from the USDA (United States Department of Agriculture).

"Is your battery still out of your cell phone and your talk and toss cell I gave you, mine is?"

"Yes."

"Please keep it that way. On second thought, now that I think about it, I need to plan a destination from here now that you've used your credit card."

"Are you being paranoid?" Sean asked.

"Better paranoid than dead and that goes for you, too."

She went to the bedroom, removed her luggage from the closet, opened it and removed her body guard, Mr. Glock 21, a .45-caliber semiautomatic pistol. She opened a box of ammunition and chambered a round and loaded a full clip of thirteen low-velocity hydrostatic rounds and shoved it into the grip and heard the click as it locked in place. She screwed on a specially made suppressor that would not clog, would suppress the sound and would not change the trajectory of the round. It had been made by one of the technicians at J.P.'s defense plant. She walked into the dining area and placed it on the table.

"What is that for? Do you know how to use it?"

"To prevent inconveniences of any type. I haven't spent my whole life with J.P. and not been aware of his abilities and how to survive, no matter what or who may interfere. Yes, I know how to use it."

"I thought you were just his confidential secretary. I didn't know you knew him your whole life."

"Until you and I disappeared, I was called his confidential secretary and everyone knew me as such because that is the way he wanted it, and as time went by so did I. He was probably grooming me to take over when he thought the time was right. But he revealed it to no one I knew, or to me either. At least I believe so. The only thing left for me to develop was his killer instinct; no one or thing was safe when he set his mind to it. He always got what he wanted when he wanted, no matter who or what. He believes he's above the law, and so far he has been."

"I didn't know J.P. was married and had a daughter."

"Your naïveté reminds me of someone who has been living in a vacuum in a cave. I didn't say he was married and had a daughter. Don't use your imagination, Sean. Don't infer. The least you know, the safer you'll be. I want to love you as you are and alive."

She opened her laptop, inserted her black and red AD3700 USB Modem into an USB port, swiveled it into place and booted her laptop. She now had global access. Lillian used software that cost J.P. millions to develop so he could do business globally and anonymously from wherever he was at the time. She sent an encrypted message to Carlos, a local friend, with the contact method to arrange a pick up. Lillian relayed it through a relay system which rendered her location and IP address hidden and untraceable. She went out to the lot behind the house. Lillian unlocked the Escape, took out the car cover and put it on. It also covered the front and back license plates.

All those years with J.P. and his clandestine methods and lifestyle would now be implemented for Lillian's and Sean's benefits. Who better than she, considering she had set it all up for him and had operated it? J.P wasn't computer literate and hadn't wanted to take the time to learn. He had made the mistake of believing she would be tethered to him ad infinitum and the money and the good life could buy her loyalty no matter the scars he gave her. Now it was going to be reward time.

# 6

**Day 4   10:00 A.M.   The White House, the Oval Office**

Two sofas made a sandwich of the coffee table in front of the fireplace. At the opposite end of the fireplace were two chairs. The president was well-dressed in his dark blue two-piece suit. He put his attractive-large build, which had blue eyes and were surrounded by a ruddy complexion into the chair on the right. Mariah sat in the middle of the sofa on the right. One of the president's assistants brought their coffee orders and set them on the coffee table in front of them.

"How have you been, Mr. President? By looking at your tie, I see you are advertising the food served here in the White House. It's enough to make the chef proud."

"Now, Mariah, I know it's been a long time since Yale. But call me Robert like you always have. And stop picking on me like you always have. I've always wondered whether your tongue or a razor were the sharper."

"Probably a tossup. Yes, about twenty-five years, plus or minus a year or two.

"If you'd accepted my proposal, you could've been first lady now."

"The only disadvantage I see in that, Robert, is I would have had to marry you. I have not seen or talked to you since you graduated from the Harvard Business School, and I was in my first year of law school. Your father must have pulled strings to get you in. If I remember correctly, there was quite a scandal when you got caught lying by your Harvard professor when you attended the business school after graduation from Yale."

"Well, to be honest with you. . . ."

Mariah interrupted the president and said, "Wait just a moment, Robert. You can use that expression with others, but you know that I know. You were amoral at Yale and Harvard and nothing has changed. You're an alcoholic, the fraternity beer keg gofer, got such poor grades you couldn't graduate and your rich dad had to visit the president of Yale and bribe him to change your grades to allow you to graduate and not disgrace the family. How much did it cost him? So don't use the words 'to be honest with you,' because as far as I am concerned you don't even know what the word 'honest' means."

"I know you don't like me, Mariah."

"No, that is not true. I do like you. I think you're charming and always have been. I don't like your policies or your lack of moral sense. You're a politician. And, when a politician says, 'To be honest with you', I know he is about to lie to me. That's you, Robert, you are what you are — a corruptician. A willing victim of the culture in which it is alright to be dishonest if you believe at the time you say it or do it you will not get caught in order to get elected or re-elected. When special interests and lobbyists give a politician money, it isn't for the purpose of good government. The corrupters want what they pay for, and when it's delivered the politician becomes a prostitute."

"Alright, Mariah, have it your way. Yes, you've got a good memory, unfortunately. Nevertheless, how've you been? Not married. No children, bring me up to date."

*Well, when he's right he's right. How can I be forty, never married, no children, wanted both and still do. Was my career and dedication worth the loss? Ah, vision and hindsight.*

"I've always loved you. You're the most beautiful and classiest lady I've ever seen, every man after you and still not married. How is that possible? I've followed your not illustrious career. Too brilliant, too scrupulous, I think. You were in the top of your undergraduate class at Yale and then Order of Coif and editor of the law review at Yale Law School. Everyone wondered why you turned down all those offers to join prestigious New York and Washington, D.C., law firms and take the big money. *I* also wondered why you didn't take the offers. You went into the military for five years. You went into the Airborne Special Operation Command under an assumed name, were trained and then assigned to a unit. I asked the Secretary of Defense to tell me about you and the unit, but he refused. He just said it was off the books. The chairman of the joint chiefs told me the same. Do you mind telling me about it now? *I'm* sincerely interested."

"It is true; it was off the books — full black. I cannot tell you anything about the unit or my activities, other than to tell you the combat and intelligence gathering training were very intense and the actions after deployment were rewarding to me for the contributions I had made. The unit made a substantial contribution to the downfall of the enemy, and I understand it is still.

"No, I don't mind telling you about why I did not join a prestigious law firm. I will give your 'sincerely' the benefit of the doubt. In fact, I am quite proud of what I decided not to do, what I have done and am still trying to do. Much more rewarding than being involved in corporate politics in big law firms, partner or not and worshipping the money god — Greed. Playing the embarrassing role of sycophant, my conscience does not permit, to big corporations and unpleasant rich clients, I don't think so. The answer is I cared then, still do and will continue to do so. I call it public service. Helping the poor in a poor part of town."

"Yes, I know I went into public service, too."

"No, you didn't, Mr. President, you went into politics because you were not qualified to get a job or hold a job. You went into politics to use it as a business to make money, became the pawn of the wealthy and you are still not performing public service. You are still on the pad."

"Being a little harsh aren't you, Mariah?"

"No, I thought I was being honest. You know, realistic. I did a dossier on you when you entered politics, sort of a hobby to see if I was right about you, and I was. I have updated it as new information came in. I may not know every bribe you took in exchange for your integrity and soul, but enough if released to the media that might, just might impede your re-election campaign. You do not represent the people of the United States; you represent yourself, your own financial interest, those of your family, family friends and your friends, your investors who put up the first fifty million dollars for you to run for president. And you have delivered and paid them back handsomely to the disadvantage of the taxpayers, your employers who you have forsaken, and with their money. This is what I detest the most about you and your administration.

"You do nothing about the lack of ethics of members of Congress. You allow them to continue to take bribes that are not even believably described as campaign contributions and other perquisites to deliver favorable legislation for big business. Members of Congress sell their souls and integrity. But you had an opportunity to do something about the corruption of Congress and you saw fit not to. You didn't even try. Besides, you could not have actually changed the corrupt culture anyway, because Congress would have had to do it, and we know the corruptions wouldn't vote for reform because they want to stay on the corporate dole. They don't want to have to work for a living. If I put corporate logos on their suits with Velcro, they would look like leopards.

"I came from a poor family. I remember my mother and father needed help. We were living in tenement housing owned by a tyrannical, despotic slumlord. I know tyrannical and despotic are redundant but I said it for emphasis; it was a terrible situation. He was taking advantage of us. No hot water most of the time, fires, bad plumbing, deferred maintenance was king, plaster coming off the walls and hazardous electrical conditions. No lawyer would represent my parents because they had no money to pay legal fees. My father called the city to get an inspector out to do something about it, but the inspectors were on the pad of the slumlord. Our complaints were used by the inspectors to extort the slumlord. Naturally, nothing was going to get done and that was just normal in the big city. The inspectors were making more money annually in bribes than their salaries.

"My mother and father were good people and loved one another dearly and were married until they died. He worked himself to death trying to support mother and me. My mother died thirty days later. So I studied hard, got scholarships to college and law school, but it was not enough to sustain me, so I worked also.

What I saw in our society I did not like; it made me care for others, and that is why I do what I do.

"No one cares about the poor or the homeless, because they are powerless and the political strategists believe they do not vote. But I care. Do you understand this, Mr. President? This is a rhetorical question. If you cared, the problems would have been solved by now. You do not even try to make a difference. You can well bet if they were a voting bloc, their conditions would change substantially.

"No one cares about the elderly poor either. These people have worked to build this nation; now they need help and there are no facilities to house them or people to take care of them, so they have me as an advocate. The problem is: there is an embarrassing epidemic for the world's richest nation.

"In the beginning I was idealistic, I thought I could make a difference, a contribution to our society, but the corrupt culture is a tsunami. Your administration does not care, and that's why I was not interested in joining you."

"I always thought you were the only lady I ever knew that genuinely cared about other people. I guess that's why you never replied to my overtures to join my administration. Too ethical for politics, big law firms and corporations. Now that I think about it, we never did have a discussion about your background. I never realized you were having so much difficulty. You never showed it."

"That's because you were always too busy trying to impress me with how rich you and your family were, like every other braggadocio and using apparent wealth as a trolling device to get laid. Fortunately for me you were using the wrong bait: how famous your father had been at Andover and Yale. You were always living in his shadow and not handling it. Besides, no one wants to hear about being poor and struggling or do anything about it when they hear it."

"Are you still a Doubting Mariah?"

"Yes, even more so now." *If the kingdom of god is in all of us, why do I need a priest, rabbi, imam or church, temple or mosque to provide me with the delusions they're peddling, what they have in stock?*

"So, Robert, you called and wanted to see me."

"I know you're honest, have a very good reputation for discretion, can be trusted and will give me a fair shake. What I want to talk to you about is: My son has disappeared or I can't find him. I think he may have run away with a girl."

"So, what's the problem? Have the Secret Service, FBI or CIA turn him up overnight?"

"They have to report things to people; there'll be public records and a possible scandal during this re-election year. What I need is discretion, secrecy. I need to find out what's going on. I don't get on well with my son. He has the same opinion of me that you do. Obviously, this creates friction. Since he started dating this girl, our relationship has gone to hell in a handbasket."

"Sounds like the kind of son and girl I would like to know. Why don't we get to it; what is it you want me to do?"

"I want you to find my son, Sean Harrison. He eluded his Secret Service detail. The service believes he flew to Los Angeles on a commercial flight. They don't know where he is. I've instructed them not to look for him, and told them I'll find him. This is where you come in. I'd like to get ahold of that woman that he's with so I can bring him home."

"What if they ran off to get married?"

"That would be most unfortunate."

"Why do you say that?"

"He's only twenty-two and that would upset his mother and my mother very much."

"Ah, yes, I remember now. You told me about how good it was to go to boarding school at Andover then Yale, and get away from the oppressive, overbearing disciplinarian you called mother. Well, do you want to find your son or 'that woman'?"

"Uhh, both."

"Bad delivery. Why don't I believe you? Is there any legal work involved, or am I just being hired as a private investigator-bounty hunter handling missing persons for the president of the United States?"

"No, there's no legal work. You want to come into my administration, office in the White House and be my conscience?"

"I think you're long past that. To start with, I do not believe politicians have a conscience or moral sense. You're a perfect example of the Peter Principle and the kind of person the Founding Fathers did not want in public service."

"I'm willing to pay you handsomely to help me out. So, I don't have to get involved in some kind of a potential scandal."

"I see. The important thing is to avoid scandal so you can get re-elected and incidentally find 'that woman' and your son. Or, is it 'that woman' and if your son is with her bring him along too, assuming he wants to come. I don't engage in kidnapping of men or women. If Sean wishes to return and needs transportation, I'll help him. If he doesn't wish for you to know where he is, I'll not tell you. What are you offering me to be the head of your missing persons' bureau? Is there a cabinet post involved, Secretary of Missing Persons O'Leary?"

"Stop picking on me, Mariah. I was thinking about twenty-five thousand."

"Well, Robert, as usual you were not thinking. You are still the king of misspeak. For a change, you should consider engaging your brain before you exercise your mouth. I guess your definition of 'handsomely' and mine are substantially different. As usual, it's always a pleasure to see the president of the United States. Thank you very much. Next time you want something done, call the head of the Secret Service aka Boy Scouts, the director of the FBI, the director of central intelligence, waste their time but do not call me." Mariah leaned down with haste to the right of her legs, grabbed the handle of the briefcase, rose from the sofa and turned to her left to leave.

"Mariah wait, I think I may've made a mistake here. What about a hundred?"

Mariah turned back, looked down at the sixty-years old seated president over the top of his salt and pepper hair and said, "If you were an honest person who needed some help and had no money, I would have done it for nothing; because this is what I do every day. But considering who you are and the insult of twenty-five, it's five hundred. Look at it as a charitable contribution to help all of the honest-poor people I represent who have not got the money to pay me. They also have not got the money to hire K Street lobbyists to buy members of Congress whom are for sale at cheap prices. My fee is five hundred thousand plus five hundred an hour, and a thousand a day in expenses."

"That's a little above your pay grade isn't it, Mariah?" The president asked with disrespect.

"The wonderful thing about being self-employed, Mr. President, is I determine the pay grade. And it fluctuates and is determined by market conditions at the time. You understand that. Anything else, Mr. Maybe, because if there's nothing more I'm leaving."

"Sit down, and I'll write you a check." He rose from his chair, walked to the Lincoln, sat, removed his checkbook from the top right-hand drawer and wrote her a check.

She sat down on the sofa and asked, "One week in advance on the expenses, seven thousand. Do you have a dossier on your son, where he goes, what he does or a photograph? What about 'that woman'? You have a name, photograph? Do you know anything about her, where she lives or who she is?"

"Yes, I have a file here with all of the information on both." The president removed a manila folder from the top-left drawer of his desk, walked to the sofa and handed it to her.

Mariah leaned back, opened the file on 'that woman', put the file on her lap so the loose pages wouldn't fall and looked through it. She didn't believe in coincidences. How was it that J.P. and Robert wanted her to look for 'that woman', Ms. McGraw, but disguised the search differently? The information on Lillian looked like a copy of the information she had in her file that J.P. had given her. It appeared J.P. had enlisted the aid of the president to find the secretary. Why, she wondered? One had a lost or misplaced secretary, and now the other had a lost or misplaced son with 'that woman' who was also known as, or aka, a misplaced secretary. Maybe, the son and Lillian were together in some exotic land. This had gone way beyond finding a secretary who hadn't shown up for work. It led her to believe the secretary knew something that J.P. and the president didn't want known by anyone. She knew Robert was still lying to her. Not unusual. It was another good reason, among many, for her not to have married him. The president's little misdirection by having her look for his son and lying about no interest in the girl. Gold and truth are so precious they need to be surrounded by a fortress of lies. What was known about fortresses? To quote Cicero, "No fortress is so strong it cannot be taken by money."

And so far from J.P. and Robert, all she had heard were lies. What is the truth? She decided they would pay her handsomely, her definition and find out. Or, to put it differently, what is the accurate information? It's a different meaning than truth, that's for sure. She believed nobody had been giving her accurate information. And, she did not know what was going on.

She read the file and asked, "There is no birth certificate in here for Lillian McGraw, why?"

"I don't know why. You have all I know." The president handed her his personal check for five hundred thousand.

Mariah looked at it, took a fee agreement from her briefcase, filled in the blanks as to the specificity for her employment. If the daily rate of five hundred an hour and one thousand a day expenses were not paid weekly, Mariah stopped working. Mariah handed the agreement to the president for his signature.

The president aggressively asked her to remove the reason for the employment, looking for 'that woman' and his son. This specificity was her friend. She refused, because she needed it there to keep her out of trouble in the future with the president and the bar association. The president was a bad poker player. When she refused, the president folded faster than folding egg whites into chocolate to make a soufflé. He handed the signed and dated fee agreement back to her. The president continued to protest, probably to assuage his feeling of not getting his way, sometimes known as an adult tantrum.

"Thank you, Mr. President. Now, all that is left is you handing me the twenty thousand in cash for my eight hours per day at the five hundred an hour daily rate for a five-day week in advance and a five-day week of expenses in advance for a total of twenty-five thousand plus expenses getting here, staying overnight at the Willard and flying home first-class. Shall we say an additional five thousand for a total of thirty thousand?"

The president picked up the receiver, asked for the thirty thousand in cash and hung up. Shortly a young lady came in and gave the president a white number ten envelope. He thanked her, and she left the Oval Office. The president handed the envelope to her; she opened it and counted the contents.

"I will only call you, Mr. President, when I have something to report. I will not call and tell you I have no information."

"Thank you, for helping me."

"Thank you, for helping me help others."

She exited the Oval Office. *I do believe I have a conflict of interest here. Who shall I give to whom when I find them, if I do? I guess I could use the Wisdom of Solomon and give J.P. and Robert one each, assuming they want to return.*

# 7

## Day 5   Raymond's Bar, Los Angeles, California

Mariah sat in her office on her cushion after she had hit the Harrison and Kennington lotteries for one million two plus the hours, expenses and travel costs. Jones walked in and again sat, not having learned anything from their last exchange.

"Good day, to you, Mariah."

"Let's get off on the right foot, shall we? Yu're a slow learner, Mr. Lack of Manners. Didya make an appointment, and I misplaced it? Next, I haven't given ya permission ta sit, call me by my first name, nor will I. It's Ms. O'Leary ta ya."

"Alright, Tight Ass. I've been fired by J.P. Now, I need a job because of you, and you owe me a job."

"Ya must stop usin' hallucinogens before ya come here. I don't owe ya the time a day."

"The first time I came here you put on a show for me, the same one you're putting on now. The bad language, the wrinkled dress with artwork by Food on it. Playing the part of the homeless lawyer. I gave J.P. a description of you, and then you showed up at J.P.'s with a different persona. He thought I had lied to him, and he fired me."

"Aren't ya the dumb ass who said I was recommended ta ya? If that was true and ya did what facilitators do, ya would've checked me out and yur incompetency wouldn't have been revealed."

"I noticed you talked like an uneducated person when we first met. You're still talking like that. But you talked like a well-educated person and were impeccably dressed when you met with Kennington. What's going on?"

"I do what Chameleons do when it comes to language, Forthwith. I adjust for the benefit of my audience so the listeners will be comfortable and accept me as one of them. I do not want my language to be a distraction to the listener. Do you think I did it to embarrass you and cause you problems because you were so dumb, lied to me and unpleasant when we first met? If you do or even imagined that I did, you would be wrong. Only I can make myself angry. Anger interferes with my clear thinking, good judgment, and therefore, I do not get angry. When you are angry, you make mistakes. I seek retribution when injustice prevails on behalf of my clients and the needy. You being neither, you have no need to fear me.

"You an eavesdropper? See, Jones, this is the way it is: I try to blend in. Be like the people I am with. When my clients from here come in, I use their vernacular. It makes them feel comfortable, and it's my way of telling them they can trust me, and I have empathy for them. See what I mean? The same goes for the well-educated. I speak their dialect too and for the same reason, sort of a Chameleon of the English language."

"How can absolutely gorgeous blend in with shit?"

"Thank you very much for the compliment. Need is blind. I would not put it that way, but maybe you are right? I am inferring from your delivery you believe the poor and needy are 'shit.' I don't believe your definition at all. I treat everyone equally. Give respect, get respect. The person's conduct brings my definition of 'shit' to the fore."

"I've some information that could help you find the missing secretary."

"I could use the help. Do you have a certified birth certificate for Lillian, or know where I could get one or find her?"

"No."

"Well, then what information do you have?"

"I can't provide that unless we start working together."

"Why would I want your help? You are probably still working for Kennington. You just want to get the information he wants, be a hero, kidnap and deliver. He sent you here to spy on me."

"No, you can call J.P., and he'll tell you I've been cashiered."

"How dumb do you think I am? I find your remark insulting. If you are working undercover for him, and now you want me to call him and confirm you have been discharged, do you believe he is not going to say yes I fired him. You really are dumb, Jones, no wonder he fired you, if he did. Any other bovine manure you wish to sell me?

"How long did you work for J.P?"

"Give or take about five years."

"Tell me. I read some background information he gave me. I saw he hadn't been married and had no children. Is this right? What's his sexual preference?"

"How should I know?"

"You do know; this was just a test to see how honest you are going to be, and I see I was right. You have not been fired. You are not going to be honest. But you do know; so, you are not going to tell me. You are a bad liar, Jones. You are still lying, we both know it, and so I would not want you around anyway."

"Alright, alright he's a womanizer. He'll do any woman who's not moving if she's agreeable. They do him in the hopes of getting pregnant and receive a reward.

He's straight. Preferably young girls, but bestows his largess, his dick, on anyone he finds attractive if they're receptive. He likes as many as he can as often as he can, he's Pfizer's biggest customer for the little blue pill. He believes he's bestowing the honorary British title of Dame upon the fortunate recipient. And the other reason, of course is: Greed."

"What has that got to do with not being married?"

"He didn't and doesn't want to share a penny of his wealth with any woman or anybody else. He's an equal-opportunity denier."

"Thank you, Jones, for your honesty, if it is. I do not hire liars. Tell him the ploy did not work. Do you have anything else in inventory you would like to try and peddle before you leave? Have I blended in with 'shit'?"

Jones took the final insult, rose from the booth, left without depositing any goodwill or leaving any amenities and slammed the front door closed. The angry and non-thinking loser displayed his dissatisfaction and gave satisfaction to the victor-viewer.

She enjoyed catching liars in the middle of their art form, or is it a science? She imagined it had to do with what degrees you held from which. Did years of experience qualify for an honorary degree? Who knew better than people like J.P., Robert, Jones and the corrupticians among us?

# 8

## Day 5   Used Car Lot, Los Angeles

Carlos arrived at the car lot with Sean in the passenger's seat and Lillian lying down on the back seat. He had picked them up at the Multiview Drive house and left a driver there to drive the Escape to its final resting place. Carlos told them, "I told the owner you were a friend of mine. I gave him no name. He's expecting you. The less you say to him the better. He knows to forget you were here, he's flexible and a deal maker." Sean got out of the car and Carlos drove with Lillian still on the back seat to a convenience store and gas station, stopped and waited.

Sean looked at the cars on the lot and made a decision. He went in wearing his mirrored aviation glasses, ball cap, driving gloves and said to the owner, "I want to buy the Ford Taurus for all cash with a bonus, if you do as I ask. Do not fill in the name of the buyer. Do you have insurance here for stolen cars?"

"Yes."

"How many days before you have to report a sale to the DMV?"

"Five."

"If I do not call you within five days and give you the name of the buyer, report it stolen. Is this agreeable?"

"Yes."

He gave him the money Lillian had given him and he received the temporary paperwork. Sean left the owner's office and drove the one mile to the convenience store and gas station. He parked next to one of the self-serve pumps. He went into the store and gave the cashier forty dollars to fill the tank. Sean walked out and started to put gas in the Taurus. He walked over to where Carlos was parked with Lillian. Sean shook his hand and thanked him for the help. Lillian gave Carlos a peck on the cheek and thanked him. She got out of the car and got into the Taurus on the passenger's side. Sean removed their luggage from the trunk of Carlos' car and put their bags into the trunk of the Taurus.

Before leaving the gas station, Sean called information and got the telephone number for the Law Office of Mariah O'Leary. He called the number, spoke to Greg, the bartender, and got the address.

# 9

## Day 5   9:00 A.M.   Raymond's Bar, Los Angeles

Sean and Lillian drove to downtown Los Angeles. They drove around Mariah's neighborhood looking for a used-clothing store and found one. They parked on the street. Sean paid cash for some old jeans, men's shoes with no laces and a gray sweatshirt with a hood to cover his ball cap. Lillian bought old jeans, men's shoes, a large sweatshirt to cover her breasts and a knit cap with cash. She took her long auburn hair and put it all under the cap so she would look like a young man. She wore sunglasses but no makeup. They put the clothes they had worn into the store into a paper bag the owner gave them. They returned to the car and drove to Raymond's Bar. Sean parked the car on the street two cars away from the bar. Lillian opened her shoulder bag and screwed the nose job onto her friend, Mr. Glock.

"I'll go in and make sure she's receptive," Sean said. Sean got out of the car, left the motor running and put money into the parking meter. Lillian moved behind the steering wheel with her friend in her bag. Lillian watched the entrance to the bar, the rear-view mirror and side-view mirrors.

Sean went into Raymond's Bar and over to the bartender and had a brief conversation with him. Greg fingered Mariah. Sean approached her table and asked, "Are you Ms. O'Leary?"

"Yes. But even though you're dressed like a bum from the hood, you're neither. Trying to pass are we? For what and why? Those are the questions. Surely not as a field agent; if you are you are a failure. You don't blend. You should have listened to the Ghettonians speak first before trying to pass yourself off as one of my people. So who are you, and what do you want, Preppie?"

"So my education gave me away. I get an A for effort, but an F for accomplishment. My father always spoke very highly of you. This is why I am here. My friend and I are in rather awkward circumstances, and we need some help. I thought I would try to discuss it with you, and maybe you would help us."

"Who's your father?"

He moved closer, bent from the waist and whispered, "Robert B. Harrison." He knew this wasn't the truth, but she didn't know his secret.

"Where's your friend?"

"In the car outside with the engine running, in case we need to leave expeditiously."

"I see. The Brighton Hotel is up the street. Here is my room key. Take your friend and belongings. Go there now and wait for me. I will be right behind you. I will tap twice quickly, pause and then tap three times. Do not let anyone in if they don't use this tapping sequence. Now go." She removed her friend from the holster which was attached to the underside of the table top, put him in her shoulder bag, looked at her watch and sat for five more minutes.

Sean went outside, got into the car, and Lillian drove them to the Brighton and parked the Taurus on the street. They got out of the car with their belongings, walked to the Brighton, took the elevator to the fifth floor. Mariah's luxurious suite was a clean and neat single room, a queen-size bed with a Tempurpedic mattress covered with an eider down-filled duvet, full bath, closet, and a large plasma television. The music was supplied by her iPod in a TRIK dock. There was a wooden rocking chair in one corner with a needle-point padded seat and back rest. Behind it was an adjustable reading lamp so she could read her law books which rested on the nearby book shelves. An Asus laptop, twenty-inch monitor that swiveled, and printer adorned a sturdy table which had a close relationship with a Herman Miller desk chair.

Mariah knew she could say to the poor and needy with sincerity, "I know how you feel." She had lived their way when she was growing up and maybe worse. She lived simply, ate simply and the poor and needy knew this and respected her, her empathy, honesty and help.

# 10

## Day 5   10:03 A.M.   The Brighton Hotel, Los Angeles

Mariah walked into the lobby and approached the reception desk. "George, is the refurbishing of the rooms on the top floor completed?"

"Yes, Ms. O'Leary."

"Are they still all vacant?"

"Yes, Ma'am."

"I will take three adjoining rooms on the east side, the quiet non-street side. No one will be registered. The rooms will be empty, as far as you are concerned. Give me the keys, please."

"I understand. So be it. Here ya are."

"Two people went up in the elevator. Were they with ya?"

"No, I am not expecting guests. Is Jerry here?"

"Yes."

"Please have him come to the lobby in five minutes. Thank you."

"I'll have him here."

Mariah went to the elevator only because George said two people went up in it. Normally, she walked up the five flights, because "Infrequently" was the nickname for the elevator, besides it was good exercise. She got off on the fifth floor and went to her room. She tapped twice, paused and then three times. Sean opened the door.

"Who has the key to your car, give it to me, what is it and where is it parked?"

Sean handed her the key and gave her the information.

"Wait here. I will be right back."

Mariah walked down the stairs and saw Jerry in the lobby. She touched his right elbow as she passed him, he followed her out the front of the hotel, and they turned right. "See that Taurus over there?"

"Sure."

"Here's the key. Do you know a nice-looking white girl with auburn hair who looks clean, about twenty-five with clean clothes and a white young man about twenty-two, clean shaven, attractive and clean clothes? And incidentally, would they like to make a hundred each?"

"Sure," said with respect.

"Alright then, pick the best two of the lot. Drive them to the Los Angeles Union Passenger Station on Alameda Boulevard in downtown L.A. in the Taurus. It's the main Amtrak station for trains in L.A., as you know. Park the car in the lot and leave it unlocked. Take the key. Go in with them and watch them buy two one-way tickets to Washington, D.C. in a compartment for departure today. Do not be visible or seen by the ticket agent. Blend in with the crowd. Have them bring you the tickets. Do what you normally do for me. Be careful. Then walk across the street to Chinatown, find a cab and return. If they are hungry, buy them lunch in Chinatown if they and/or you wish. As usual, tell them nothing. If you must, tell them you are just helping a friend. After you are back, call me and leave a message with Greg and say done. If there is a problem of any kind, call me on my talk and toss; here's the number." She wrote the number on the back of one of her cards and gave it to him. She removed a roll of Benjys from her shoulder bag contained in a flexible band with diamonds attached. She peeled off layers of bills and said, "This five hundred is for you. This additional should be more than enough for the two imposters, train tickets, food and taxi fare back here. Thank you. Be careful, as usual. I do not want to lose you, my friend."

Mariah returned to her room. She tapped the code again and Sean opened the door. Lillian sat in a chair with her right hand in her shoulder bag and on Mr. Glock and his wife, Ms. Suppressor, and the love of his life. The piece was still inside the bag but pointed directly at Mariah at all times.

"Alright, Sean, Lillian, pick up all your things. Leave nothing behind. No waste either, if there is any. Follow me."

They left Mariah's room in the ghetto castle and took the elevator to the tenth floor. They got off and followed Mariah to room 1012. She opened the door, went in, and they followed. She then opened the connecting door to 1010 and 1014. "We will use 1012, this middle room, for talking. You two may have either room for sleeping, and then I will take the other."

Sean and Lillian walked through the newly remodeled and refurbished rooms. They were cheery and were furnished in earth tones. Plenty of light came through the east windows. The clean sheers and curtains that covered the windows were in good taste. The furniture in each room was overstuffed and of good quality.

Lillian and Sean chose room 1014. "Here is the key to 1014. If you need two keys, here take this one to 1012, and I will sleep in 1010 temporarily until I can move you two to a safe location. Please make yourselves comfortable. I am going to call a friend and arrange for passage and safety. I will be right back. She went to 1010.

Mariah removed her talk and toss from her shoulder bag. She punched in the appropriates, pushed send and heard it ringing. The ringing stopped, no one said hello, nor did she expect it. "I need some help. Are you, a couple of friends with the necessaries and the safe house available for some personal attention for two people?"

"Yes, of course. For you, whatever. When?" He asked with a low voice.

"How soon can you be here?"

"Tomorrow morning at daybreak, if nothing unusual happens."

"Tomorrow at daybreak it is. Thank you. The pickup will be the usual place?"

"Absolutely. You embarrass me when you thank me. I owe you big time already. I can never repay."

"Just being considerate and letting you know how much I appreciate the help."

"You're welcome." They disconnected.

Mariah returned to the center room where they waited. "Do not unpack completely. You will be leaving at dawn tomorrow morning. Be prepared. Now we can talk."

The three of them sat around the small desk in 1012 and put three chairs around it.

"I want you both to know something before you talk, because you will need to make a decision. I have been hired by Jonathan P. Kennington to find Lillian. I have been hired by Robert B. Harrison to find Sean. Though I must admit, I believe Robert is more interested in finding Lillian than he is you. As you can see, depending on what you want me to do, I may have a conflict of interest. In both cases, I have agreed to find you. If I do and you wish to return to your respective homes, I am to provide transportation if you need it, but no kidnapping. If you do not want to return home, I am to inform them of your whereabouts, but *only* if you wish. So, now I have found you both. Do either one of you wish to go home?"

"No," they said a cappella.

"Do you wish for me to inform my employers where you are?"

"No." They stared into Mariah's eyes with conviction when they said it.

"Now that I have your answers, I have earned my fees and my obligation to them has ended, except for informing each of your decisions, which I will do.

"Sean, Geoffrey MacIntosh, my investigator who was formerly with the National Security Agency and a computer wizard the likes of which no one has ever seen, found your location in Los Angeles ten seconds after you swiped your card at the supermarket. Why would you do such a thing under your circumstances?"

"Stupidity. Stopped thinking for a nanosecond. I did not plan ahead."

"If we are to go forward, may I count on you sending your stupidity on vacation in some far-off exotic land with a one-way ticket, so it will fall in love with a native girl called Think, marry her and stay forever? These people who are after you will do anything, and I *do* mean *anything* to get what they want."

"I guarantee it."

"Thank you. So, do you want my help?" Mariah asked.

"I do," Sean said. "My father had said you could be trusted and you cared.

Considering he is a politician, it might be the only honest thing he said."

"I do, too," Lillian said. "I believe we've a serious problem here, and I need guidance and help." Lillian opened the Victorinox and removed a manila folder labeled "Personal." She gave it to Mariah. In the folder, there was an agreement titled "War Plan" signed by the president and J.P. The agreement called for J.P.'s chemical company to develop a colorless, odorless poisonous gas that had no antidote. The gas would be used to kill thousands of poor black Americans. The blame would be placed on terrorists from the Middle East country J.P. decided to have the U.S. invade and conquer for the purpose of his and the president's financial interests. Mariah finished reading it.

Lillian said, "J.P. wished to expand his oil holdings. The president can actually go to war if the U.S. has been attacked or is in imminent danger of being attacked with an executive order. This would be such an attack, and he'd get the CIA to confirm the terrorists were from whatever country Robert was told to select by Kennington. J.P. and James McDonald, the vice president, suggested this plan and the president signed off on it. The war would bring more profits to J.P.'s defense firm. J.P. and his wealthy friends wouldn't help the president get re-elected unless the president signed the agreement. The plan's good for all three of them, only if the president's re-elected."

Sean said, "I have read it, and I cannot believe my father would do such a thing. I can see why he did. He is down in polls, wants another term and needs a dramatic event. His political advisor, Richard Rigor, had told him he would not get re-elected unless he had a war."

Mariah was incensed when she saw it, sat in silence and contemplated what she should do. "I have both their signatures on the two fee agreements they signed. These look genuine."

"My father's signature is."

"I agree. It's J.P.'s for sure." Lillian said with sincere and deep concern, "Kennington is obsessed with putting another zero on his financial statement and being the richest man in the world, no matter how he does it or how many people have to die for his benefit."

Sean got up from the desk and went into 1014's bedroom, the one he and Lillian were going to share. He closed the door and went into the bathroom.

Lillian grabbed two folders from the Victorinox with speed. One was labeled "Lillian McGraw" and the other "Lillian McGraw Harrison" and gave them to Mariah. "Please read these now on a confidential basis and give them back to me. Sean knows nothing about this, and this is another problem I need for you to help me solve."

Mariah read the contents of the folders including the Paternal DNA Reports and handed the folders back to Lillian and said, "So, J.P. is your father by Victoria Kennington. Victoria is the daughter of J.P. and the then sixteen-year old Lillian McGraw before she married Robert. He probably does not know about Victoria either. You are pregnant thirteen weeks plus and the president is the father. You are also the granddaughter of Lillian McGraw Harrison, the president's wife. And the final is: J.P. is the father of Sean and the mother is the president's wife, Lillian McGraw Harrison. I wonder if the president knows? I am sure Ms. Harrison does, but may be in denial and never had a DNA done because she did not want to know the truth. And, if she did, never told Robert."

"No, she's not in denial. Everything else is true. I've the VHS tape of J.P. and Lillian McGraw Harrison having consensual sex so she could try and get pregnant. The date and time are there and date of birth of Sean coincides with the sexual activity of J.P. and Ms. Harrison."

"I am going to need the Wisdom of Solomon to solve this collection. Also, I believe I am getting a headache from the complications of these circumstances and the solutions, figuratively speaking. There are so many unknowns, I cannot count that high. What do you want to do about it?"

Lillian put the folders back into the Victorinox, turned the combination wheels and locked it. "I'd like to get an abortion without Sean finding out about it. The question is: What can *you* do about it?"

"There are free clinics here. They will do it for you without any cost or obligation. I know the doctor, and there will be no record if this is what you want."

"I need to resolve this pregnancy situation someway before I start to show. I paid six hundred dollars for the DNA report. There were three candidates for fatherhood. I gave the lab the chewing gum the president discarded in order for them to determine the father. I used a tissue from one of the men who blew his nose into it and a bandage with blood on it from the other. J.P. doesn't know I'm pregnant. If he finds out it's the president's, he'll have an additional way to extort him for his financial benefit. This is the way it works.

"J.P. was using me as a call girl. When he needed a contract or something done he couldn't get done the normal legal way, he'd use me to set up a honey trap with the decision-maker. It was at the estate; a special bedroom with audio-video recording capabilities. He'd give a party and invite the target. The targets were government officials, members of the military and defense department or anyone else he needed to extort to get what he wanted. I'd inveigle the target into the bedroom. All one had to do to start and stop the recording was to push a button behind the night stand.

"So, there was a possibility three men could've made me pregnant. Then J.P. would have the DVDs to extort the targets and get what he wanted. I took the digital recordings, downloaded them to DVDs and placed them on a dedicated computer that I controlled. Then I put the DVDs in the vault. The targets never knew I was working for J.P. or was his daughter and Lillian McGraw Harrison, the president's wife's granddaughter. No one but J.P., you, and I know I'm his daughter. Even my mother, Victoria, doesn't know in her mental state. I've the three DVDs, the rest of the DVDs, VHSs and all the computer data with incriminating documentation. I downloaded it all from the computers, the server, and it's on my laptop. All of those sexual encounters with married men, evangelicals, archbishops and other vulnerable men and women were captured by digital recordings and put on DVDs. Then I scrubbed the files from the hard drive. Now J.P. no longer has access to any of the extortion materials.

"I also took all of the manila folders that are incriminating to J.P. With the information I have, he could go to prison and at his age die there. I also took all the cash in the vault. Now, you know it all."

"You realize stealing from J.P., daughter or not, is a crime, a felony?"

"Yes."

"Why would you be willing to be a 'call girl' as you call it? So, what do you want to do?"

It was not a pretty story. When she was little and weak, life was not easy, and she wasn't able to do what she wanted. J.P. forced her into sexual relations with him at age thirteen. He raped her the first time. Then after that, he had sex with her at his convenience. After a while it made no difference. When she was eighteen or nineteen, he lost interest in having sex with her because she was no longer a young girl. It's amazing how the human being can adjust to adverse circumstances. One day she decided to get even. She was still thirteen at the time. Lillian waited twelve years before she was ready to get even. She learned all about him and his businesses and didn't believe he knew anything she didn't. Lillian had the ability to retrieve anything from any of his companies' computers worldwide without leaving a trace of her penetration.

"I want to remove him from all of his wealth and power, then send him to prison, make him homeless and set him adrift for all of the evil he has done to others. And, now he's descended into the deepest form of infamy; he's conspired to commit treason and murder with the president. We must stop this plot, expose them and have the president resign. If he won't, impeachment, conviction by the Senate, and then have them both sent to prison. This is what I want.

"Money and power are the only two things he loves. He doesn't love me. Can you imagine a loving father turning his daughter into a prostitute, for that is what I was? To be a prostitute, you need to receive a financial benefit. Mine was retribution, board, room and a business education no Harvard Business School could ever teach. Then I want to take over all of J.P.'s businesses and run them legitimately."

"I do believe I have seen some tall orders in my life, but this may be walking up Mount Everest backward," Mariah said.

Sean returned to the room, sat at the desk and asked, "What is a tall order?"

"Doing what the two of you want to do: stop J.P. and the president from committing treason and murder," Mariah said. She looked at Lillian with a look that told her that her secrets were safe with her. Lillian responded with a slight nod not seen by Sean.

Mariah told them it was her belief they were going to be involved with people who would do bad things to good people. No J.P. Kennington or a Robert B. Harrison, president of the United States of America, the most powerful nation on this planet, was going to allow three nobodies to interfere with their apparent plans. They would put them into a meat grinder at some sausage-making plant and some pigs would eat them if they were lucky. Unless, of course the plants did what they normally did and that was to make sausage with meat they knew was contaminated and sold it to the unsuspecting suckers, called customers.

She explained the war plan may be just another step in putting together a One World Order. Who knew? She didn't for sure. The three of them decided to quit for the day, took the rest of the day off and contemplated the grave considerations of the future. Mariah told them the questions they should ask themselves were: Did they want to risk their lives, because this was what they were going to be doing? Next, did they want her to help them?

Mariah told them she was forty years old and had peace of mind. Which meant: she had no fear of dying, controlled her desires, and her desires did not control her. But they were young. She provided them with the reality of the quest. If they wanted to go forward, they should do so with the understanding one or both of them were going to die. Their opponents didn't kill and leave. No funerals. They would disappear in a stripper vat of sulfuric acid in a chrome-plating plant, be turned into dog food or thrown into a pig's sty. Friends and relatives wouldn't know if they had eloped, gone to some exotic island for the rest of their lives, hid out in a monastery or something else they did voluntarily. No one would look for them. Friends and loved ones would wait to hear from them.

Mariah told them she inferred from the expressions on J.P.'s face, his delivery and the same with the president when she met with them, neither had any interest in getting Lillian or Sean back alive. Maybe Sean's mother or grandmother did, but Robert did not.

Mariah believed J.P. and Robert lied to her. When she had asked J.P. if there was anything missing and she had mentioned a list of possibilities, he had looked at her and had said no. She knew he had lied.

"I assume, Lillian, you took it all. Right?" Mariah looked at her.

"Sure did, I have it all."

"Robert will arrive at desperation shortly. Desperate people make poor judgments. I believe right after I see him, if you want me to help you, he will find someone to find you two and the materials. The person he hires will not be a humanitarian, have no interest in the Albert Schweitzer Humanitarian Award, and no interest in leaving you two alive.

"J.P. on the other hand is just your normal, ruthless modern-day robber baron who will stop at nothing to get what he wants, because he believes he's above the law. His ruthlessness makes the robber barons of the U.S. in the past look like children playing in a sandbox.

"I want you two to sleep on it. Tell me in the morning your every wish and desire. If you decide to do so, do you want me to help you?"

"If we do want your help, what would you charge us?" Lillian asked.

Mariah smiled and sat for a moment and said, "I haven't given it any thought. I have been too occupied with the quest, the monumental task and trying to decide if I'm the right person to help you. If you decide to go forward and you want me to help, I will need to talk to you both and then with your help put together a plan. I don't know the answer to your fee question at this moment. I too need to think about it overnight. Let us talk in the morning after you have decided, if you have. Remember, dawn is the moment."

# 11

## Day 6  The Brighton Hotel, Los Angeles

First light had not started to light or warm room 1012. Sean and Lillian sat and waited for Mariah in two of the chairs at the desk. She walked in and asked, "Well?"

"I have," Sean said. "I do not wish to return to the White House. I am ashamed to bear his name. I will make peace with my mother somehow, ask for her forgiveness and live with her answer. But, I think she will understand. I am sure she does not know about his treachery. Speaking for me only, I would like your help."

"I agree," Lillian said.

"The legal fee's going to be one dollar. You each will need to sign my fee agreement; the bar association requires it." Mariah filled the blanks in her printed fee agreements; they signed their respective ones and each gave her a dollar. "I am now your attorney. I can now have in my possession all of your materials and anything you say to me will be protected by the attorney-client privilege.

"If we were in the military, they would call our uncertainties fluid. Which means chaotic, unstable, and we do not know what we are doing. So, I'm going to suggest I stir the pot. I'm going to see the president and then J.P. I'm going to tell them what we have agreed.

"First, I intend to tell Harrison I have found Sean, Kennington I have found Lillian and neither of you wish to return. Second, I have discovered the 'War Plan', and I do not want them to go forward with it. I probably should wear earplugs. Their laughter will be so loud, it will hurt my ears. When they stop laughing long enough to speak, they might say so what, and what are you going to do about it? Or, threaten me. I want to see if I can put a stop to this insanity of gassing innocent Americans to go to war illegally for profit, like the previous administration did in the Middle East. Let's see what they do." *I will not be telling anyone what I can do about it. For now, it'll be my secret if they don't cease and desist this insanity.*

"Next, while you're driving to this new location, please do not speak about anything except the beautiful weather, how green is my valley and the latest movie you have seen. This is all that is alright but nothing else. No holding hands, no show of affection. We're on a need-to-know basis and these people at this moment have no need to know. All they are supposed to do is house you in pleasant surroundings, gourmet food and see that you do not die or leave the premises unwillingly. Like all things, they will assume they know. No reason to confirm their suspicions, right?"

"Right," they said.

"They will not know your names. Get used to any two new names you want, but do not use your names. The probability is: None of these people will know who you are. If they find out, I will worry about it. Having said this, please give me anything that has your name on it or any means of identifying you. Keep the cash you have. Give me all of the documents, VHSs and DVDs. Put everything I have asked for in the Victorinox and give it and the combination to me. I need us to prepare for our trips. How much money do you want to take out of here?"

"I'll take a thousand." Lillian slipped it from a package of ten thousand.

"When my friend and your protectors arrive, we will be going out the back door. There will be two SUVs there. They will be specially made and armored. They will be dropping me off at a location and then taking the two of you to your new home for the duration until our plan has come to fruition. Then, I am going to see the president first. When I return, I will see J.P. Then I will meet you two in your pleasant surroundings. Be vigilant. Here, Lillian, I will not need your friend with the suppressor and the ammunition. You keep it, you may need it, but if all goes well you won't. There's first light, let's leave."

The three of them went down the back stairs, out the back door of the Brighton and into the waiting SUVs. No acknowledgements were made, no amenities exchanged.

# 12

**Day 7   6:30 A.M.   JPMorgan Chase Bank, Los Angeles**

Mariah and Harry Burstein, the manager of the branch, sat in his office.

"Good to see you, Harry. Thank you for the accommodation. I know it is very early, but I need your help."

"Good to see you, Mariah. The only complaint I have is: I don't get to see you often enough. Everything you asked for is ready, and he's in the next office waiting."

"Thank you, and thank you again for all of the financial information you gave me on J.P."

"Glad to do it. I owe you." Harry escorted her through a door and seated at the table was her handwriting expert, William C. Morse, who had recently retired from the CIA.

"Hello, Bill, thank you for coming."

"You look great, Mariah. Still hot. How do you do it?"

"Doing good things for good people and doing bad things to people who do bad things to good people." They laughed.

"That's what I hear. You're my hero."

"Thank you for the compliment. Here's my fee agreement with Kennington. I saw him sign this in my presence. Here's my fee agreement with Harrison, and I saw him sign it in my presence. Now, I am going to give you a document. There are two signatures at the bottom which are purported to be those of Kennington and Harrison. I want you to see if this document was signed by Kennington and Harrison, or are the signatures or one of them a forgery. It's important you don't see the contents of the document. So, I am going to fold it and ask you for your expert opinion. When you are finished if the signatures on the document are genuine, I want you to sign this opinion document I have prepared and Harry will have a notary verify your signature. Is this agreeable?"

"Yes, of course."

She gave him the two-fee agreements and the folded "War Plan" document. He examined them with his equipment and said, "There's no doubt. The same person signed Robert B. Harrison on both documents, and the same person signed Jonathan P. Kennington on both documents. Give me the document you want me to sign."

Mariah asked Harry to come in to notarize Bill's signature. He read it and signed it. Harry notarized it and left.

"Thank you, Bill. Here is your fee. Sorry about the cash." They laughed, and he left.

Mariah took the VHS tape of J.P. having sexual relations with Ms. Lillian McGraw Harrison and put it into the duplicator Harry had provided. She left the room and went into Harry's office and asked, "Would you please step in, Harry?"

Harry came into the office where she and William had been and the VHS was duplicated. She removed the original and the duplicate and put them into the Victorinox. "Harry, I have some birth certificates and some Paternal DNA Reports. I am going to make copies of them in here on the copy machine in your presence. You will look at each document before I copy it and then check it against the duplicate, and as I mentioned to you yesterday you will certify for me they are true and accurate copies. What you see will be between the two of us only."

"Sure."

Mariah copied the birth certificate of Sean Harrison that showed Robert B. Harrison was the father and Ms. Lillian McGraw Harrison was the mother. Then she copied the Paternal DNA Report of Sean Harrison which showed Jonathan P. Kennington was the father and Ms. Lillian McGraw Harrison was the mother. She placed the original and the copy on the table.

She followed the same procedure with the Paternal DNA Report of Lillian McGraw demonstrating that Robert B. Harrison was the father of her unborn child. Harry examined the originals and the copies, rubber-stamped the copies on the back guaranteeing they were true and exact copies, and then signed his name to the guarantees.

She picked up the original VHS, the original documents she copied and returned them to the Victorinox. She put the VHS copy and the copies of the documents into a nine-by-twelve manila envelope and put the envelope into her shoulder bag. "Now, Harry, I need to visit a new, anonymous, unregistered large safe-deposit box that does not exist. I want to empty the contents of this bag into it."

"I have arranged it for you. I have the key. It isn't rented and won't be; also, I've taken it out of the computer." They went into the Safe Deposit section. He opened the door and removed the box for her. They walked to a cubicle, and he left her alone with it. She emptied the contents of the Victorinox into the box and returned it.

"Thank you, Harry. This envelope has instructions regarding the distribution of the contents of the box to be carried out in case of my death."

"I don't want to lose you, but I'll do as you ask."

"I do not want to lose me, either." She left the bank, got a cab and went to the airport for her flight to Washington, D.C.

# 13

## Day 8   10:00 A.M.   The White House, the Oval Office

*Divide and conquer, breed dissension and make my small contribution to public service.* Mariah sat on the sofa to the president's right, where she had sat previously. He sat in the chair on the right near her. She put her open shoulder bag on her left and between her and the sofa's armrest. She reached into the bag and activated her digital recorder. She pulled out her handkerchief, feigned a sniffle, dabbed her nose and replaced her handkerchief into her bag.

Mariah showed the president a guaranteed copy of the "War Plan" signed by Harry Burstein, her banker. He looked at it for a second and placed it between them on the coffee table.

"So, you found Lillian McGraw? And your banker saw the document and signed the guarantee?"

"Yes he did. But he is not a politician, and he can be trusted. You mean did I find 'that woman' and incidentally Sean? Yes, I did. He does not wish to return."

"Where is he? I'll send his Secret Service detail to bring him home."

"I don't believe you heard me, or you did not read my contract with you. He doesn't want to return, and I have no obligation to give you his whereabouts, assuming I know where he is at this time. The terms and conditions of our contract have been fulfilled, and I am no longer your attorney. I am now representing Sean. I am also here to tell you I am here as a U.S. citizen trying to bring some sanity into the life of the president and this administration.

"You have conspired to commit treason and murder. I want you to know I had the best handwriting expert compare the signature on this 'War Plan' document with your signature on my fee agreement you signed, and they are signed by the same person, you. Also, the expert compared the signature of Jonathan P. Kennington with a known signature of his, and this is his signature beside yours at the bottom of this document.

"Robert what has happened to you? Here's the signature of the expert witness on the document verifying the signatures are genuine. The expert's signature has been guaranteed by the bank. What are you going to do about this so I don't have to? So, please do not deny you did not conspire with Kennington to commit treason and murder for your joint financial gain and to keep the power you have by being re-elected.

"Do you believe erroneously like the marionette, George W. Bush, and his puppeteer, Cheney, and Richard Nixon when he said, 'When the president does it, that means it is not illegal.' So far, Bush and Cheney have not been indicted and prosecuted for going to war illegally in Iraq so Bush could be re-elected. Congress and the media just rolled over and put four paws in the air, but this could change with a new president. Also, hopefully some justice-minded state attorney general or county district attorney will indict the two of them for the murder of military personnel from their state or county. For murder is what they committed."

Mariah gave the president a bank guaranteed copy of the Paternal DNA Report designating him the father of the unborn child Lillian McGraw carried. He read it and looked back at Mariah and she said, "Congratulations, Robert, you are going to be a father. You must be very proud. I guess you showed all those friends of yours who thought you could not take care of business."

"I want a second opinion."

"You *are* the father of Lillian McGraw's child. This is your second opinion. I have a DVD with me showing you and Lillian having sexual intercourse. You attended one of J.P.'s parties in Bel Air, went into one of the bedrooms and performed for the world to see. Do you want to watch it? You are the male lead, a star. I call it the 'President Does Lillian'. Also, you had sex with her on other occasions which are documented. Let us get on with it."

"No, I mean I want her to go to my doctor, and I don't want to watch it."

"Robert, you've just insulted me. How dumb do you think I am? You should not judge other people by yourself. Just because *you* cannot chew gum and walk at the same time, because you played too many football games without a helmet does not mean I am in the same condition. I am not going to allow you to isolate her with a doctor of your choice. You want her to go to your doctor not to get a third opinion which will be the same as the first opinion and my second. You just want her to show up at your doctor's office so your goons can pick her up and have her disappear. But the documents proving your paternity will be available even if she disappears or dies not by accident or natural causes. And of course, your audition DVD as a porn star will live on, and on, and on."

"Politics is a dirty game and a lot of bad people are going to be upset if you meddle with their financial plans and potential profits. I think I made a mistake in hiring you. I knew you were independent, but I didn't realize you wouldn't do just what I asked. We'll have angry special interests which will find your conduct unacceptable and wish to take matters into their own hands. And, I'll not be able to help you. These are men and women who are driven by greed only. They have no other god and aren't Bible thumpers, not even Deists."

"I will assume that is not an oblique threat to my life. Is this correct? But a direct one, right?"

"I can't control the actions of others."

"You can, but you do not want to. Their will is J.P.'s and your salvation for re-election. Just do not tell them. Don't go forward with this treason and murder, and do not sign an executive order to go to war at a time and place of J.P. Kennington's direction by having the CIA use forged or fabricated intelligence like they did during the Cheney administration. The previous president and his cabal should have been prosecuted for conspiracy to commit murder of our military personnel and the civilians in Iraq and other crimes.

"Next, what are you going to do about your son Lillian is carrying, for it is a son. It has been verified by her obstetrician. Should I have her give birth, bring it to the White House for TLC? Have your wife take care of it?"

Without hesitation he said, "I don't think that's funny."

"Then tell me something that is not funny."

"I want her to have an abortion immediately."

"But she loves you and wants your child desperately. She does *not* want an abortion. She is already fourteen weeks pregnant." *There is nothing wrong with providing disinformation to the dishonest among us. But this will not erase the fact that you are the father of this child, and I have the records to prove it.*

"I don't give a fuck what she wants, this is what I want," he said with anger. "I'm the president, and what I want, I get."

"Very well, Robert. Knowing how pleased you would be, I had prepared a document for your signature. It basically says you acknowledge you are the father of her unborn child. You waive your right to have an additional Paternal DNA Report done. You agree to pay to me five hundred thousand dollars on signing. This money will go into my trust account and will be disbursed to her. Next, I will set up a trust over which I have control for her benefit, so she will receive the sum of two hundred and fifty thousand dollars a year for twenty-one years. She in turn will have an abortion immediately upon my receiving good funds into my trust account in the amount of $5,750,000. So, if you will give me a check now for that amount, sign and date this document I have prepared, you can have this matter behind you, and it will be your little secret. Also, I want you to know I only charged her a dollar as a legal fee. You must make up the difference, two hundred and forty nine thousand." She handed the document to him.

He read the brief agreement and asked, "How do I know I can trust the two of you?"

"Trust *me?* You are the wrong person to be asking a question that involves integrity, moral sense and the word trust. Sign it or read about it on the front page of the New York Times and the Washington Post in the morning; your choice. I can see it now: a photograph of your choice which I will take with me to the Times and Post alongside hers and the full story of your adultery and collusion with J.P. to commit murder and treason."

Robert signed, dated the agreement and gave her the two checks for the full amounts.

"Thank you, Mr. President. May I use your VHS player?"

"Why?"

"I want to show you something that may be of interest to you."

"Oh, alright."

She put in the copy of the VHS tape that showed J.P. having sexual relations with his wife and pressed the Play button. Robert leaned forward, stood, went to the monitor and stared at it.

"Recognize the participants, the date and time of the consensual sex between your wife and J.P.?"

"Yes, what the fuck!" He sat back down and watched the tape to the end. He looked at her and asked, "Who's Victoria?"

"She is your wife's daughter with J.P. when she was sixteen. Her name is Victoria Kennington, the mother and sister of Lillian as a result of J.P.'s incestuous relationship with Victoria. Were you aware that Lillian was J.P.'s daughter? And J.P. is a pedophile?"

"What? You mean he put his own daughter into a conspiracy to extort me?"

"Yes."

"I thought she was a virgin. She didn't tell me this. J.P pretended all these years to be my friend, but all along he was laughing behind my back and using my office for financial gain."

"Spare me, Robert. If your wife was the love of your life, why were you having extramarital sexual relations? You gained financially when he gained as a result of his bribes to you. He gave you millions for your assistance with government defense contracts. I have the records to prove it."

Mariah rose from the sofa, removed the tape and replaced it into her shoulder bag. "Here, look at this." She handed him a bank guaranteed copy of Sean Harrison's birth certificate. Then she showed him the Paternal DNA Report designating J.P. as the father of Sean Harrison and the mother Lillian McGraw Harrison. Robert sat in stunned silence.

"J.P. has cuckolded and suckered you into doing his bidding like every other marionette he has. He's a master puppeteer. You and the previous president will go down as the worst presidents in the history of the U.S. What are you now going to do about the cease and desist of J.P.'s 'War Plan'? For your peace of mind and my safe passage to the world beyond, what I have shown you today are just copies. The original of all this material and other which prove your treason, attempted murder, selling of the office of the president and other crimes are in a safe place that only *I* control. I know you cannot control others, but I suggest you do. You must tell them about reality. If you go down, they will go down."

"Please help me."

"What do you suggest?"

"Somehow get rid of J.P., J.P.'s ability to manipulate me, and replace all the money he's going to give me for my re-election campaign."

"Robert, you are beyond help and redemption. He is no longer in possession of any DVDs or VHSs to extort you. You can help yourself by getting some spine, stand up and be a patriot for a change instead of an embarrassment to yourself and the nation. Resign and force the vice president to do the same  I will await your answers until tomorrow morning before noon. If you do not call me by then, I will believe you and the vice president are going forward with the 'War Plan' and are not going to resign. Your conscience and moral sense are elastic, malleable and adjustable to fit your benefit — financially speaking of course and this includes the vice president, McDonald."

She rose from the sofa, left him sitting there with his head hung down and resting in his hands. She left his office and turned off the recorder. *Did I do all I could? I hope so. Maybe, I have separated the twins, and they will defeat one another. I sowed dissension. If they do not comply, I for sure will defeat them, with a little help from my friends.*

# 14

**Day 8   3:00 P.M.   The White House, the Oval Office**

The president called J.P. on the phone. "I know you sleep late so I waited. I want to talk to you about fucking my wife when she was only fifteen, and a child by her named Victoria Kennington before I married her when she was only sixteen, you pedophile. And, sex with my wife when we were married and your son Sean with her. Now I know why my wife was always urging me to go along with your positions on the different issues, whatever they might have been. Extorting her too, J.P.?

"I thought you were my friend. Obviously, you're not. I'm just calling you to let you know that you can't expect any consideration from me in any area at any time. As far as I'm concerned, our 'War Plan' is off. I'm not going forward with you."

"Well, Robert, if that's the way you feel about it. It's alright with me. Sorry you feel this way."

"Also, J.P., I'm tired of you using me and laughing behind my back. You cuckolded me. You set me up with that Lillian McGraw woman, she got pregnant so you could extort me. And then I got extorted by her attorney. You used your own daughter as a prostitute — from an incestuous relationship to set me up. You're lower than a street pimp; even those scumbags don't use their own daughters. I finally see you for what you are. You're lower than a drug dealer or a politician. The way I look at our relationship is: You're getting everything you want, but that has come to an end. Now that all of the DVDs and VHSs have disappeared, I don't see that you have any hold on me at all. The fact is: I think you're impotent."

"Who told you all the DVDs have disappeared. What does that mean?"

"Your man Jones told me Lillian was missing and some important materials too. So, the DVD with Lillian and me doing it has disappeared and you can no longer extort me." *Unfortunately, Mariah has got all the documents to prove I made her pregnant, but J.P. doesn't know this.*

"Again, Robert, I'm sorry you feel that way. I've always admired you."

"That's bullshit and you know it, J.P. The only thing you admire about me is what I can do for you."

"But the 'War Plan' is essential to you getting re-elected. You know, like George W. Bush. Karl Rove told him the only way he could be re-elected is if he went to war in Iraq. So Bush did illegally."

"In the beginning, that's what I thought. But now, I've learned from W I know I can get my director of the CIA to give me any excuse I want, like Cheney and Libby did for W with Tenet. They'll just fabricate or used forged documents as an excuse that says the U.S. is in imminent danger of being attacked, whether it is or not. Imminent being in the mind of the beholder, me. And I'll pick the Middle East country instead of you. My friends'll get rich instead of you and yours. Just wanted to let you know you're not calling the shots anymore. And don't count on any more government contracts from the Department of Defense. We'll see how much longer your financial empire'll stay together without being on the dole from my administration and the DoD.

"Also, I'm having the FDA look into your pharmaceutical company because you've been bribing doctors to use your medications that have been approved but for treatments of problems that have not been approved. Your company knowingly sold cheap-prescription drugs you had made in China, knew they were tainted and are killing Americans. I'm going to refer the matter to the U.S. attorney general's office for consideration for criminal action. I'm going to put an end to this business where pharmaceutical companies just pay fines for misconduct and prosecute a few CEOs, one of which will be you, asshole, for the crimes committed. Have a good day, J.P."

# 15

**Day 9   9:00 A.M.   The White House, the Oval Office**

Robert B. Harrison sat behind the Lincoln and Tom Jones sat in a visitor's chair in front. Jones had reached into his right-hand coat pocket and activated his digital recorder before he had walked in. It was connected to a wireless microphone pinned to the back of the left lapel of his suit coat.

"Thank you for coming, Mr. Jones. When you were here last and before you gave me your card with your telephone number, you alluded to the fact you had some people. Let me see now. You said something about, 'final solution', 'discreet people who operate on a need-to-know basis', 'exceptional skills' and 'how a good illusionist can make a person disappear without a trace.' Does this sum it up?"

"Yes."

"Are these accommodations still available and reliable?"

"Yes."

"I believe a matter of national security has presented itself, and I need someone with special skills to handle the situation. My administration will be grateful to have a patriot like you handle this delicate matter. I'm going to authorize you to see if you can help your country — with discretion and anonymity. Are you up for this challenge?"

"Sure am."

"Do you know a woman by the name of Mariah O'Leary?"

"Yeah, sure do unfortunately."

"Do you know a woman by the name of Lillian McGraw?"

"Yeah. Her, too."

"Do you know a young man by the name of Sean Harrison? He's no relation to me."

"No, sir, I don't."

"Well, one of these three people I believe has in their possession a top-secret code word document labeled 'War Plan' that has been stolen and needs to be returned to *me personally* and no one else. Do you understand this? Also, there are other materials that were stolen from J.P. by Lillian McGraw. I want them all returned to me personally also. Do you understand, *to me personally?*"

"Yes, sir, I do understand."

"If in the process of getting the document and J.P.'s materials anyone or all three of these people happen to meet their maker, that would be alright with me. If I were you, I'd start with the attorney O'Leary. I believe she has all the documents and other materials under her control. Do you understand me, Mr. Jones?"

"Yes, I do. And, how grateful is the United States Government going to be, monetarily speaking of course, to this patriot for this great service to its national security?"

"This is of such secrecy, I'm not telling anyone but you. You'll need to tell me the cost and then I'll arrange the money. You understand that no payment of any kind can be made until the matter has been brought to a successful conclusion. That's the delivery to me of the original document and J.P.'s materials. Also, if they're in possession of any other documents or materials that might be harmful to my administration, to me, or our country, I'd be pleased to pay a bonus for those materials. What would be your fee for handling this situation?"

"To get the document, other materials and return them to you — considering the sensitivity of the matter two million. For each person who's no longer with us, let's say five hundred thousand each. So, if the worst took place, three million five hundred."

"That'll be satisfactory. Thank you for coming and please keep me posted. And, try to get this concluded at your very earliest convenience."

"I'll need an executive order to act on your behalf."

"That and the money'll be available to you when you return with the document and the other materials."

"Thank you, Mr. President."

Jones left the Oval Office and turned off his recorder.

# 16

**Day 10  The Prague Castle, Prague, Czech Republic**

Two men had signed the Strategic Arms Reduction Treaty (START). Then they spoke to a full hall about their agreed position on Iran and the need for the United Nations to move toward stiffer sanctions. The ceremony ended. The guests, members of the media and security people had left. They sat alone in the massive hall. One was in a black lounge suit, white shirt and red-striped tie and the other a blue lounge suit, blue shirt and a blue tie. They were about the same age. Each sat in an upholstered-high-back chair with partial upholstered armrests. The maroon pattern was in good taste, and the exposed wooden portions of the chairs' frames were carved and stained a light off-white. The left armrest of the man on the left and the right-front side of the armrest of the man on the right were at an angle which allowed them to talk sotto voce and look at one another.

The man on the right said, "You and I've a mutual problem, Islamic extremists, fundamentalists and terrorists. They even kill Islamic moderates, their own people. You fought the Muslims in Afghanistan. I've been supporting Russia's Islamic war in Chechnya, Dagestan, Kabardino-Balkaria, North Ossetia, and Tatarstand. This is so, even though your country's responsible for killing all of the Islamic hostage takers, 41, and the hostages, 129 of the 800, at the Dubrovka Theater just down the street with fentanyl gas. The international community with my lead seemed to rationalize the situation as justified, and therefore, no outcry for the benefit of Chechnya's independence. At your request, I had the State Department declare three of the Chechen organizations terrorists to prevent their being able to finance their activities from the U.S.

"This declaration, along with the backlash among the Chechen populations in Chechnya, Georgia, U.S. and other communities around the world is most important to you. This backlash'll prevent the terrorist organizations in Chechnya from gaining financial and political support for their misconduct. I could've gone the other way and supported the Chechens as separatists and nationalists. After all, your terrorist is another man's patriot, a freedom fighter and a nationalist.

"I, too, have a Muslim problem. Therefore, it's time for you to repay my decisions on your behalf. This is what I intend to do. I've been advised by Richard Rigor, my political advisor, I need to motivate the American public to support a war against Islamic religious extremism, terrorism. This can be done, he says, by arranging the deaths of thousands of Americans and blaming it on Muslims. Or, do what Bush did and have my CIA director use forged documents to justify a preemptive strike against Iraq.

"This'll allow me to declare war on any country or area that has religious extremists, terrorists, no matter the religion. But specifically Islam, the anti-Christ," Robert B. Harrison said, with conviction and dedication.

"Has Rigor suggested a target city and target in the city?" Petr Petrokov, president of Russia, inquired in English with a Russian accent without concern for the murders.

"Yes, he has. We've a white paper called National Vulnerabilities prepared by the Department of Homeland Security. It sets forth the cities and the targets in those cities that are the most vulnerable. I'm thinking about these cities and the parts of these cities with the highest concentration of poor blacks. This'll reduce welfare payments, crime, and prison populations substantially."

"There is no doubt you are the president of the Jingoism Society of the United States for the benefit of your financial interests and that of the military and industrial companies," Petrokov responded with a smile. "Do you believe killing just thousands of Americans will be sufficient?"

"Maybe, I don't know, but I'm told by Rigor that the answer is yes. If he's wrong and I need more motivation, I'll arrange more 'Muslim' attacks. You see, I've a cadre of Evangelicals, sheeples, who are unquestioning followers and they'll do what I ask when I ask. I give them money, bribes, for their faith-based organizations, and they deliver the consensus and the votes. Not my money; so I give them the taxpayer's money that's necessary."

"So, what do you want from me?"

"I want you to support me in The Final Solution to the Muslim Question with enthusiasm, vigor and without hesitation. This crusade will spread Christianity across the land, will accelerate the Tribulation, the second coming of Christ, and the guaranteed ascension of the true believers. I want you to get the countries in your sphere of influence to back this war, this is what I want. Is this agreeable to you?"

"Going to church doesn't make you a Christian the same as going to the kitchen doesn't make you a chef. Am I to understand you are mounting the Tenth Crusade, Milites Christi, Knights of Christ? Do you have a letter from the Pope and/or a letter from your religious king requesting this journey?" Petrokov asked and laughed at him with disrespect and sarcasm.

"No, I don't." Robert didn't realize he had been denigrated and continued as if he had been given a compliment. "But I've the backing of the televangelists who represent the moral majority, and this is enough for me to do what I want. If the citizens object or don't agree with me, I just brand them un-American or unpatri-otic. Also, I tell them, 'You're either with me or against me'.

"Why hell, I'm not even religious, but the suckers need to believe I am. So, I became apparently religious and aligned myself with the televangelist and the Evangelicals right after I found out there were thirty-two million of them as a part of the Moral Majority. The only thing I worship is money. Are you going to help me?"

"Yes, as long as you go to war against my terrorists also." Petrokov affirmed.

"I agree. Shall we have an accord prepared for our signatures?"

"Yes, I will appoint Andre Lunev, from the FSB, the Federal Security Service, as my liaison person with yours. He can be trusted implicitly. I will have him draft the accord for our signatures. Shall we call it The Prague Accord?"

"Yes, that'll be fine. I'll have him work with someone in the Department of Homeland Security. I'll take care of it when I return to Washington. There'll only be two copies. One for you and one for me, is this correct?"

"Yes. I see that neither one of us has learned that the only way to kill an idea is with a better idea, not with force. But we keep trying. What method are you going to use for the extermination of the black people you hate? For everybody knows you and your family are racists and anti-Semites too, with bigotry added for flavor."

"What do you suggest?"

Petrokov responded with a sadistic smile, "Tularemia. We have a laboratory in Obolensk, near Moscow, that can provide you with the formula. We will need to genetically engineer it differently if you want to target African Americans. For a price, of course, paid to me personally."

"Of course, paid to you personally." Robert smiled and knew he had been extorted. *At least when you deal cash to a politician you always get what you pay for.*

"Before we adjourn, Robert, I've always wanted to ask you why you take off your lounge-suit jacket and roll up your sleeves below the elbows when you visit blue-collar workers? Do you actually believe this transparent pretense leads the people to believe that you believe that you are one of them? Isn't this just another form of political dishonesty — acting, you know pretending to be one of them."

"I'm doing Abraham Lincoln. You know, 'You can fool some of the people all of the time, and all of the people some of the time, but you cannot fool all of the people all of the time'."

"Yes, but the question is: are you fooling anyone any time? Whenever I see you doing this, I laugh out loud. Americans must really be buffleheads to have elected you. We in the international community are always amazed at the people they elect in the U.S. The voting public, lemmings and sheep, is driven to slaughter by advertising and marketing.

"President Harrison, what is on your agenda for the Middle East and its oil reserves as a result of your Tenth Crusade?"

"President Petrokov, it's only to stop terrorism. The U.S. doesn't have any desire for a permanent presence in the Middle East. What about Russia?"

"My desire is your desire. I just want to stop religious extremism, religion–based violence, terrorism, caused by the fanatical Islamists in violation of the Quran."

# 17

## Day 10   1:00 P.M.   Raymond's Bar

Mariah returned to her office after depositing her check from Robert into her bank account and his other check for the benefit of Lillian into her trust account with her banker, Harry Burstein at JP Morgan Chase. Also, she had downloaded the recording from her digital recorder of her meeting with Robert to a CD, deposited it and the original of the agreement in her new, nonexistent safe-deposit box.

She sat in her booth. There were no other customers, but Greg was behind the bar doing what bartenders do when there are no customers. She had not heard from the president regarding the "War Plan" and her request for him to cease the implementation of it.

Mariah removed her cellular telephone she used for secure calls only from her shoulder bag which was on her right side. It had been prepared by her friend, Geoffrey MacIntosh, a former deputy director of NSA. He had done programming at MIT and the NSA. He was the best of the best, according to his peers.

"Good day to you. How are things in Glocca Morra?"

"All is well. No problems."

"I believe there is a lady there, and she is due at the pick-up location tomorrow at nine A.M. Is this good for you?"

"Yes."

"Thank you, even though you do not want me to say it."

"I don't mind. It's always good to be appreciated, and I know you do." He disconnected.

She called on her regular cell phone and made an appointment to see J.P.

Two new clients came in and needed some help. She arranged to help them without fees or expenses, they were grateful, and they left. She had lunch and considered going to the Brighton to overcome jet lag.

Jones walked in with two colleagues. The colleagues walked over and sat on two bar stools across from her booth, leaned their backs against the bar, put their elbows on it, feet on the foot rests and stared at her, not with admiration of her beauty. Jones sat opposite her in her booth, uninvited.

Mariah reached into her shoulder bag and activated her digital recorder. "Well, well it's the well-mannered Mr. Jones. Not a surprise to see you, Jones. What are you going to do for me this time, give me cancer? I see you brought two assistants to overcome your incompetence. Must be important."

"Listen, Smartass, my employer has asked me to retrieve some documents and other materials you have in your possession. So the sooner you give them to me, the sooner we can part and never enjoy one another's company again."

"What documents? Do they have a name?"

" 'War Plan' and all the others are described as having been stolen from J.P. and '. . . any other documents or materials that might be harmful to my administration, to me or our country'."

"So, you have switched allegiance, moved into the big time. You are now the gofer for Robert B., and you brought two assistant gofers to carry the heavy load of all those documents. They must weigh tons if you want '. . . any other documents or materials that might be harmful to my administration'. Do you have an eighteen-wheeler parked out front, a forklift, palettes and a properly licensed truck driver to handle it. Because the two sequoias, General Sherman and General Grant, you brought, do not look like driving trucks is in their line of work. Besides, their muscles are making the buttons and cloth on their cheeseball suits scream for mercy they fit so tightly. They could be arrested for torturing. Stretched to the max of technology, I'd say. Instead of tailors, maybe they should switch to tent makers. What would you say?"

"Are you going to give them to me, or am I going to have my two gentlemen colleagues remove you from here, take you to a non-vacation resort and spa and massage your body with a Little League aluminum ball bat until you do? When I'm through, even Greg won't recognize you."

"Unfortunately, Jones, you have arrived without an appointment, and I just have not got the time to assist you and enjoy your company. Maybe another time. In addition to this, I don't have any documents."

Jones nodded at the two barrel-chested symbols of American manhood from Gold's Gym and not finalists at the Mr. Universe competition who were having a bromance, a close platonic male friendship. They removed their elbows from the top of the bar and leaned forward to unload their obesities from their stools.

"Keep your seats, gentlemen, or I'll paint the inside of my bar. Clasp your hands on top of your heads," Greg said, with a southern accent and the authority of a former Special Forces officer who was lusting for an enemy combatant to disobey his order. Greg had a double-barreled. sawed-off shotgun pressed into the back of the goon on his right. The gentleman on his left turned, saw the shotgun and nodded to the other.

The sequoias did as they were told. Jones turned immediately and looked at the two with their hands clasped on top of their heads.

Mariah put her hand under the table while Jones sat distracted by looking at the beleaguered. She grasped the grip of her friend which was resting in a rotating holster that allowed it to be fired from within the holster and pointed it at him. Jones turned his head back, looked at Mariah and moved his right hand toward his left lapel.

"Do not do that, Jones. Freeze, as the police are wont to say. How do you get suckers to hire you, you incompetent? And the people you hire, the two waddlers at the bar, must be more incompetent than you."

"You're bluffing. You're not going to shoot me and them in here."

"How much money do you have with you this time?"

"I don't know, why do you ask?"

"I thought we would make another bet."

"Yeah, I'll bet."

"Thumb and first finger only, or *I'll* paint some artwork on the partition behind you."

He reached into his inside coat pocket with his left hand and brought out his wallet and put it on the table between them.

"Now, with thumb and first finger of your left hand, remove your piece from under your left bicep really slowly. Then when it is uncovered, grab the barrel with your right hand, and give it to me grip first. I am not a licensed paint contractor. I do not want to be in violation of any building codes by splattering this booth and walls red."

He did as he was told. He placed the Smith and Wesson .38 caliber four-inch barrel revolver into her left hand. She placed it into her shoulder bag and demanded, "Count your money."

He counted the Benjys and said, "It looks like seven thousand and change."

"I have only four, so I'm going to be light. I'm betting seven, but three light. If I lose, I owe you three. Greg will give me three as soon as he dispatches the incompetents. In case I don't pay you, you can send the two gentlemen at the bar to give me a massage. I don't want you to be empty." She put her money next to his. "You can look now."

When he looked under the table, she grabbed all of the money, the same as she had done the last time. She looked at Greg and nodded. He struck each of them at the base of the skull with the butt of the shotgun. They fell from their stools and hit the hard floor unintentionally, imitating two three-hundred pound sacks of Russet #1 potatoes. "Greg, empty their pockets and bag the contents. Look outside and see if there's a waiter. If there is, tell it Jones wants to see it."

Greg went through the front door looked, around outside, came back in and said, "No one."

"Where is the car parked, and what is it?"

"It's out front. It's a black Navigator."

"Who's the owner?"

"J.P."

"Give me the keys."

Jones handed her the car keys. She gave the keys to Greg and said, "Bring his Navigator around back. Lock the front door and put the closed sign up, thank you. Secure the two sleepers before you go."

Greg locked the front door, put up the closed sign and then walked to the store room in the back and returned with quarter-inch line. He cut lengths of line and hogtied the two. Then he dragged one at a time to the store room. Then he went through the front door, locked it and drove the Navigator to the rear door of the bar.

"You see, Jones, this is the way it is. Greg was in the military, Special Forces, and then a tour with LAPD. He wanted a bar where his friends in law enforcement, Special Forces, Rangers, SEALs could meet, enjoy themselves, talk and have a good time. His problem was he needed some help financially and other. So I assisted him. Now and then, he assists me as you have and will witness. He now has what he wanted, and I have what I wanted, an office. Face down on the floor, Jones, you're next."

"You can't do this to me. I'm under orders of the president of the United States pursuant to a Presidential Executive Order."

"Show it to me."

"I haven't got it yet. He told me I'd have it when I delivered the documents and all the materials stolen from J.P. by Lillian."

"You *are* dumb. You actually fell for that old trick. How much money were you to get?"

"Depends on how many of the three of you were still alive when I got all the documents. Three million five if all three were dead."

"Who are 'all three'?"

"You, McGraw and Sean Harrison, his son who he told me was not related to him."

"If we gave you the documents and the materials, if we had them, were you to kill us?

"Yes."

"Are you telling me he authorized you to kill three people if necessary to get the documents he wants, and after you got them kill us anyway?"

"Yes. That's what I believe he wanted done and had planned on doing."

"Do you have any proof of this?"

"What will you give me in exchange for the proof?"

"Better than what you were going to give the three of us — your life. Where's the proof?"

"In my pocket. It's recorded on my digital."

"Again, with thumb and first finger give it to me very slowly, or I'll make you look like a hemophiliac with a leak. There will be no medical attention available, because I don't know any medical people. These low-velocity hollow point rounds are very effective in close. When they exit, they'll remove your back."

He removed the digital recorder from his pocket and put it on the table between them and pushed the Play button, turned up the volume, and they listened to it.

When it was over, Mariah took the recorder and placed it into her bag and said, "Telling me the truth for a change was a smart move on your part. Next, you're working undercover for J.P. right?"

"Yeah, sure."

"We are making progress. How did you get to see the president?"

"J.P. sent me to tell him about a change of circumstances, and he wanted to enlist the president's help in locating Lillian McGraw, Sean Harrison and get J.P.'s documents back. When I was about to leave the first time, I gave him my card and told him if he needed help I could be of service. He called me and authorized me to get the documents and kill you, Lillian and Sean for money."

"Does J.P. know you are doing this for the president?"

"No. I don't think so. But with those two, who knows?"

"So, you went into business for yourself?"

"Yes."

"Greg, hogtie him, and let him join his friends."

"What're you going to do with us?"

"Better than what you were going to do with us."

Mariah turned off her recorder and kept her Glock 21 pointed at him under the table.

Greg removed him without gentleness from the booth, slammed him as hard as he could face-down on the hard floor, which consisted of aged, small, octagon-shaped grayish-white tiles, and drove his right knee into the small of his back and simultaneously tied his wrists behind him with the line. Then, he bound his ankles and attached a line between his ankles and wrists and pulled the line until the heels of his shoes made an impression in the seat of his pants and his arms were stretched to the limit. He removed everything from his pockets and put them in a bag. He gave him the same special consideration he had given the sequoias when he put earplugs in, Gorilla tape around his head covering his mouth, another length of tape around his head covering his eyes and put a black bag over his head and sealed it around his neck with tape. Need-to-know means transporters do not need to know what their three transients look like. Greg dragged him to the store room.

Mariah removed her secure cell phone from her bag and pushed redial. The male voice answered, "Yes."

"Do you have any of your people here in town?"

"Yes, always; how can I help you?"

"I have three who need to be picked up in back of my office immediately and placed into incommunicado-secure accommodations for an indefinite period of meditation. When I'm finished with this project and it's time to allow the guests to leave your facility, they'll be delivered to the police after I've arranged it. Is this alright with you? Also, I have their Navigator and the keys. Please take it with you."

"Are you talking about Dungeons and Dragons?"

"Yes, absolutely."

"I'll have two SUVs there in twenty minutes and a driver for the Navigator." He disconnected.

"Greg, the three and the Navigator will be picked up in twenty minutes in the back. Was there anything of interest in the pockets of the three incompetents?"

"The two thugs were empty and Jones had trash."

"Burn the trash and wallet." Mariah walked to the Brighton, went into the lobby and asked George, "Is Jerry here?"

"Yes."

"Please ask him to come down, thank you."

Jerry arrived and asked, "What can I do for you?"

"I need a ride. Are you available now?"

"Yes."

They walked to the hotel's underground garage, got into his car and drove to JP Morgan Chase. She went to see Harry Burstein. She used his computer to burn a CD backup of the president's orders to Jones and another of her conversation with him. They walked to her non-registered safe-deposit box and put Jones' digital recorder and the two CDs inside. Mariah left the bank and rode back to her office with Jerry.

# 18

## Day 11   9:00 A.M.   The Brighton Hotel Rear Entrance

A gray SUV with all the windows darkened behind the driver and the front passenger seats stopped in front of Mariah. The passenger got out and opened the right rear door behind his seat. Lillian stepped out and said hello to Mariah.

"And to you, too. Come with me, please. Thank you, gentlemen." The SUV drove away.

They started to walk, and as they did Mariah explained to her what had transpired with the president. They walked for two blocks and arrived at a nondescript building, opened the door and went into pleasant and quiet surroundings.

"May I see Dr. Riggins, please? I have an appointment. The name is Rogers," Mariah said.

"You may go right in, the doctor is waiting for you." They walked into Riggins office.

"Good morning, Mariah." He wore the traditional white smock and stethoscope on his short-medium frame.

"How are you, John? Thank you for handling this for me."

"No thanks necessary. This free clinic wouldn't be here if it weren't for you and your help."

"Speaking of that, I have another check here for you." She gave it to him.

He looked at it, looked at her and said, "You must have hit the lottery."

"I did, three times as a matter of fact. Take care of her. When will she be ready for me to pick her up?"

"Around noon will be fine."

"Noon it is." She looked at Lillian and said, "I will see you at noon."

Lillian nodded and Mariah left the building and started walking to her office.

"You're very fortunate to know her," Riggins said.

"Yes, I know."

"If it weren't for her, I wouldn't be able to help you. Many people in and out of this community owe her so much. I wanted to call the clinic the 'O'Leary Free Clinic' because she set me up here, but she refused. So, 'Neighborhood Free Clinic' it is. She sees needs and plugs the holes."

# 19

**Day 11   2:00 P.M.   The White House, the Oval Office**

Harrison returned from his meeting with the Russian president in Prague. He had his secretary summon Richard Rigor and James McDonald to the Oval Office. Rigor arrived first because his office was near the president's. Rigor's porcine face, almost bald, bespectacled, short and portly made him look older than his fifty years. He was the deputy chief of staff and the president's political advisor. He had worked on political campaigns for twenty years.

"Richard, here's one of the two originals of The Prague Accord. Please place it in your safe. Please return when you are finished. McDonald's coming over."

Rigor left and placed the Accord in his office safe. He returned to the Oval Office. The president sat behind the Lincoln Desk.

James P. McDonald, the vice-president, arrived. McDonald had served in different capacities in previous administrations and had been the CEO of a company in the private sector before becoming vice-president. The two stood in front of the Lincoln.

Robert made them stand in his presence to get childish revenge for telling him what to do all of the time. He did not enjoy being a marionette. He believed this little bit of revenge and plotting to rid himself of these two yokes kept him sane. He knew McDonald was sixty-six years old, not in good health and hoped he was accelerating his demise.

"Petrokov signed The Prague Accord. He's going to join with me in the Final Solution to the Muslim Question. I'm now ready to go forward to use a bioweapon to kill poor black Americans, blame it on the Muslims, and unite the Christian people in the war against Islam, the anti-Christ."

"Well done, Robert," McDonald said with his Midwestern accent. "This way we can invade Iran, own the oil reserves and have a permanent presence there. We'll now be able to control the distribution of the oil from the Middle East that moves by tanker in the Persian Gulf. This'll prevent China, India, and other nations from getting their hands on our Middle East oil under their sand unless we allow it." McDonald and Rigor laughed. "Now, we'll be able to get all of it and run the sand niggers dry."

"Whoa. Wait a minute," Robert said with surprise. "Richard, did you know anything about starting a war with China, other nations or World War III?"

"Yes, I knew about the overall plan," he said without an accent but with embarrassment and looked at the floor.

"I told President Petrokov it was only to stop terrorism. I told him the U.S. didn't have any desire for a permanent presence in the Middle East." *No reason to tell them about the "War Plan" document I signed with J.P. I'll disparage them.* "You two have set me up. I lied to Petrokov."

"Robert, you didn't lie to him," McDonald looked at him through his spectacles below his bald head with a white horseshoe-shaped band of hair which ran from temple to temple and told him with exasperation and arrogance, "A lie's a statement made to another, believing the statement's false and with the intent to deceive. Therefore, if one makes a statement to another, believes the statement to be accurate and without the intent to deceive, but the statement's inaccurate, one hasn't lied, just provided inaccurate information."

Robert thought for a moment, attempting to absorb what McDonald had just said through the haze provided by enjoying being an alcoholic since his college days. "Okay then, what pretext are you going to use, Jim? It's my understanding the only ways we can go to war legally is by being attacked, defending ourselves against an attack, being in an imminent danger of an attack or by the approval of the United Nations Security Council. What do you know that I don't?"

"Mr. President, I'm a little hungry," Rigor interrupted. "Why don't you order lunch for the three of us, we can eat uninterrupted, talk and set the foundation for going forward."

"Good idea, I'll take care of it. I'll have the chef prepare a surprise. He knows Jim has a bad heart, is way overweight and other miscellaneous. So I'm sure whatever he prepares will be acceptable to you and your snake-charm rattling doctor at Walter Reed." Robert called the White House chef and ordered lunch for three. He looked forward to adding additional advertising for the White House food to his tie.

"Robert, let's talk while we wait for lunch," Jim McDonald said in the form of an order. "To answer your question, '. . . defending ourselves against an attack . . .' can be interpreted in many favorable ways to us. As an example, you can have the director of the CIA provide you with tailor-made false and/or uncorroborated intelligence. This would lead you to believe that Mahmoud Ahmadinejad had conspired with terrorists and attacked us. Or, is conspiring with terrorists to attack us again, or he's developing nuclear weapons to attack us or an ally. This way we can bypass the U.N. We can go it alone. This way we don't have to sell bullshit about the 'coalition of the willing' propaganda.

"If Britain or any other nation wants to join us and reap the rewards of an oil supply, supporting oil services infrastructure and reconstruction contracts paid for by Iran and American and other nation's taxpayers, so be it. After the war starts, and if someone finds out the intelligence was rigged to support our invasion of Iran, you can ask the DCI to resign clandestinely. He'll resign, and then you can give him The Presidential Medal of Freedom for his '. . . especially meritorious contribution to the security or national interests of the United States . . .'

"As an alternative, we can get the CIA to paint one of our old F-14A Tomcat planes like the ones used by Iran with their military markings and have it bomb a kibbutz in Israel. Dress the pilot in an Iranian Air Force flight suit. So, when the Israelis shoot it down or we do, whichever comes first, we'll have our excuse to go to war. It'll work."

"Jim, are you suggesting we kill Israelis, shoot down one of our planes, kill one of our pilots and blame it on Ahmadinejad?"

"Absolutely! I don't believe Israeli lives, one plane and pilot to reach our goal is of any moment. Based upon economic projections I've received from learned economic professors the true cost, direct and indirect, of the war and occupation will be in the trillions, depending upon how long we stay. And this will only include the costs to the U.S., not Iran or any nation that may join us. Also, it doesn't include the lifetime care of the veterans who will be injured during the conflict."

"Trillions?" Robert responded with a raised voice. He rose, paced agitated behind his desk chair. "No one's going to accept this. Are you nuts? What are we going to tell the public and Congress?"

"We'll do what a previous administration did when it went to war illegally in Iraq. We'll continue to do what we always do, just lie to them. We'll find someone in the Office of Management and Budget or our economic advisor to give a low number, say sixty billion. If neither does, we'll fire them and get someone who will. We'll get the chairman of the Joint Chiefs of Staff to go along with it or replace him. I don't believe he'll resign in protest and go public. Once Congress appropriates the money and the costs continue to escalate, they'll have to keep giving us more money, chasing the old with the new, to complete the job no matter the costs, or how long it takes or the number of lives lost."

The vice president ordered Robert to set up a meeting with the DCI and arrange for him to provide the intelligence needed for the pretext that demonstrated the U.S. was defending itself so it could go to war. The pretext would be the bioweapon attack that killed many thousands of our poor-black citizens. Then the DCI would provide additional intelligence to Robert which demonstrated the terrorists were members of the Army of the Guardians of the Islamic Revolution, sometimes called the Revolutionary Guards, which is attached to Iran's military.

McDonald gave Robert a dose of reality when he told him their investors, corporations and wealthy persons were making the decisions for this administration. These investors were the donors who contributed the initial investment of fifty million dollars of venture-risk capital to Robert's campaign for president. They were pleased how quickly Robert paid them back with the tax cuts, beneficial legislation, eliminated bureaucratic regulations and deregulation that impeded their profits. The investors had been assured by McDonald, the investor's pawn and watchdog, they would continue to receive favorable treatment from this administration. The investors were Harrison's father, family, and J.P. Kennington and his friends from Texas who were in the oil business. This was the foundation for their fortunes, Middle East oil, Kuwait and Saudi Arabia.

McDonald said to Robert, "What's good for our investors and us is good for America. This is what we want done. This is what you want done."

The investors, the decision-makers for the administration, had discussed the possibility of war with China. They decided that war was an acceptable risk, because they would make more money if there was a war. The U.S. would win the war as far into the future as it could be determined at this time. The investors would have to take some risks in order to progress with the building of their fortunes. This decision was made by them without any useless consideration for the loss of lives of U.S. military personnel, civilian deaths or bankruptcy of the U.S.

"After Iran, there'll be Syria," McDonald said. "Then onto Lebanon to root out Hezbollah. It's the only way to remake the world as I see it."

"I agree with McDonald, Mr. President," Rigor said with conviction. "McDonald sees it correctly."

Robert sighed acceptance and with a slight nod of his head acquiesced, looked at Rigor and McDonald and said with a smile, "Sounds good to me." Robert was always outwardly pleasant. The principle was: never threaten your enemies; just act to dispose of them when the appropriate moment presented itself. Always be pleasant to them just before you kill them.

At this moment, there was a knock on the door of the Oval Office. The gourmet lunch arrived that had been prepared by the White House chef. The three men changed the meeting's subject. But the setting's animosity was pervasive. Robert did not appreciate their attitudes and tallied them on his list.

Neither McDonald nor Rigor wished to embarrass the president publicly, but private abuse, reproofing and impugning his intelligence was standard fare and their favorite game.

Now, the conviviality and friendship performance was presented to an audience of one. The steward placed three chairs at the table and rechecked the table to determine that all was correct. "Enjoy your lunches, gentlemen," the steward said and left.

Robert said to Richard, "Have Raymond Neilsen at Homeland come and see you, and when he arrives, I want to see both of you as soon as possible."

"I'll see to it, Robert." The three men enjoyed and concluded their fine dining.

Raymond Neilsen, the deputy secretary of the Department of Homeland Security, known as Homeland or the DHS, arrived at Rigor's office about an hour and fifteen minutes later. "Raymond, I'm going to give to you a copy of the National Vulnerabilities document prepared by DHS Secretary Wheat. Keep it safe. Show it to no one."

"I won't," he said with a New England accent.

"Let's go see the president." Rigor then escorted Neilsen into the Oval Office. They stood. Neilsen was about forty-two years old, short and wore a suit and tie.

"Mr. Neilsen, I want you to work on a special project which will encompass national security. You're not to discuss the overall plan with anyone except Rigor. Richard you'll give him whatever support he asks for."

"Yes, Mr. President; I've already started."

"That's all, gentlemen." Rigor and Neilsen started to leave. "A moment, Mr. Neilsen." The president told Neilsen privately about the project he and Petrokov had agreed upon, but did not tell him about the Prague Accord or Petrokov's involvement.

"I'll be pleased to engage in this crusade, Mr. President," he said in the conduct and speech of the most egregious sycophant. "I'll select the right city and area for your incident."

# 20

## Day 12  9:00 A.M.  JPMorgan Chase

The day after Lillian met with Dr. Riggins, she felt fine. Jerry drove Mariah and Lillian to Chase. Mariah was dressed elegantly in her go to the bank outfit, a designer-dark blue pants suit and dark-blue pumps with two-inch heels. Her Glock was comfortably ensconced in her shoulder bag.

Lillian appeared to have just left the ranch in her jeans, Levi work shirt, sheepskin vest, cowboy boots, mirrored sunglasses and ball cap. Her friend with a suppressor on its nose was still housed in her shoulder bag. The safety was off and a low-velocity-hollow-point round was in the chamber. The clip was filled with alternate rounds of hollow point and Teflon-coated. Her right hand caressed its grip and her first finger engaged in foreplay on the trigger.

They strode with Vigilance, their other protector, through the lobby joined by Authority and Determination. Mariah's head turned and moved constantly. Her eyes looked through her dark-brown curved sunglasses with Silhouette frames and surveyed the lobby and her surroundings for potential hurdles to their forward progress.

Mariah stopped and then Lillian. They faced one another but both continued to look about. Mariah said, "Before we go upstairs to see our banker. I want to ask you about something. How much cash did you remove from J.P.'s cash locker?"

"I never counted it, but there were about sixty packages of ten thousand dollars each. I used some of the money to buy a car. The dealer will report the car stolen and receive the money from the insurance company plus the money Sean gave him. I bought some old clothes for us at the used clothing store near your office and took a thousand before I left. I think that's about it. Why?"

"What is your position on counting the money when we go upstairs and offering to return it to J.P.? Take some of the money you received from Robert and make J.P. whole? Cannot be much. What, maybe less than ten thousand? I know he said nothing was missing, he's a liar and worse, but I thought I'd ask."

"You've posed a question I hadn't considered. But I'm surprised and grateful for what you've done for me with the president. Are you sure you don't want more than the one-dollar fee I paid you?"

"Why did you change the subject? Sounds like a bribe. Pay me a large fee, and I will not consider returning the money to J.P., keep it for myself or what?"

"No, I was just trying to show my gratitude."

"I hope so."

"What do you suggest I do with the money?"

"I do not know at this moment, I will think about it. The answer to your question is no. I received the fee I requested. If in the future you have a need for my legal services, we will talk about it. Causing the downfall of corruption is called public service. Causing the downfall of the corrupters is called retribution. Back to my question."

"Let's see what he says. If he says no cash is missing, I will ask you to consider its disposition."

"Alright. This is what I suggest. Let us go up and count the cash. If it is short and not sixty packages, then we'll make it sixty packages or whatever it was when you took it. I have an appointment with J.P. this afternoon. When I see him, I am going to confront him with the lies he told me about the documents, DVDs, VHSs and cash that was taken. I am going to offer to return the cash only, because all of the other items are the only things that will keep you, Sean and me alive at this time. When we are finished with this project, I will dispose of them in a manner that best serves the interests of the American people. You have my word on it. What do you think?"

"I think you're the caring person Robert said you were. I think you're noble. Too bad he didn't learn anything from you when you knew him at Yale."

They went up in the elevator, got off and went to Harry's office. Harry's secretary escorted them into his office. "Harry, this is my client Lillian McGraw. Lillian this is Harry Burstein, your banker. The two of us will be handling your affairs for as long as you want us to."

"Good to meet you, Ms. McGraw. Would you like to open an account at this time and have Mariah transfer funds from her trust account to your account?"

"Harry, Lillian and I wish to go to a room with my box."

"Of course." He removed his safe-deposit box key from his desk drawer. He escorted Lillian to a cubicle and asked her to wait. Mariah and Harry opened the box. Harry returned to his office. Shortly Mariah returned with the box to the cubicle.

"Please count it."

Lillian went through each package. There were ten one-hundred dollar bills held together with currency straps for a total of one thousand dollars. There were ten bundles of one thousand to a package held together with a currency strap for a total of ten thousand dollars. There were sixty-one packages. "I only opened one package of ten thousand. So, there were sixty-two packages. Six hundred and twenty thousand."

Mariah and Harry locked the box and returned to Harry's office with Lillian. They sat in the two visitor's chairs in front of Harry's desk.

"Mr. Burstein, I want to give to Mariah, ten thousand dollars in cash at this time. Can you arrange it now for me?"

Harry made a call. A man came into his office ten minutes later with ten currency strapped bundles of one thousand dollars each and gave it to Harry and left. "Here you are, Ms. McGraw."

"Here." Lillian handed the ten thousand to Mariah.

"Harry, I hate to bother you again, but you and I need to make a guerilla raid on my box again, no cubicle needed." He and Mariah went to the box and she put the ten thousand in. They returned to his office. Lillian told him she will speak to Mariah about the disposition of her money and call him with instructions. Mariah and Lillian left Harry's office.

# 21

## Day 12   10:30 A.M.   The Brighton Hotel Room 1012

Jerry drove them back to the hotel. Mariah and Lillian went to the room they used as a conference room. They were seated at the desk.

"How are you feeling today? Have your friend with you?" Mariah asked.

"I feel good. Yes, all the time."

"Do you want company? There is a fellow who lives here who is a friend of Greg's, the owner of Raymond's Bar. He is a former CIA operative with high skills. He performed special tasks and janitorial services. He is also a man I have and do rely on. You met him this morning, Jerry. He will join you here if you wish while I go see J.P. I would feel better if he is here."

"Alright, if you say so."

Mariah went to the phone and called George, the desk clerk, and asked, "Is Jerry around?"

"Yes, he's in the lobby reading the book you gave him."

"Will you call him to the phone?"

"Just a moment."

"Yes."

"Jerry, can you come to 1012 prepared?"

"Yes, I'll bring my book and be right there," he said with a slight Midwestern twang.

A few minutes passed, and there were two taps on the door of 1012, a pause and then three. Mariah looked through the eyepiece and opened the door.

"Thank you for coming. I need to be gone for an hour or two. If you want lunch, here is some money. Order takeout please and have it delivered to 1012." She gave him a Benjy.

"No problem, we'll be fine."

Mariah left them alone.

# 22

**Day 12   12:00 P.M.   The Kennington Estate, Bel Air, West Los Angeles**

Mariah sat in the library in the chair she had used during her previous visit while her cab waited outside. Again she admired the extensive mahogany bookcases that were all filled. She sat with her right hand in her shoulder bag.

J.P. walked in unannounced by Humphries.

She activated her digital recorder.

He approached her, she extended her right hand and again he took it in his right hand, did not shake it but kissed it lightly while looking into her eyes and sat down opposite her at a forty-five degree angle in front of the fireplace.

"So you found Lillian, congratulations, expeditious. So when may I see her?"

"She does not wish to return, and she does not want you to know where she is, assuming I know. Therefore, I have fulfilled my agreement with you. I now represent her.

"When last we talked, I asked you if there was anything missing and had you done an inventory. You answered no and yes to those two questions. It appears to me you provided me with inaccurate information. Did you do the inventory?"

"Yes."

"Why the subterfuge?"

"My reasons are my reasons. The reasons are the same as why off-ledger transactions are off-ledger transactions. You remember those don't you? You've no need to know."

"Yes, I do remember them. How much cash was missing?"

"Who said there was cash missing? I didn't."

"If I can find the cash that is missing, do you want it returned?"

"Again, I didn't say cash was missing."

She opened her briefcase so the top blocked J.P.'s view of the contents. She pulled an agreement from under her friend, Mr. Glock, and said, "Very well, there is no cash missing. I have prepared this document for you to sign. It states there is no cash or any other personal property missing of yours, from any of your companies or from this estate after the date of Lillian McGraw's disappearance. It also states in case you have made a mistake as of this date whatever property you have found missing belongs to the person in possession of the missing property at the time of the discovery. Finally, you will not pursue any criminal or civil action against any party under any circumstances." She handed it to him with a pen.

J.P. read the document, signed it and returned it to her. She replaced it into her ostrich briefcase under her bodyguard and comforter which she also used as a paperweight.

"Lunch has been prepared in anticipation of your visit. Shall we adjourn to the arbor, enjoy the landscaping and some gourmet food? We can talk some more."

"Yes, thank you. So you serve lunch to guests, but no high tea?"

They walked through the ten-feet high double French doors, out into the garden, entered the arbor and sat at a round table with a linen table cloth. The flatware was sterling, the rolled linen napkins were individually embraced in the middle by Georgian sterling rings.

Two servants in uniforms served lunch and left. The Chilean sea bass was wrapped in spinach leaves, dressed with salsa with parmesan cheese on top and asparagus prepared al dente then buttered and seasoned.

J.P. asked, "You need to tell me how much money you need to give me the DVDs and VHSs that I want and need for my businesses."

"You told me nothing was missing, J.P., and you signed a document to that affect."

"I signed the document because I don't want anyone to know certain items are missing. I need deniability. I've businesses to run. My financial future's in jeopardy; I need to correct this situation now. I've had another inventory done, and there are things missing. For now, it's the DVDs, VHSs and the 'War Plan' document."

"J.P., you must do business with a lot of dumb people. 'I've had another inventory done, and there are things missing.' You expect me to believe this? You are really a bad liar. You have been lying to me from the moment we met. What makes you think I have them? And if I did, why would I sell them to you?"

"The president called, and he was upset when he found out about Lillian McGraw's pregnancy, his paternity and the hush money he had to pay. He blamed me for setting him up."

"He paid no hush money. He is the father and he assumed his financial responsibility as a father. The same as every father does and/or should. Spare me your insinuation of extortion. After all, you should; you are an expert at it."

He had not acknowledged she had spoken an insult, because it was not an insult to him. He had skin thicker than layers of elephant and hippopotamus. His silence had been an acknowledgment of the compliment. "He was also upset about the sexual activity of his wife with me and our two children, Victoria Kennington and Sean. I believe I've you to thank for my temporary inconvenience."

"You should not blame others for the problems you created. After all, I infer from your anger, you and the president have had a falling out as a result of your misconduct. You have only yourself to blame. Your victims of extortion will feel much better after they learn your puppeteer's strings have been removed from their bodies. The president knows you are now vulnerable, and it is going to be payback time."

"So, how much is it going to cost me to get back what was stolen?"

"Stolen? Nothing has been stolen. For if it had, you would have called the police, and I would know about it."

"Give me a number and stop being obstructive."

"I know you are wealthy, believe you can buy anyone and believe you are above the law. But you must understand, sometimes you will meet a person who is not for sale. The person I have in mind is your luncheon companion who believes you are hearing impaired."

"I want to know if you'd like to work for me. I'm very impressed with your performance. By the way, have you seen Tom Jones?"

"No, to answer the last question first."

"I understand the president sent him to see you. Jones decided to go into business for himself I understand. He misled the president. The president made a serious error in judgment again. I do believe he's as dumb as he's reputed to be. The president asked me to inquire as to Jones' whereabouts and his mission."

"What was his mission?"

"The president didn't tell me."

"J.P., you have just done it again. I am sure Jones will turn up at my office if the president asked him to."

"Yes, I'm sure he will. Robert's a real wimp. He saw some sexual activity, collected some information and folded like a four-flushing gambler. Jones was supposed to have vetted you and he didn't. I made a mistake in hiring you for the job. Then to top it off, Robert hired you without asking me. Now, the two of us are in awkward circumstances."

"The public always gets what they voted for. I assume you have a back-up candidate, because the 'wimp' as you call him, is not going to be re-elected."

"We'll see. I want to discuss with you working for me. What's your thought about that?"

"I want to discuss you discontinuing trying to bribe me. I want to discuss not going forward with the 'War Plan' document you and Robert signed. You two are already guilty of conspiring to commit treason and attempted murder. The conspiracy has gone past the talking stage and signing the agreement is an overt act in the furtherance of the commission of the conspiracy. I do not want you and Robert to go forward with this plan. Become the 'richest' some other way.

"What kind of a person would send his daughter out as a call girl to set up honey traps so her father could extort the targets who became entangled? Next, what kind of a person would send his daughter to have continual sexual intercourse with the president of the United States until she became pregnant by him so he could control the president by extorting him into increasing the father's wealth? All of this for the money you worship.

"A psychiatrist would say you had an anti-social personality disorder with narcissism. You will do anything for the money you worship. You are alienated from people and seek friends and you have none, according to my dossier on you. You need treatment.

"What kind of a person is it J.P. who had sex with his friend's fifteen years old daughter, Lillian McGraw Harrison, made her pregnant and had a daughter. I believe the name for this person is a pedophile. Then when his daughter became a teenager, got her pregnant, had a daughter by her and then had sexual relations with the second teenage daughter? Do you call this person an incestuous pedophile or just an incestuous bastard? Please leave Lillian McGraw, your daughter and the sister of her mother, your other daughter and Sean Harrison, your son, alone."

"You *are* damn well-informed. There's no benefit to you in discussing my personal business again privately or publicly with another."

"That was not even a subtle threat, J.P. Your eyes said more than your mouth."

"I like you more already. So what do you think? Back to my question. Lillian's gone, and I need a replacement."

I am an attorney, not a 'confidential secretary' or a prostitute."

"She wasn't a 'confidential secretary' either. She did it all."

"Yes, I am sure she did. But I would not be interested in doing it all. I would not be interested in having any type of intercourse with you, sexual or social. I would not be interested in being loaned out as a 'call girl' so you could get richer by corruption and extortion. As far as you are concerned, I am giving the suckers who were doing your bidding or risked the myriad consequences you would impose a permanent vacation."

"So, what about working for me, not having sex with me or being a 'prostitute-call girl', just business."

"It would be a conflict of interest, I am afraid. You see, I have ethics and a moral sense. I am anti-corruption, and I sleep very well every evening. I do not believe your culture would be to my liking, but thank you for the compliment. I am sure you already have attorneys now who do your bidding, sold their moral sense, worship their money god Greed, do not ever look into the mirror, but spend a lot of time in the confessional with their favorite priest at the end of every day paying their premiums to the church's Absolution Insurance Company."

"I pay well. Say, best office and location, full staff, base salary of five million a year, plus benefits, expenses, travel, making big deals and taking a piece. What do you say?"

"It sounds like an augmented bribe. But the unknowns frighten me. Also, I believe your ability to pay me would be short-lived. I know I will never be able to prognosticate the unknowns to my satisfaction, so I will pass. But again, thank you for the compliment. I have to go. Please, excuse me. A two-hour lunch is most unusual for me, thank you."

"I believe you've mistaken my kindnesses toward you as suggestions and a weakness. I'd prefer you give me my DVDs, VHSs and documents back before you leave. I'm sure they're in your briefcase. We can talk about the return of the cash after the delivery of my requests."

She looked at him. She rose from her chair, picked up her ostrich brief case and shoulder bag.

"I'll not permit you to leave without my requests. I don't wish to escalate this matter by calling my security people."

"I see what you mean." She replaced her shoulder bag onto the blue stone floor of the arbor. She placed the briefcase onto the table. She sat in her chair and put the briefcase on her lap. She opened the top, removed her paperweight, comforter-friend and placed it under the table with the tablecloth resting on top of it. It was the same paper weight which Mr. Tom Jones had met on his first visit to her office and had lost twenty Benjys, and then again when he lost seventy. She pointed Mr. Glock and his muzzle's companion, Ms. Suppressor, at the abdomen of J.P. "I can see from the servants you run a fine five-star hotel. Maybe, I can have Lillian's old room now that it is vacant. But my schedule is tight, I am overdue for my next appointment, and I must leave. So if you will excuse. . . ."

He interrupted and said, "I don't think you understand. You're not leaving until I get my requests, and when I do we'll talk about other matters."

"No, J.P., 'I don't think *you* understand'. This friend of yours, Tom Jones, did he ever tell you about losing two bets to me in the amount of nine thousand?"

"No."

"Well now, here we have it. I have a friend of mine, a paperweight and comforter, pointed at your abdomen. I do not wish to harm you as you have wished to harm me. There is no doubt in my mind that the president asked Jones to visit me at your insistence. I do not believe he was going to bring the Welcome Wagon to my office."

"You're bluffing."

"That's what Jones, your lackey, said. You must have the same script writer. You have called me a liar, and that is unacceptable to me. Please do not do it again, or your lunch will be on the bluestone floor. And because my friend under the table has a suppressor, your staff probably will not hear me kill you. I have only a small amount of cash with me. I think it is about five thousand. I'll bet you five thousand. Put up or I am leaving."

J.P. picked up the intercom handset that was on the table and ordered five thousand in cash. A type showed up wearing the black two-piece suit, white shirt, black tie, Oakleys and black shoes with rubber soles, a real blender this guy. No one could possibly suspect he was trying to make a living in security. He left the arbor. J.P. put the money on the table.

Mariah continued to look into his eyes as she reached into her bag with her left hand, grabbed a roll of Benjys bound by a flexible band with ten five-carat D flawless marquis cut diamonds attached to it and placed the roll on top of his money and said, "Look under the table and under the tablecloth." When he did, she grabbed all the money and placed it into her bag.

"I see I've made three mistakes with you. Hiring you, misjudging your character and now this. What am I going to do with you, Ms. O'Leary? You caused Robert to be very upset with me because Sean and Lillian McGraw are my children, and I had sex with his wife on more than one occasion. He called me a pedophile. You called me a liar, pedophile and an incestuous bastard. No one speaks to me like this, including the buffoon in the White House or the buffoon from Texas before him. You've caused my marionette to bolt. His alienation will severely jeopardize my future. You've meddled in my affairs, the affairs of other powerful people and that's unacceptable conduct to us. You must pay for your meddling. The only solution now is not to sell me the 'War Plan' document, DVDs and VHSs but give them to me."

"Leave me alone."

"I can't do that until I have my requests."

"I am going to leave. Please do not interfere. I do not wish to paint any portion of this lovely home. Desperation is the father and anger is the mother of poor judgment and you have surely displayed all three today. Pass me the handset." He did. She rose from her chair and threw it about ten yards into the landscaping. "Good day to you, J.P." Mariah placed her friend into her shoulder bag with her right hand on the grip and first finger on the trigger. She picked up the briefcase. She kept her eyes on him as she backed out of the arbor and into the library. She turned off her recorder. She replaced her right hand onto the grip of her friend, walked through the library, the foyer, the front door and down the steps to the waiting cab. She entered and gave the driver directions. She plugged the ear buds into her ears, pushed the lever to Play on the recorder and listened to it. She was satisfied.

*Lillian told me the money and other items were removed from J.P.'s vault without his permission. Theft is a felony and Lillian is guilty of it. If I do not report her to the police, I am guilty of compounding a felony, a felony. I could be disbarred. But is there a crime? He said nothing is missing, and he signed my agreement. Then he said there was and threatened my life.*

She knew if she informed the federal authorities or the justice department, the FBI, of the "War Plan" document and turned all the materials over to them, the president would have them put all the materials into the circular file, the burn bag.

She did not know how to stop this "War Plan" and not get prosecuted for compounding. Not reporting the crimes of a conspiracy to commit treason and attempted murder is compounding. Disbarred came to her mind and not living happily ever after, too. Now, there was a Trifecta. She hoped she could afford the bet?

Her real fear was: J.P. would go forward without the president. He would manufacture the poisonous gas, murder the people, provide the terrorists by kidnapping the citizens of the country who live here he had chosen, kill them and plant them at the site of the murders with the appropriate documentation. Use his media connections to force a war.

# 23

**Day 12   12:15 P.M.   The Brighton Hotel**

Jerry and Lillian sat and faced one another across the table in 1012 with their backs to the adjoining doors of 1010 and 1014. Jerry motioned to her to come near her and he whispered, "Did you hear that?"

"Yes, it was a footfall in the hallway outside."

"Get ready. We may have the uninvited."

Jerry and Lillian turned toward the front door of 1012. She removed her friend, Mr. Glock, from her bag, screwed on the suppressor, turned toward the door and pointed the pistol. Jerry did the same with his Beretta M9A1 9mm, but it had no silencer. Their peripheral visions allowed them to see through the open connecting doors to 1010 and 1014.

The sound of the key turning in the lock of 1012 alerted them. They watched the knob turn. Then the door opened wide. One man came through the door of 1012. He started to lower his four-inch Colt .45 which was pointed at the ceiling to fire. But before he could get it into firing position, Lillian shot two rounds of .45 caliber into his chest. His body lifted from the carpet and went backward. As it did, she put one round into his forehead. The body of the intruder slammed into the wall on the opposite side of the hallway and slid to the floor. Jerry did not get off a shot.

An intruder came through the front door of 1014. Jerry whirled around to his left, rolled out of his chair and flung himself toward the connecting door to 1014 and the floor.

Lillian saw Jerry move toward the connecting door between 1012 and 1014. She turned in her chair to her left when Jerry moved toward 1014. She acted as cover for him.

Half of Jerry's body traveled halfway through the connecting doorway. He fired two rounds into the exposed left side of the assailant's torso while he was in the air. Jerry landed on the carpet in a prone position with his firearm still pointed at the assailant. The hollow point Parabellum rounds entered under his armpit at the same level of his heart. As they traveled to his right side, the rounds created such trauma as they passed through his heart and tissue he was not able to use his weapon. The assailant turned toward the sound of the shots and Jerry fired another round into his right eye. His body lay immobile in 1014 with fragments of the back of his skull caroming off the walls and ceiling like billiard balls.

Lillian sat in her chair facing 1014. She heard the door open behind her in 1010. She forced her chair backward. As she was falling to the floor, she saw the overhead light fixture, then the ceiling passed, looked back over the top of her chair, saw the top of the door jamb and through the connecting door into 1010. She saw a man with a revolver. He stood framed by the jamb of the connecting door. He had not adjusted to her action and left himself exposed. When he fired the first round, it went high and would have struck her if she had remained seated. She shot the man twice in the chest. She rolled her head forward toward her chest before the back of the chair hit the carpet and let her back take the impact. The man moved backward smartly and hit the wall behind him. Lillian rolled out of the chair. Then she fired one round from the prone position into his head.

When it was over, they were silent for a few minutes. Jerry rose from the carpet and asked, "Are you all right?"

She got off the carpet, stood and looked at him. "I think so. Just my ears. They're ringing. I wish you'd used a suppressor."

"Mine too, and I should've. That was some shooting. Where did you learn to shoot like that?"

"This man I know is in the defense contracting business. He arranged for me to go to Fort Bragg in North Carolina for some combat lessons. A Special Forces instructor tutored me. The man then used me as a body guard because I didn't look like one along with other duties when he traveled."

"Shooting backward as you were falling is maybe the best I've seen."

"Thank you. Better him than we."

"I'm going to call some friends and remove the garbage."

# 24

## Day 12   10:00 A.M.   The White House, the Oval Office

"Mr. President, Mr. Cliff, the DCI, is here for his appointment," the president's secretary announced.

"Ask him to come in, Rosemary." Roger Cliff had been the director of the Central Intelligence Agency for two years and had been appointed by Harrison. Cliff was sixty-three years old, a graduate of Yale, and the former CIA director of the Directorate for Operations. This directorate had the responsibility for retrieving foreign intelligence. He was well dressed in his dark-blue three-piece suit, white shirt, and conservative red and blue tie. He was a striking figure at six feet three, two hundred pounds and handsome.

"Good to see you, Roger."

"Good day to you, Mr. President."

"Please sit, Roger." Roger took a seat in one of the two visitors' chairs in front of the Lincoln. "Roger, what information do you have at this time regarding any activity on Iran that would lead me to believe that there may be a national security problem?"

"Nothing at this time, Mr. President."

"Do you really mean that?" He asked not as a question, but as a suggestion for Cliff to change his evaluation. "Don't you have any intelligence that the dictator's a sponsor of terrorism and is a threat to our country? Any citizens of that country involved in funding, training, or providing terrorists with intelligence?"

"No, Mr. President, just rumors and speculations. Nothing firm or confirmable. Besides, Ahmadinejad was elected by the people. Though I do admit it appears to be one vote one time. So, I guess you could call him a dictator considering he's suppressing the opposition with fear and murder, not what one would call a liberal democracy."

"Do you really mean that?" He asked again. It was not a question, but an order after Cliff did not take the hint to fabricate the first time. "Can't you interpret the rumors and speculations on the side of caution as far as national security is concerned? Isn't a dictator's saber-rattling rhetoric to wipe Israel, our ally, from the map enough to pose a continuing threat to destabilize the region, our oil supply and our ability to control the distribution of oil from the Persian Gulf and therefore our national security?"

"I don't see Mahmoud Ahmadinejad's braggadocio or his misconduct as an imminent danger to us, to his dissenters for sure, but not to us. Again, we have rumors. Defectors and informants trying to sell forged information to us for their financial benefit. But so far, none of it has turned out to be authentic. We do know he's developing nuclear weapons and missiles with capabilities which could change the balance of power in the region." *The man is not even subtle or tactful when it comes to ordering me to fabricate and using flawed intelligence.*

"And endangering the U.S. troops in the area, don't forget, and that's good enough for me. I don't think 'imminent danger' is necessary. Our ally Israel's being threatened on a continuing basis. We're in danger in the future; that's if he's planning any type of program that'll come to fruition. That'll be good enough for me. Don't you think we should do something about disposing of him now? You know, preventive maintenance with insurance attached for the peace and stability in the region? Our major corporations have invested heavily in the region, we need to protect their interests, and we need to maintain the status quo. What's your thought on this?"

"We've been funding opposition parties and organizations with the idea of overthrowing his regime by coup or revolution, but to date we have been ineffective because of his ability to infiltrate and dispose of dissenters. Protecting the business interests of big corporations is not within the purview of the CIA."

"Sounds tenuous to me at best. What about assassination?"

"Assassinating heads of state is against the law."

"What about having one of his bodyguards kill him? You know, like Indira Ghandi's two Sikh bodyguards did to her?"

In 1976, President Ford issued Executive Order 11905 to clarify U.S. foreign-intelligence activities. In a section of the order labeled Restrictions on Intelligence Activities Ford concisely but explicitly outlawed political assassination: 5(g) Prohibition on Assassination. No employee of the United States Government shall engage in, or conspire to engage in, political assassination. Then again in 1981 President Reagan, through Executive Order 12333, reiterated the assassination prohibition: 2.11 No person employed by or acting on behalf of the United States Government shall engage in or conspire to engage in assassination.

"I don't believe it is legal under any circumstance." His attitude and delivery told the president to forget it.

Robert was not pleased with Cliff's professorial attitude toward him and lack of respect. This lecture reminded him of his authoritarian mother's punishing admonitions when he had done something wrong even when he was an adult. The rage and anger built in him like a tsunami about to come ashore. He was agitated and moved about in his chair as if he had to use the toilet desperately. It was enough that he had to endure the degradation by McDonald and Rigor, but this was unacceptable.

"Well, shore up the rumors and speculations. Give me an analysis that supports and verifies the rumors, speculations, defectors, and informants' intelligence that gives me solid grounds for disposing of him any way I see fit, assassination or invasion."

"I know the vice president is determined to go to war with Iran. He and his chief of staff visit with my analysts on a weekly basis. Even the analysts believe he has already decided to invade Iran and is looking for an excuse to make a preemptive strike. If he goes to war illegally, it must be only for his personal financial benefit. It surely has nothing to do with our national security or consideration for the murder of our military personnel. Maybe he has decided to have a permanent presence in the Middle East. Is this correct; McDonald has decided to have a permanent presence in Iran so the U.S. can control the Persian Gulf? Has he discussed this with you?"

"No, Roger, he hasn't. As far as McDonald and Iran are concerned, he has never discussed with me having a permanent presence in the Middle East or in Iran and/or going to war with Iran. Remember, Roger, I'm the president, and I decide what to do about Iran based on my perception of our national security. I'm the decision-maker in this administration. Do you understand this?" The tsunami had come ashore and wreaked havoc. The bright red-orange magma flowed from the volcano and it was visible.

"Yes, Mr. President." Cliff responded with submission.

"As far as the vice president is concerned, he fails to realize he works for me. He does what I tell him to do or he's history. Do you hear me? The American people pay his salary and supply his extraordinary benefits. He believes erroneously that he isn't accountable to the people, above the law and superior to the people. He believes erroneously what's good for him personally is good for the American people. Once again, I'm the president, I make the decisions, you do what I ask, not what the vice president asks. Do you understand this?"

"Yes, Mr. President, I surely do. Having said what you just said, I'm led to believe that only you want me to fabricate intelligence so you can go to war. If so, you'll have to find another pretext or source of intelligence that supports your belief that Iran is an imminent danger to our national security by preparing nuclear weapons or is amassing weapons of mass destruction intended for an attack on the U.S. This way, you can pick and choose intelligence which fits your agenda and that of the vice president and the other members of your cabal. This conforms to your policy of a preemptive strike."

" 'Fabricate, pick, and choose' are not words I would use." Robert told him with eruptions and histrionics. The magma gave off a red-orange color as it moved down the side of the mountain. He pounded Lincoln with his fist as the magma moved. "I would phrase it: interpret intelligence in the most favorable and beneficial light for the benefit and at the request of your president so he can act with maximum latitude without restrictions or encumbrances to protect our national security. This is the way I would put it. How would you put it?"

"There's no national security issue here. 'Fabricate, pick, and choose' to justify an illegal pre-emptive strike still comes to mind."

"The only reason you have this job is because you were one of my roommates in college. Your resignation comes to mind when I hear you tell me, 'Fabricate, pick, and choose to justify an illegal preemptive strike still comes to mind'." Robert rose from his chair, paced, and was one nanosecond away from a tantrum. His face flushed, clenched his fists and waved his arms.

"You determine how to defend the intelligence, Roger, if it becomes necessary to defend faulty or flawed intelligence. I don't care how you do it. I'm not in the defending of intelligence business, you are. I'm in the defending of my country's business. You give me the intelligence I want. You do what your president tells you to do to protect this nation. I decide how to protect this nation, not you." The content of his castigation was obvious disingenuousness. His patience was at an end with this servant, who refused to take orders even if they were oblique.

"Yes, Mr. President. Again, I want you to know that the CIA can't confirm that Iran is preparing a nuclear weapons program, has weapons of mass destruction or is a threat to our national security."

If fabricated and/or flawed intelligence was used as a pretext to go to war in Iran based on pretending to defend national security or without the U.N. Security Council's approval, the world would know that the U.S. violated international law and had gone to war without rules again.

The president's engagement in vainglorious misconduct propped up by his cabal was in the mistaken belief that he would extricate himself from the shadow of his father, and for once in his life accomplish something worthwhile, in his opinion, on his own, so his father would be proud of him. Going to war illegally for the purpose of maybe getting re-elected was a crime of monumental proportions. He would go down in disgrace and infamy, the same as a former president had done, if he pursued this flawed method of self-aggrandizement and pseudo-foreign policy.

"Are you on my team, Roger?"

"Yes, I am. I'd be doing you a disservice if I told you otherwise. It's my responsibility to collect information that affects the national security, determine its accuracy, and advise you. You, Rigor, and McDonald aren't using the intelligence to make a decision. You three have already made the decision to invade and are now looking for intelligence to justify and support the decision. The strategic intelligence assessment I have and can confirm is that you're going to be inserting this nation into a maelstrom of another killing field without an exit strategy, because there isn't one.

"The only exit strategy you're not going to enjoy will be similar to Napoleon's humiliating defeat and humiliating and embarrassing retreat from Moscow. The U.S. humiliating defeat and humiliating and embarrassing retreat from Korea, and the humiliating defeat and humiliating and embarrassing retreats from Vietnam, Lebanon and Somalia.

"Then, of course, there's the British occupation of Iraq pursuant to the mandate of the League of Nations and their humiliating and embarrassing early withdrawal in 1936. The thoughtless and ill-planned British withdrawal spawned a dictatorship, more violence than during their occupation, and a loss of all of the progress they had made in trying to stabilize the country.

"The international disgrace and embarrassment will make you the current international bully and pariah for some time to come. A bully's a bully. You start with Iran, what nation is next, Lebanon, Syria, North Korea? Whatever nation you don't like at the moment and for which there's a financial benefit to you and your investors whom know you for what you are?

"Remember, no nation wants us to be the world's police force and invade as we decide. Your assassination comes to mind. Do *not* believe you're indispensable. Engaging in an illegal war means you are not smart enough to find a diplomatic solution satisfactory to all parties concerned. Americans will not be able to travel abroad safely.

"Oh, you'll win the conventional war easily, but the aftermath of the war will be horrific. There will be no plan for law and order after the war is won. Urban warfare's the most dangerous, a lot of young American men and women are going to die because of your greed, and the civilian collateral damage will be incalculable. You're putting your personal financial interests, those of your family, McDonald, and your campaign contributors before the national security of this country and its citizens. This I firmly believe.

"Finally, Mr. President, you'll be a traitor. You'll be committing treason, a high crime for which you can be impeached. A traitor is one who violates a trust, confidence, faith, or is false to an obligation or duty. You are violating your allegiance to this nation. Also, corruption in office is treason."

"Roger, but you. . . ."

Cliff rose from his chair, interrupted the president, looked at him with disrespect, shook his head, turned toward the door that exited the Oval Office and left. He walked along the hallway.

*Harrison has always been a bad liar. Do I resign? What about my oath of office? What about integrity? What about having no integrity like the cabal of the president, McDonald, Rigor and the others who want to invade Iran and control all of the oil from the Middle East? Do I become one of the boys, a team player, roll over, give him what he wants, and my integrity be damned? Probably get The Presidential Medal of Freedom if I cooperated. Look good on my résumé.*

## 25

**Day 12 11:00 A.M. The White House, the Oval Office**

James P. McDonald, the vice president, walked through the door unannounced and uninvited, which was normal and demonstrated the high regard he had for Robert. The president was alone. "I understand your meeting with Cliff didn't go well, what happened?"

"How did you know?"

"Robert, what happened?"

"What happened is: Cliff doesn't want to cooperate and give me the pretext to invade Iran on the basis of defending our national security. All he talked about was flawed and fabrication of intelligence. He told me Iran wasn't a national security issue and the CIA will not confirm it is.

"He told me with conviction, if I violated international law I'd be indicted by the International Criminal Tribunal at The Hague for crimes against humanity, murder, and maybe assassinated or impeached if the citizens become too aroused by our deceit. He told me you and your chief of staff had been pestering him weekly, wanted to go to war in Iran for financial benefits only to yourself and others. He called me a traitor, and told me I was committing treason, a high crime, and could be impeached. An altogether unpleasant confrontation. What do you want to do?"

"I want to invade Iran and have a permanent presence there, that's what I want you to do," McDonald responded with arrogance. "We'll not be able to get a resolution from the Security Council, that's for sure."

"What about my being assassinated, impeached, indicted, arrested and tried at The Hague?"

"I wouldn't worry about it."

"That's easy for you to say. They may indict, arrest, and try you if I provide them with the necessary information that I have. Remember, *Mr.* Vice President, if I go down you, Rigor, the cabal and our investors all go down."

"Robert, you have just become expendable to your family, our investors, yourself and me."

"What does that mean?"

"Look it up in the dictionary," McDonald told him, as he walked out of the Oval Office.

# 26

**Day 12   3:00 P.M.   The Kennington Estate**

One of those people wearing black two-piece suits, black tie, white shirt, black shoes with rubber soles and Oakleys to let every viewer know he was a member of a security detail and not a guest, entered the library and approached the Louis XVI desk and chair J.P. used and said, "Mr. Kennington."

"Yes, Roberts, what is it? What happened at the Brighton? Have you got the documents, if so, where are they?"

"I don't know, sir, the three men I sent haven't reported in or come back. They're probably KIA. I've tried to raise my man on his cellular telephone, but there's no answer."

"You mean killed in inaction don't you, Roberts. Seems to me you're having some difficulties following orders. I want my property back no matter what. If during the retrieval process an unfortunate loss of life should take place, it will be fit punishment for stealing from Jonathan P. Kennington. It's bad for business to allow people to steal from me and get away with it.

"Jones didn't return with my Lincoln Navigator, nor did two of your men who you sent with him to retrieve my property from O'Leary at her office. Have you heard from him? What about my SUV? Where is it?"

"I've tried to contact Jones and the other two, but they've not been found and your SUV is gone."

"Are you sure you're qualified for this job, Roberts?"

"Yes, I am. Seem to be having a run of bad luck or better competitors. Pursuant to your orders, we've located Sean Harrison. Lillian McGraw is probably with him. He used his cell phone and called his mother, Ms. Harrison. I've a transcription of it for you to read, if you want."

He handed it to J.P. It read: "Mother, I wanted to call you. I'm not supposed to use my cell, but I wanted to tell you I'm safe and tell you how much I love you."

"Oh, Sean, I've been so worried. Your father's trying to find you so he can send your Secret Service detail to bring you home. Your grandmother is beside herself."

"That's the other reason I called. I found out my father isn't Robert, but J.P. Kennington. I watched a VHS with the two of you having sex. I saw my birth certificate and the DNA Paternal Report. I know you have another child with him, Victoria Kennington. I forgive you, Mother, it's alright."

"We all make mistakes, my son. When will you be coming home?"

"I don't know if I will. Lillian and I will live together out here. Because of our relationship, marriage is probably out of the question. I don't know; I'll have to look into it."

"You're too young for marriage. Please, be careful, my son. There are bad people looking for you and Lillian."

"I will, mother, I love you. When I'm located, I'll call you again. I love you."

J.P. folded the transcription and put it into his inside coat pocket. *So, she made a mistake having Sean with me. And I'm a member of the bad people looking for him and Lillian. Her idea and she blames me. Well, at least she didn't use my name. Now Roberts knows my private business, and I'll have to get rid of him now. When is this nightmare going to be over?*

"Afterward Sean called O'Leary's office and talked to her. He wanted to leave where he was. She told him he was stupid for using his cell phone. What do you want done, Mr. Kennington?"

"I think we should accommodate Sean. If he wants to leave where he is so be it. You know what I want done. I've given you your orders previously. He or others he's aware of have my property that was stolen from me, while you and your minions were sleeping and not doing what you got paid to do. Not only did you allow McGraw to leave here with my property, but you then sent three people to the Brighton to do a simple job, and now they haven't come back. What happened to them?" He asked with anger.

"As I said, Mr. Kennington. I don't know. They should've been back long ago."

"Get Sean Harrison and my property back. It appears I made a mistake in hiring O'Leary. You met her when she was here at the house. She has become a problem. Then if he hasn't got my property go see O'Leary and get my property anyway you can. If she won't give it to you, dispose of her. Get one of your ruffians dressed as a homeless person, go to her office and just shoot her. Here's her file." Roberts took it.

"Yes, Mr. Kennington, I'll get right on it."

"See that you do. You know the penalty for failure."

"Yes, sir, I'm to mete out 'fit punishment' for both. Dispose of them after they have or haven't got your property. If this is what you want, it'll be extra."

"According to your contract with me, you're supposed to take orders whatever they may be, remember?"

"Sure, I remember. But under the circumstances, it'll be a hundred." He paused, "For each, Harrison and O'Leary."

"I do believe your 'under the circumstances' leads me to believe you believe you can go into business for yourself and extort me." *I do believe Mariah was right when she said, "Desperation is the father and anger is the mother of poor judgment, and you have surely displayed all three today." I do believe I'm about to make it four.*

"I'll give you cash. Meet me at the vault in five minutes. Give me the address of the location where he is." Roberts handed him the piece of paper with the address on it. "Go ahead, I'll be right there."

Roberts left the library and walked toward the stairs to the basement which was as large as the footprint of the foundation, fifteen thousand square feet. He reached into his lapel pocket and pushed the stop button on his digital recorder. This was his standard procedure when receiving orders from J.P. so he could protect himself from the false accusations: he had not followed orders. He would download the conversation to his computer and make a CD backup of it and place it in his safe after he retrieved the cash and went to his office in the house. *I'll need to call a meeting and set the plan for the abduction of Harrison.*

J.P. thought a moment, rose from his chair and followed two minutes behind Roberts. Roberts was standing by the vault door with the O'Leary dossier in his hand when J.P. arrived. J.P. stood close to the keypad to shield Roberts' view, put in the combination, used the retinal eye scanner, opened the door, the light went on, and he pushed the door until it was open far enough for him to enter. Roberts remained outside the vault. J.P. walked in, took out his key, opened a stainless steel locker door and removed a metal box from inside, placed it on the table and said, "Here it is. Count it out and meet me in the library for further instructions." J.P. walked out of the vault.

Roberts went in, sat at the table, put the folder on the table, opened the box, saw the packages of ten thousand held together with currency straps, pulled out a package and started to count.

J.P. closed the vault door, the light went out and he locked it. *If I remember correctly when I had the safe built, the specs said there was enough air in there to last one person for two days. I'll see if the manufacturer lied to me. So much for entrepreneurs. When are people going to stop going into business for themselves at my expense?*

Roberts sat in the dark, had plenty of money, more than he had asked for, but his inconvenience was impeding his gratification. *I do believe I have made serious errors in judgment: giving him the transcription of the cellular call, telling him about Sean's call to O'Leary and asking for the two hundred. Oh yes, letting him close the door with me inside. So what do you do now, dummy?*

He removed his Blackberry from his inside coat pocket and turned it on. There was no signal. Roberts opened the folder and used the light from the cell to read O'Leary's particulars. He opened his contacts' folder, entered her name,

Email address and saved it. He selected the email address and composed.

He pushed the send button. He knew if the cell was recovered and turned on, the message would be sent automatically. He turned off his cell. He got out of the chair, turned around and placed the recorder on the top of the shelving behind the chair on the Westside.

# 27

The twelve hundred square foot, two-bedroom house sat on a knoll on five thousand acres of agricultural land. It had a view of the Figueroa Mountains and the valley below. The Figueroas changed colors as the sun rose and set. It reminded one the colors changing in the Painted Desert in Arizona.

The house was not visible from the main house which sat back a quarter-mile from the highway. But the dirt road to the guest house was visible for about a mile. The house was constructed of adobe with a Spanish tile roof and a massive front door. The architecture was Southwestern. It was a duplicate in style, construction and was complementary to the main house, a sprawling one-story hacienda of twenty thousand square feet. Cattle, goats and sheep grazed on grass produced by the fertile land. A windsock and small hangar with an aircraft maintenance area were near one another about halfway down the nine thousand feet concrete runway equipped for day and night landings.

Oak, acacia and eucalyptus trees swayed in the soft breezes that cooled the land. The water fountain in the courtyard out in front of the guest house was in keeping with the haciendas of California. The house was decorated in earth tones and was a relaxing atmosphere. A king-size bed was in the master bedroom and rested on a Southwestern area rug and had a large bathroom. A queen-size bed on a Navajo area rug adorned the guest room with a full bath. The large living room had a fireplace. A full kitchen, utility room and a two-car garage detached completed the house's accommodations.

Sean sat in one of the saloon-style chairs that surrounded the six-foot diameter round dining table made of black walnut and under a wagon-wheel chandelier. The table was adorned with roses cut from the landscaping that surrounded the little house.

Foster Thompson walked in without knocking, saw Sean holding his personal cell. He walked over to where he sat, pulled him out of his chair by the front of his shirt, held his face close to his and said with anger, "Mariah just called and told me you called her on your cell to whine about missing your girlfriend and wanted to know when she was returning. You stole it from my office after I confiscated it from you. I told you not to make any calls. Who else did you call?"

"Leave me alone, you can't talk to me like this. I'm the president's son. Let me go."

"Who'd you call other than Mariah?"

"My mother to tell her I was alright."

"I know who I'm talking to. You're an elitist brat who has endangered yourself, my employees who are my friends, and who have served with me in Iraq and Afghanistan. Your stupidity's going to get us all killed. If you don't care anything about yourself, that's alright with me if you want to commit suicide. But you've no right to endanger my friends. You're a pariah as far as I'm concerned. When you see your father next, you can tell him I said so. If he has a difference of opinion, you can tell him how to contact me, preferably in person. You're some piece of two-legged garbage, Sean Harrison. If you weren't here under the protection of Mariah, I'd drag your dumb ass outside, shoot you dead and give you an exalted burial somewhere on my five thousand acres under some cattle pies. Make you disappear without a trace. Look, I don't enjoy babysitting the likes of you any more than you enjoy being here. So, stay out of trouble." Foster pushed him hard down into his chair, grabbed the cell from Sean, walked out of the house and drove back to his headquarters. He gave the cell to one of his men to put through the ranch's recycling metal shredder.

# 28

**Day 12  3:15 P.M.  The Brighton Hotel**

Mariah returned to the hotel. She walked in and saw George behind the desk with a bandage on his head and his hands in casts. His white hair barely showed below the bandage. The eighty-years-old man had weathered worse. She knew that, much worse in fact. The numbers tattooed on the inside of his left arm told it all.

"What happened to you?"

"Three men came in. Grabbed me and took me into the office. The biggest one pistol-whipped me into unconsciousness, because I wouldn't tell them your room number or anything else. Then they revived me and broke both my hands, and I gave it all up about the three rooms on the tenth floor and your room on five. Mariah, I love you like a daughter, and I'm sorry, but they were going to kill me, and I was surprised they didn't. I didn't report it to the police. I went to see Riggins and he fixed me up."

"Thank God you're alive. Do you need to see him again? What about Jerry and Lillian?"

"No, he said I'll be fine. Just time to heal and take the casts off. They're both fine. That Lillian and Jerry are some team. They're upstairs with Greg and some friends of his. When they're finished, I'll have the three rooms refurbished. I'm afraid they're not habitable at the moment."

"Thank you, George, God love you. I will need two new rooms, and I will take care of the refurbishing of the rooms. I will have my people get on it. You may forget about it. They will be as good or better than they were before."

He gave her two keys. "Thank you. Class always shows."

"Thank you, George. How nice of you to say so."

Mariah went upstairs to 1012. The door was open as were the front and connecting doors to the other two rooms.

In a jovial manner trying to lighten the depressing sight, Mariah looked at Jerry and Lillian, "It appears I cannot leave the two of you alone without refurbishing the rooms. You two are some house painters. Bad interior designers, too. Red is just not my color for wall adornment."

They smiled at her. "This lady's some shooter, Mariah," Jerry said. "She got two to my one. I didn't realize she was packing and her piece had a companion on its nose. Me, mine just made a lot of noise. The good news is there are no tenants on nine and ten and the windows were closed. Lillian and I concluded our continuing education class with A-pluses."

There was blood on almost every wall. Three bodies rested on the floors in two rooms and one in the hallway. Parts of the carpets in each room and part of the runner in the hallway were blood-soaked. Greg and his two friends had body bags and were in the process of bagging the incompetent uninviteds.

"Greg, I see you brought the cleaners."

"Yes, you know Roger and Clemenza."

"Yes, good day, gentlemen."

"Hello, Ms. O'Leary," they said in unison.

"I'll have them out of here in ten minutes, Mariah," Greg said. "Roger, Clemenza and I'll take care of them from here."

"Greg, speaking of taking care of them, will you put a crew together? Here are the three keys to these rooms. I want these three rooms stripped. Clean the furniture first if possible, and move the furniture to the rooms across the hallway and store it temporarily. Then remove all of the carpet in the three rooms and the hallway. Clean the walls, ceilings, repaint the entire three rooms and hallway, put in new carpet and pad and return the furniture and/or replace it on an as-needed basis. How long will it take you?"

"Three days max."

"Good. Let me know how much money you need as you need it. When you are finished, give me the bill for labor and anything else you needed to do the job. I want this place better than it was before. Thank you." She reached into her bag and handed him ten Benjys. "This is to get you started."

"I'll take care of it. Who's responsible for this bloodbath?" Jerry asked.

"I do not know, but I am willing to bet everything but my life I had lunch with him today. It is always good to have an alibi from someone who hates you, very believable. As opposed to a friend who nobody believes. We all know what liars friends can be. How do you feel, Lillian? Do you recognize any of these three people?"

"I feel fine, thank you. Sure, the one who made the blood smear on the wall above him and is sitting on the floor resting his back against the wall in 1010 is one of your lunch date's employees. He works for a guy by the name of Roberts. He's head of security for J.P. at the estate."

"Oh, yes, I met him. What about the other two?"

"Never seen them. Probably two subcontractors for deniability purposes. I don't know."

"Jerry, Greg, do you know these people?"

"Never seen them," they said, stepping on one another's lines.

"How did they find us?" Jerry asked.

"They tortured George."

"We'll put them in the body bags, take them down in the elevator to the garage and tonight dispose of them," Jerry said.

"When you get back, Jerry, I would like to speak with you, Greg and Lillian for a moment.

"Sure."

Greg, Jerry, Clemenza and Roger removed the filled black body bags from the three rooms and placed them in the elevator. They took them to the underground garage and placed them into Clemenza's SUV. Roger and Clemenza were Greg's military buddies from their Special Forces days. They hauled the "garbage" away.

*How can I have been so stupid? He duped me. He didn't want to have lunch and offer me a job. It was a charade. He did want to threaten me to get his property back, but that was not the reason for lunch. Was he being considerate? He might have thought killing or kidnapping an attorney might not have been good for him or his businesses. Who knows what Niccolò di Bernardo dei Machiavelli Kennington thinks and is up to?*

*I assume Greg means by that he and his two friends will be depositing the employee and subcontractors in circumstances so they will not be found. Probably turned into another form. You always need to be careful if you have a pet. Food contamination is a hazard. I guess this is one reason I do not eat sausage in a casing or otherwise or bologna either, by the way.*

Jerry and Greg returned. "Clemenza and Roger are on their way to the appropriate garbage dump," Greg said. "They'll let me know when the three have been turned into a different form, but not what form or where interred. I'll say one thing for the two of them: they've respect for the FDA and USDA regulations regarding our food supply. But it doesn't mean they won't use a heavy-duty wood chipper or large operation meat grinder feet-first at a processing plant even if they were still alive."

"Let us move to our new very temporary location. I have two new rooms down the hall." The four left the arena of carnage.

They went into 1020 and 1022, looked around, saw the rooms were furnished in the same design of earth tones as 1010, 1012 and 1014 and opened the adjoining doors. They brought chairs up to a small desk and sat.

Mariah told them the first order of business was: she would need new quarters for Lillian and her. They would need to leave the Brighton so George would not be tortured again. She thought she knew of a place, but would have to call first and see what the accommodations were. Greg and Jerry would be safe in the hotel where they were. They were not targets.

"Now, down to business. As usual, this is need-to-know only. I had not intended to include Lillian into this fray. But, Jerry seems to be impressed with her skills in certain areas, I in other areas and she is essential to my plan, because she knows all about J.P.'s business and is a computer wizard. So, I have decided to include her if it is alright with her, and then if it is alright with you two. Lillian?"

"As they say in Texas Hold'em, I'm all in. What are we going to do about Sean?"

"He is safe where he is and not qualified in any area to do what needs to be done; in fact, a liability."

"I'll take Jerry's and your word for it, Mariah," Greg said. "If you two like her, I like her."

"Jerry?" Mariah asked.

"I've seen some shooting in my time. She can be my partner in a shootout anytime. As to the rest of what you have in mind, I'll rely on your good judgment. So far, you, Greg and I are batting a thousand."

"Very well, it is the four of us against them. And therein, good people, lies the sticky wicket. One for sure is none other than Jonathan P. Kennington. Presently a billionaire, not in first place as the world's richest man but wants to be. What I do know is: if you let your desires control you and drive you, you stand a good chance of falling into a tiger trap, onto sharp bamboo stakes with dung on the points, a slow painful death. His above-the-law attitude is his weakness; this we will exploit and take him down."

Their goal was to give a slow painful death to their opponents. Death meant death as they knew it, and death meant deprivation of power and wealth. Either being satisfactory as long as they could do it anonymously or as close to it as possible without the victims knowing who was responsible for their permanent inconveniences. The forum was opened for discussion as to the best way to bring acclamation to the downfall of the deserving. Two candidates came to mind immediately, the president and marionette, Robert B. Harrison, his puppeteer, Jonathan P. Kennington, J.P. and their lackeys.

"During lunch today, J.P. said something very interesting. I didn't think much about it at the time. But riding in the cab back here it came to me. I believe he is in financial trouble. He said, 'My financial future is in jeopardy, and I need to correct this situation now.' He wanted to buy the DVDs, VHSs and get the original of the war plan. Actually he wants all of his property back, cash included. There must be one or more of the DVDs that hold the key to his financial future. Lillian, do you have an idea about this?"

"Yes, I think so. It was one of those honey-trap situations. He's addicted to debt. When someone controls your debt, they control you. His bank has loaned him more money than he or his companies are worth. He's collateralized with all of his stock and other holdings. In effect the bank owns his companies and everything else he owns, including his jets, yacht and estate. In my DVD collection there's one with Edvard Lavananski; he's the CEO of International Investment Bank and Trade, or IIBT, and J.P.'s prime lender. He's married to a prominent woman in international society. The DVD shows him having sexual relations with a young boy.

"The only reason J.P. was able to continue to borrow was because of the DVD and the supporting financial documentation of the bribes he gave to Lavananski not well disguised as loans. He also represented to the CEO he would have new government contracts with the Department of Defense because of his relationship with Harrison and DoD decision-makers. Based on all this, the CEO loaned him money illegally. If J.P. goes down, the bank will be insolvent. Considering the fact it's the world's largest bank, it could be a global financial nightmare.

"I have DVDs that show the secretary of defense, Glen Goodman, in compromising situations and the documentation of the bribes given."

Lillian told them J.P's pharmaceutical company was under investigation by the Federal Drug Administration for importing cheap, tainted prescription drugs from China the company knew were tainted, but didn't care and sold them to the public knowing the products could cause and did cause deaths. He had bribed doctors to prescribe drugs approved by the FDA for specific problems, but had expanded the use of the drugs for problems not included in the approval and had been another act of illegality.

These acts of illegality confirmed his weakness: his above-the-law attitude. Mariah knew how to cause his downfall. Her first order of business was the "War Plan" devised and signed by J.P. and signed off on by the marionette, Robert. She believed J.P. and Robert had had a falling out. She realized when Kennington said that to her at lunch her sowing of dissension between them had been successful.

Since the president had gone to Prague and met with Petrokov, the Russian president, one could infer Robert had been manipulated by Richard Rigor and James McDonald to go to war without J.P.'s approval or selection of country for their own personal financial benefits. Mariah believed Petrokov had given his word he would not interfere, and maybe he had signed an agreement to that effect. If an agreement had been signed, they needed to find it.

The president's cabal could accomplish two things. The war would probably get Robert re-elected, their major concern, and the cabal would disguise the illegal war of greed as a fight against terrorism, a flexible definition depending on the politician who spoke at the time.

Mariah explained a friend of hers would be joining them. He was Geoffrey MacIntosh, a former deputy director of the National Security Agency, or the NSA. He had done computer programming at MIT, or Massachusetts Institute of Technology, and the NSA. He was considered by his peers to be the best of the best computer wizards of all time. She quoted Cicero: "Nihil tam munitum quod non expugnari pecuna posit." Translation: "No fortress is so strong it cannot be taken by money." As to Geoffrey, a slight change of the quote was appropriate: "No firewall is so strong it cannot be penetrated by MacIntosh without leaving tracks." She thought: *At this moment we are a band of patriots who are willing to give our lives for what we feel is the right thing to do, that is, climb Mount Everest backward.*

"I like the idea of using his own money to cause his downfall, irony it is," Mariah said. "After all, he said it wasn't missing. So therefore, it isn't. And the possessor of the money has the right to spend it any way the possessor sees fit. So, let us use his cash to pay all of our operatives weekly. If there is any left over, we will give it to John Riggins' clinic. Is this good for you, Lillian?"

She hesitated for a second caused by the surprise question and said, "Yes, whatever it takes."

"Once the operatives get their first cash, each of them will hire me for a small retainer fee, no hourly rate, sign my fee agreement and a receipt for the money paid. This way I can collect the information they gather and it will fall into the attorney-client privilege, which I will not violate."

Greg would be the paymaster. He and Jerry would be the recruiters. They knew all the ex-CIA operatives, police officers and Special Forces people. Greg would ask them not to drink during the operation. They would come into the bar to socialize. Greg and Jerry would not hire anyone they have not known for a very long time, and knew he and or she could be trusted and to expect attempted infiltration. All these people would be dedicated to their cause against the "War Plan" and the downfall of J.P. and Robert. Mariah outlined her plan and the others agreed to it.

"We will need to prepare a dossier and set up surveillance around the clock on Rigor," Mariah said. "Lillian, you and Geoffrey will do the dossier. Jerry, you will put teams together to track him. I want full electronic and humint. I will arrange for hotels and cars. Geoffrey will set up the tracking of his cell, but you will need teams to follow him and see who he meets. If he makes a mistake, we will interrogate him and find out what is really going on with the president's and vice president's war plans, and then we will turn him."

"I believe there's a way for us to get a little help from the inside. This is what I have in mind." Lillian explained her plan. The three agreed.

# 29

## Day 13  9:00 A.M.  The White House, the Oval Office

"J.P., I have not heard from Jones, have you? He doesn't answer his cell."

"Shut the fuck up, Robert. I'm handling it. You were a dumb fuck to hire O'Leary and Jones. Because of you, O'Leary knows that we're after her and our "War Plan" document. Jones, two of my security people and my new Navigator are missing."

"So, what happened, J.P., when you sent your people to the Brighton? Are our problems over?"

"They have disappeared also and didn't do the job or get any of my things back. No one has found anything."

"Speaking of 'a dumb fuck', you're not so smart after all. You said you were going to hire a dumb lawyer in the ghetto so you could set her up to take a fall whenever we wanted. So far, it appears she has outsmarted both of us, and you hired Jones."

"But not for long. Why don't you hire some former CIA operatives like Nixon did? Some black baggers. Get the documents and all my property back and be done with it."

"I don't think another Watergate would be of assistance to my re-election campaign if they got caught."

"No risk, no gain. You've always been a wimp, Robert."

# 30

## Day 13   10:15 A.M.   Geoffrey MacIntosh's Home, Los Angeles

Lillian and Mariah moved in with Geoffrey MacIntosh on Charing Cross in Holmby Hills, south of Sunset Boulevard.

The three of them sat in his office. He had been listening to Bill Evans *Symbiosis* album. Mariah said, "Geoffrey, I have given you the background on why we are going to be your guests for a few days. I will still be going to the office. It is now obvious the president is not going to cancel his plan to go to war, so we need all the information we can retrieve from every source to defeat him and J.P.

"We need to monitor the progress of the manufacturing of the gas and stop the plan and expose it before any Americans are killed for greed, maybe a little comeuppance at the end and give J.P. a taste of his plot.

"Lillian, this is my thought. Because the world is run with ones and zeros, I would like for you to supply Geoffrey with all of the information you have on all of J.P.'s businesses worldwide and his computer system at the estate in Bel Air. The only firewall that can keep Geoffrey out is if the computer is off. But corporations do not turn their servers off."

"All the work stations and the server at the estate are on all the time," Lillian said. "Probably with one of the DVDs we have I can get Lavananski, the president of IIBT, to cooperate with me. He's a pillar of the community, an evangelical and married with three children. He has been having sex weekly with young boys, another religious hypocrite. It'll have to be done swiftly; as soon as J.P. finds out he's out of business he'll threaten him with exposure. Lavananski will not know J.P. doesn't have the DVD any longer." Lillian had information regarding J.P.'s staff and the management of his businesses on her laptop. All of his secrets were digital.

"I'll be able to install key logging and key stroking onto all of the computer work stations in the house of J.P," Geoffrey said. "I can read all of his communications. I can penetrate the server and shut down the computers with a Trojan, worm or virus if we need to? I'll go into the telephone master control panel and see if it'll allow me to turn every handset into a microphone and listen to conversations. I can also tap the phones and record the conversations. Global satellites will allow me to use the Random Frequency Tracking System. The system will capture cell numbers. I'll put in key words and an alarm will activate when the key word is used, and I can listen to the conversation and see if it will help us. If Lillian can get some inside help, we'll not have to train an antenna onto J.P.'s home on the estate."

Mariah said, "Geoffrey, the principle involved is: to cause the downfall of this corrupt administration and J.P. Kennington. These acts will save the U.S. from the president's cabal, the tyrannical ambition of McDonald, prevent the murders of Americans so Harrison can be re-elected, not go to war for greed and to defeat the egregious ambition of J.P. Kennington. As you know, members of the previous administration conspired to go to war illegally in Iraq, and because of that they murdered our military personnel, the military personnel of other nations, its civilians, and they have not been held accountable, yet. I am hoping one of these days they will be indicted and tried for their war crimes. They squandered billions of dollars that could have been used to improve our infrastructure and the lives of our citizens. We are calling this project 'Operation Downfall'."

# 31

**Day 14   11:55 P.M.   The Kennington Estate**

J.P. had placed a call to Daren Dirk after the entombment of Roberts and asked him to be at the estate with two colleagues. J.P. sat behind his desk in the library and Dirk sat in one of the visitors' chairs. The two colleagues sat in the foyer.

"Pursuant to our earlier conversation, I've a job for you. I need a new head of security here. Are you interested?"

"Of course."

"Here's an address. There's a man there by the name of Sean Harrison. He has or had knowledge of the whereabouts of my property. I want all my property back. It consists of cash, documents, DVDs and VHSs. Be discreet and don't be caught. Use the best of the best for this job.

"Then there's a lawyer by the name of Mariah O'Leary who may have the cash and documents. She's to be interrogated and get all my property back. I'll look at the documents to make sure all has been returned. If she hasn't got them, there'll be a woman with her by the name of Lillian McGraw. If she's not with her, make O'Leary tell you her whereabouts. Get the cash, documents, DVDs and VHSs from one of the three and then terminate them.

"Next, there's a man in the vault downstairs who's dead. He needs to be removed from there and disposed of. Are these assignments agreeable to you?"

"Yes, I've two reliable men, and I brought the body bag you requested."

"Good, what's your fee?"

"The same as last time six months ago. Each assignment will be a million in cash."

"Done. When all three are finished, you'll be stationed here as head of security and as of now interim head of security. This is all need to know. No discussion with any of the other security people here or anyone else. Agreed?"

"Yeah, sure let's get at it."

J.P. and Dirk walked from the library to the foyer. Dirk motioned for his colleagues to join him. They got into the elevator and went to the basement. They approached the vault. J.P. stood close to the keypad and obstructed the view of the three. He put in the combination and used the retinal eye scanner to release the lock and the green light went on. He opened the door and there was a foul odor of human waste. The two colleagues placed Roberts into the body bag and zipped it closed. J.P. then asked Dirk to have his people remove the fecal matter and the urine from the floor with the rags and dustpan nearby. They put the used rags and fecal matter into the body bag after they cleaned the vault floor.

J.P. went back in and retrieved a black-medium size piece of luggage with soft-sides. He picked it up, carried it from the safe and handed it to Dirk and said, "Pursuant to our previous arrangements, here's your request."

"Thank you."

J.P. and Dirk got on the elevator and rode it to the foyer. The two colleagues carried the body bag up the stairs to the foyer, went through the front door and placed the bag and its contents into the rear area of their SUV.

"I'll be in touch with you, J.P., as soon as I have Harrison in hand, I'll put the question to him with vigor, and then you can give me instructions as to when and where his disposal is to take place."

"Look forward to hearing from you, Dirk."

Daren and his colleagues left the estate.

J.P. retired to his bedroom. *Now, for a good night's sleep for a change.*

# 32

**Day 15   2:00 A.M.   The Mojave Desert Off California State Route 138**

Two men in an SUV pulled off the highway and into a barn that needed repair. They put on their lightweight MV-14BGP Dual Tube night-vision goggles attached to a PVS-7/14 head mount. The goggles provided excellent vision and depth perception. One of them lifted the rear door with his gloved hand. They removed the body bag filled with Roberts, rags and fecal matter from behind the last seat. They had removed him from the Kennington Estate two hours earlier. They took it twenty yards behind the barn into the desert. Randolph and his partner dug with two shovels for thirty minutes and were satisfied with the depth of their performances as amateur grave diggers. They removed Roberts and the rags from the bag. Randolph searched him and removed Roberts' Blackberry, his Rolex watch, wallet, money and stripped him of his clothes. The clothes were placed into a garbage bag.

Randolph's partner returned to the SUV and retrieved five-gallon bottles of sulfuric acid. The partner filled Roberts' mouth with acid, poured it onto Roberts' palms, fingers and face. Then they pushed him in the grave with their shovels. The partner poured the remainder of the acid from the bottle and another bottle onto the entire body from head to toe.

Randolph shot his partner twice in the heart with his Smith and Wesson four-inch .38. He stripped him of his night-vision goggles and head mount, all of his belonging and his clothes. The clothes were placed into the garbage bag. He poured acid into his mouth, on his palms, fingers and face and pushed him with his shovel into the grave on top of Roberts. He proceeded to pour all of the remaining acid from head to toe on the two of them and the body bag. He dropped the five empty bottles into the grave. He shoveled the dirt and covered the bodies. He leveled the dirt on top of the grave and threw the remainder of the dirt in every direction. *The wind will be coming during the day and will distribute the dirt. The grave site will look like its surroundings by later today.*

Randolph walked back to the SUV. He placed his partner's things into his gear bag along with Roberts' Blackberry. Then he opened the rear door and placed the bag inside. He removed all of the money from the wallets and put them in the bag. He put the money into his wallet. He took off his watch and put it in. He put on Roberts's Rolex. He closed the rear door and entered the driver's seat. He started the drive back to Los Angeles. *I'll keep the Blackberry, donate the clothes to the Thrift shop, take all of the contents of the wallets and shred them. Discard the empty wallets into a Dumpster along with the gloves I'm wearin'.*

# 33

**Day 15   6:00 P.M.   The Apartment of Roger Preston, Los Angeles**

Lillian sat in the living room with Roger. He was the Internet Technician, or IT, for J.P. at the estate.

Roger and Lillian sat in his living room. "Roger, I'd like to help you with your financial problems you have mentioned to me in the past. Are you interested?"

"Yes, of course."

"Money in exchange for information. Anything interesting happen since I've been gone?"

"You bet. J.P.'s been more unpleasant since you left and is looking for you. Hired an attorney by the name of O'Leary to find you, spent a lot of money but is unhappy with her. I guess she didn't find you. Jones and two security thugs went to see O'Leary, and they've disappeared along with J.P.'s brand new Lincoln Navigator. Three other security people disappeared along with another car of J.P.'s. The man's fit to be tied.

"And the topper, Roberts disappeared very suddenly. His car's still at the estate. He didn't say goodbye to J.P. and has wages due. He didn't take his final check. Also, evidently there was an odor J.P. didn't like in the vault. So he stood and watched someone deodorize the vault with some kind of aerosol. Very strange goings on after you left. J.P. hired a guy by the name of Daren Dirk as his new head of security."

"Interesting. I'll try to reach Roberts on his cell phone; I've his number on my laptop. Maybe he can help me. Any change of passwords or anything unusual with the server or work stations?"

"No. J.P. didn't order any changes, and I haven't suggested it because I thought you may want to penetrate and look around. Though I know new passwords or firewalls aren't going to keep *you* out with your skills. Anyway, I thought I'd leave well enough alone and make it easier for you."

"Thank you. Here's an envelope with cash which should take care of your debt. If you should see any penetration, call me first before you get alarmed. I'll give you my number. It's for a talk and toss. Don't call unless it's a must. Otherwise, I'll call you daily here at home. I'm going to try and rectify some ills."

"Lillian, I've always loved you. Thank you, for all you did for me when we were working together for J.P. What are you going to do?"

"What I should've done a long time ago, but didn't have the courage or the support. Thank you for the compliment. I'll be in touch."

# 34

**Day 16 3:00 A.M. The Foster Thompson Ranch, San Feliz, California**

Daren Dirk, Randolph and six of their operatives arrived in three black Humvees at the barbed-wire fence. It was the farthest distance from the main house of the five-thousand acre ranch. Two of the operatives got out of the lead vehicle and cut the wire between two posts. The armored Humvees had been prepared by AM General at the request of Kennington Industries, J.P.'s defense contracting company, for the purpose of testing. The Humvees had a hybrid-electric drive train for improved mileage and the ability to run almost silently for tactical surprise and a blast-bucket inner shell to protect the operatives. Each had a Browning .50-caliber machine gun mounted on the roof with a protective shield to protect the torso of the shooter when he stood in the firing position. A .50-caliber round could put a hole in a cinder block about the size of a tasty Ruby Red grapefruit. The ammo belts hung from each .50, and there was one in each chamber.

All the operatives wore the MV-14BGP Dual Tube night-vision goggles and head mounts over their black balaclavas. The dual tube design was excellent for driving a vehicle in the dark, because of the ability to achieve accurate depth perception so the vehicles and their operatives could move through the terrain without headlights to the setting on the GPS devices on the dashboards.

Each operative wore black coveralls, Kevlar bullet-proof vests and combat boots. The operatives communicated by radio. They were armed with sleeping-gas canisters, .45-caliber Glock 21s with suppressors and ranger knives. Each carried an automatic Alliance Armament Saiga 12 Conversion shotgun with an eighteen-inch barrel and a thirty-round drum loaded with Triball shells. Each shell held three pellets that weighed three-quarters of an ounce and was 15.24mm in diameter. The shotgun carried an Eotech sight with a forward pistol grip.

The night watch commander at Foster's headquarters awoke Foster and alerted him. The commander told him of the movement he saw on the infrared monitor toward the guest house of three vehicles with eight personnel. Foster said, "General quarters for everyone. Institute 'Infiltrations Plan A'." The information was passed to all of the personnel on duty through their receiver-transmitter communications systems. The off-duty personnel were awakened and alerted in their quarters by a Klaxon.

The Humvees moved toward the guest house and dodged the cattle, goats and sheep as they proceeded. The three stopped on top of a knoll and looked down at the dark guest house. Dirk looked at his infrared monitor and said, "Two occupants of the guest house. It appears they're sleeping in two different bedrooms. No guards on duty. Alright, proceed according to the plan, and see if one of the occupants is our target. If not, we'll proceed to the main house and or the interrogation and detention center if necessary."

Randolph approached the guest house and parked about five yards away. He and an operative got out of the Humvee and walked to the back door. Randolph tried the knob, but the door was locked. He removed a pick lock gun and a torque wrench from his pocket and unlocked the door. The operative put on his gas mask, walked to one bedroom and sprayed the sleeper with the sleeping gas. The gas had been prepared by Kennington Chemical and Pharmaceutical to put people to sleep for thirty minutes without any after-effects. It was to be used to prevent hijacking of commercial aircraft by releasing the gas into the passenger compartment. The operative determined the sleeper was not the target. He exited the house and got into his Humvee and waited for Randolph.

Two of Foster's guards approached the operative who waited for Randolph with stealth. They came from an outpost to the east and were unseen by Dirk. They wore night-vision goggles and carried P226 SIG Sauers. They removed the operative from the Humvee and subdued him. Then gagged him, plugged his ears, put a black hood on and bound his hands behind him and his feet with plastic zip ties. They connected the tied wrists and ankles with an adjustable web belt and pulled it so it was taut. They carried him to their SUV and placed him into the rear cargo compartment. They walked back to the Humvee and waited.

Dirk and the others watched the action in the guest house on the infrared monitors in the other two vehicles. Dirk announced, "Five vehicles approaching from the main house at speed. See if the target's there and get back to your vehicle. Your partner's been captured. We're going to need all the firepower we can muster."

Randolph put on his gas mask and went into the other bedroom. He sprayed the sleeper with the gas. He turned on his penlight and saw the sleeper was Sean Harrison and said, "I have the target. Pull the transportation to the front." He removed him from the bed, went through the front door and deposited him in Dirk's Humvee. Dirk's operatives gagged him, put ear plugs into his ears, put a hood on him and pulled the drawstring tautly. They bound his wrists together behind his back, his ankles together and placed him in the rear. Dirk made a U-turn and drove as fast as possible to the entry point in the barbed-wire fence. The other Humvee followed.

A rocket-propelled grenade struck the trailing Humvee and it exploded killing the three occupants. The .50-caliber gunner in Dirk's Humvee returned fire at the approaching vehicles. The tracers, every five rounds, lit the paths. The devastating fire from the .50 ripped into the engines and unarmored SUVs. They exploded and killed six men. Dirk and two of his operatives escaped through the perimeter of the ranch with Sean Harrison.

Randolph looked through the guest house for documents, DVDs, VHSs or anything that looked like it belonged to J.P. He found nothing and prepared to leave.

One of Foster's guards who had subdued the operative in the Humvee waited with his back flat against the outside wall of the guest house on the hinge side of the door. He knew there was another person inside, because the operative who was captured had waited in the Humvee. He turned his head to the left, looked at the rear door and waited. Randolph walked through the door with his shotgun at the ready. He didn't see the guard, because he was hidden by the solid door. The guard greeted Randolph with an unwelcomed assault. He struck him at the base of his skull with his SIG. The two guards bound him hand and foot, placed plugs in his ears, a hood on his head and hogtied him. The guards put the two unconscious bound and hooded operatives into the Humvee.

"Base, this is Three. Two prisoners, Humvee, gear, gear bags and weapons. Destination interrogation and detention. Be prepared. Three out." The other guard drove the SUV to the detention center.

Foster dispatched two men to the point of entry of the intruders to repair the fence. He also had installed a sensor that would alert headquarters to a repeat of the breach along the length of the fence in that area.

# 35

Tom Jones and the two thugs captured by Mariah and Greg at her office were in the detention area. They were dressed only in two pieces of clothing. But, they were runway ready in sartorial splendor with designer-tailored pullover shirts and baggy drawstring trousers made of unprocessed wool for maximum comfort and no footwear.

Each enjoyed his own six by six feet five-star solitary cell with a ten-foot high ceiling and it was monastic in its décor. The cells were soundproof to produce the maximum benefit from contemplation and meditation. They were constructed of hardened steel on all six sides. The steel door in the front side had a rectangular door at the bottom with a locking bolt on the outside. It was just large enough to slide a food bowl into the cell; sterling flatware was not in attendance. The old-fashioned method was available, fingers. The bowl was four inches in diameter and one inch high. A one-way eyepiece adorned the door that allowed a guard to look into the cell if the light in the middle of the ceiling behind bullet-proof glass was turned on from a switch next to the door on the outside of the cell. Otherwise, the occupants remained in the dark without sensory stimuli, except for the constant scratching caused by the softness of the unprocessed wool clothing, to improve contemplation and meditation but were monitored from the master control room by infrared.

There was a toilet, basin and cold water unit in one corner of the cell opposite the door. It was made of stainless steel and anchored to the floor and to the two steel walls that were in juxtaposition. The bed was made of hardened steel and had no mattress, sheet, blanket or pillow. The water drain was covered by a six-inch grill. The cell was steamed-cleaned and sanitized after the departure of the occupant or on an as-needed basis.

Randolph and the other operative who were captured at the guest house were brought into the facility and put into separate interrogation cells. The cells had concrete floors covered with lime-green epoxy paint and with a water drain in the middle of the floor covered by a grill. The four walls, ten-foot ceiling and door were hardened steel. A rectangular-steel table and two bare-steel chairs were anchored to the floor. A single fluorescent light fixture covered by bulletproof glass was in the middle of the ceiling and controlled from a switch next to the door on the outside. The temperature in the room was sixty-two.

Randolph sat in the nude on the steel chair facing the door. His wrists were bound behind him. His ankles were bound and joined to his wrists by a taut web belt which ran under the seat of the chair and to his wrists. He had been in this condition for about an hour. The other operative was in another cell and in the same circumstance.

An interrogator walked into the cell and the door closed. He wore mirrored aviator's eye glasses, desert camouflage fatigues, desert boots and a vest filled with eider down, the mottled brown feathers from the female eider duck. He placed a folder on the table. He sat in the chair opposite Randolph.

"During your unconscious period, our forensics people rolled your fingerprints and took your picture. We took some blood for DNA sampling. You're Randolph Waters. I ran your prints and photo through the FBI's Integrated Automated Fingerprint Identification System, aka IAFIS. It turns out you're a Soldier of Fortune wannabe, just another incompetent thug without skills. You've convictions for assault with a deadly weapon, robbery of liquor stores and other muscle and no-brains' arrests and convictions against innocent and helpless victims who couldn't shoot back. You're a coward and a dirtbag. Whoever hired you must be desperate. Your colleague, the other incompetent, told me you were hired by Daren Dirk to do wet work and kidnapping at the request of J.P. Kennington. Dirk's another notorious sadistic mercenary. Is this right? Did he tell me the truth, or do I have to pull out the fingernails on his other hand?" *No reason to tell this dirtbag the truth. Let him think about his fingernails. Torture's not a method to get reliable information, anyway.*

"So, what's the answer, Mr. Waters?"

"What do I get if I tell you?"

"Your life. Now, what's the answer or do I go for the pliers?"

"Can I get out of here, put on some clothes and get warm?"

"Yes, right after you tell me all, and I confirm it."

"Alright." Randolph told him Kennington hired Dirk, about the removal of the body of Roberts from J.P. Kennington's vault in Bel Air, and that J.P. supervised it. He related Roberts' burial but not the killing of his partner. Randolph said Dirk hired him to remove Roberts from the vault, buried him and where, participated in the kidnapping of Sean Harrison and the planned return of Harrison to the Kennington estate.

"You'll be leaving this morning with two men. You'll identify the site and uncover the grave for them. Both men are forensic experts. If you've lied, wasted my or their time, you may look forward to the probability of hiding in the Mojave under hard pack, never to be seen again. So, if what you have told me isn't true, tell me now or join your ancestors at the site."

"It's all true."

"Are you going to cooperate?"

"Yes."

"I went through your gear bag and retrieved a cell phone before we started to enjoy one another's company. Is it yours?"

"I took it from Roberts before my partner and I buried him."

"Why?"

"My cell's a cheap one, and I knew the Blackberry was high quality. I intended to have the service transferred to my name."

"I also found a revolver that has been fired recently. Two pair of night-vision goggles. Why? Who belongs to the other pair?"

"They belonged to the man who helped me bury Roberts. The gun is mine."

"Where's that man? What's his name?"

Randolph looked away and did not answer.

"I'm waiting; answer me," he said, with firmness.

Randolph did not answer. "So you shot him with this revolver and dumped him into the grave with Roberts, right? I know the revolver's yours. Our forensics dusted it and the prints match yours. I'm led to believe you killed your partner, right? Who ordered you to do it?"

"Daren Dirk. He told me J.P. Kennington told him he wanted no witnesses."

"Why didn't Dirk kill you when you returned?"

"He needed me for this Sean Harrison job?"

The interrogator turned on the cell and set it on the table beside his folder. It received a full signal. "It is listed to a man by the name of Cornell Roberts." The interrogator looked through the contacts and emails. He saw Mariah O'Leary's name. At that moment, the interrogator saw that an email had just been sent to her by Roberts. He read the message and said, "I'll be right back."

He left the cell and locked the door. He went to a telephone and called Foster and said, "Foster, can you come here for a moment. You need to see this."

Foster arrived. The interrogator told him about the burial of Roberts, the interrogation to date, and the message on Roberts' cell. Foster read it and said, "Thank you. I must call her at once and tell her about all of this and the kidnapping of Sean. Stay with your detainee and wring him out. Make sure you have video and audio. Then have it transcribed, signed by the interrogee and notarized by Rachel. Get two men to take him to the site and verify the information. If Roberts and the detainee's partner are in there, call me and I'll give you instructions. And then place him in solitary after you return. When you're finished with the other detainee, make sure you get his signed confession, and then put him into solitary until I decide what to do with them after I talk to O'Leary."

# 36

Mariah opened her email account on her laptop and read the message from Roberts. "Ms. O'Leary, you're the only honest lawyer I know. If you read this message, I'm dead. J.P. Kennington has locked me in his vault in the basement of his house in Bel Air, and I've suffocated.

"There's no cell signal in here. Have one of your techs find this phone. The person in possession will probably be the person who disposed of my body and may know J.P. murdered me, if you can make him talk. Whoever turns it on will automatically send this message from storage. It's dark, but I'll write a brief note by the light of my cell and put it under the table in here so you'll know I was here and this story is true. Also, if I defecate I'll do so in the vault, but will put some fecal matter under the table near the note so you can check my DNA and confirm my story.

"J.P. knows the whereabouts of Sean Harrison. He's going to kidnap him and make him return his property. Or, hold him hostage until he gets his property back. He may or may not want to kill him at the time he finds out Sean doesn't have his property. He also wanted me to get his property back from you if Harrison didn't have it, and then when I got his property I was to dispose of you. The digital recording of my conversation with J.P regarding you and Sean is in the vault with me. I'm going to place the recorder on the top of the shelving on the Westside. All of J.P.'s orders to me have been downloaded to CDs with the dates and times and are in my safe in the office. The combination is Left 4 times to 25, R 3x17, L2x77, R to 96 and stop. Whatever you can do to cause J.P. Kennington any inconveniences for all of the evil he has done and my murder will be greatly appreciated. He'll probably hire someone else to get Harrison, and if he's held hostage it'll probably be at the estate. Roberts."

"Greg, will you call Jerry and have him join us for a moment, please." Ten minutes later, Jerry walked into Raymond's and sat in the booth opposite her.

Greg walked from behind the bar and sat in her office next to Jerry. "We may now have two plans which we will implant simultaneously. Something unusual has happened. It appears J.P.'s desperation has caused him to use poor judgment, and he may have shot himself in his pocket book. If what I believe is true, we will be able to accelerate his downfall. Sean Harrison has been kidnapped by J.P.'s goons. Also, it appears J.P. has murdered his former head of security and had two goons bury him in the Mojave Desert of Los Angeles County. Greg, do you have one of your friends in the sheriff's department in homicide?"

"Sure," he said with the small remainder of a southern accent. "You know him, Christopher James. He comes in here all the time. I introduced you to him about a month ago."

"Good, I am waiting for a call from Foster. If the information he believes is right, Mr. James will need to view the remains with a coroner to determine the cause of death if he can before an autopsy. He will need forensics there, too."

"When you know, I'll take care of it."

# 37

## Day 16   12:00 P.M.   The Kennington Estate

J.P called Mariah at her office. "Ms. O'Leary, Mr. Kennington here."

She reached into her shoulder bag and removed her digital recorder. She plugged the device into her cell, activated it and said, "Yes, Mr. Kennington, what can I do for you?"

"I've something you want, and you've much of what I want. I'm willing to exchange no questions asked as long as all of my property's returned."

"What is it you believe I want, and what makes you believe I have anything of yours?"

"I've Sean Harrison. He'll be my reluctant guest until I get the return of my property. He'll be enjoying the confinement in his girlfriend's former room."

"You kidnapped him from the resort where he was living. That is a felony. And I am not aware I am in possession of any of what you want. What do you think I have of yours that you want back?"

"So he was kidnapped. So what? Do you really believe I give a shit what some D.A. or law enforcement officer thinks? I buy and sell politicians by the dozen. I want back my DVDs, VHSs, the 'War Plan' document and my money, about six hundred thousand plus of it. And, I want it all now."

"What you want and what you are going to get are two different things. First, I have no interest in Sean Harrison other than as a client. I am sure the president and his wife may have an opinion different from mine, so you should call them. And I did not take your property, and therefore, I cannot return it."

"I suggest you develop an interest in Sean. I suggest you find my property and return it, or there may be another celebrity disappearance."

"I cannot help you, Kennington. You must do what you are going to do. Call the president and see if you can exchange him for what you want. Ask the president for your property back. After all, you own him. Order him to return your property." She disconnected.

To say J.P. was furious when he slammed the handset into its cradle would be a euphemism. It is sometimes called an adult tantrum.

Mariah called Lillian at MacIntosh's home. She related the conversation with J.P. to her. Lillian said, "I'll take care of it. Is Jerry in town?"

"Yes."

"Would you please ask him to pay me a visit?"

"Yes."

Foster called and told Mariah there were two men in the grave in the Mojave Desert. He asked her for instructions and she provided them.

# 38

## Day 16   9:00 P.M. Washington, D.C.

Jerry had assembled three surveillance teams of two men each and sent them to Washington, D.C. Six former CIA field agents had Richard Rigor under electronic and human surveillance, or humint, twenty-four hours a day and seven days a week. Team One penetrated his D.C. apartment and installed audio-visual equipment that transmitted to their laptops. They placed small wafer-thin GPS locators into the cuff of each pair of his trousers. Each team's laptops acted as a tracking monitor.

A laptop sat on Rigor's desk in his den-office. The tech booted it and saw it was connected to the White House network. He removed a flash drive prepared by Geoffrey MacIntosh and inserted it into a USB port and followed his instructions. This allowed Geoffrey and Lillian to have access to the data and download what was needed to Geoffrey's server to assist in Operation Downfall.

When Richard Rigor returned to his apartment after work, Team Two placed a GPS locator into his car along with a miniature audio transmitter above and behind his head where the headliner met the rubber seal for the driver's door. They retrieved his cell phone number from his telephone bill in his apartment and used it to track him and listen to his conversations. They tapped his landline. It was called belt and suspenders. Electronics designers called it redundancy, insurance. From his desktop, Geoffrey backed up his pornographic videos of child pornography to a ten-terabyte external drive. Then they installed key logging and keystroking software. They were able to read all of his emails. One of Team Two's members downloaded all of the contacts with their attendant information from his database.

Team Three's members, Simon Spencer, and his partner, saw Rigor take a young boy into a public restroom. Rigor was dressed in a business suit. The boy wore tennis shoes, jeans, shirt, jacket, and carried a backpack.

Spencer waited a minute, walked on his black rubber-soled shoes and followed them in. He determined the stall they were in. He went into a stall next to them.

He listened for a moment, heard their engagement and then stood on the toilet.

He retrieved his high-resolution JVC GY-HM100U compact-handheld camcorder which was capable of recording in reduced light. He rose and moved to the partition that separated Rigor's and the young boy's stall from his. He removed his small mirror, placed it in a position to see the activities of the two. Rigor was engaged in orally copulating the boy's erected penis and masturbating himself. Spencer moved the camera into position and recorded the sexual activity. The camera didn't make a sound. He stopped the recording, checked the reproduction and transmitted the images to his laptop in his car. The transmission arrived and Spencer heard from his partner through his communications' transmitter-receiver in his ear, "Good transmission." He left the stall silently, placed the camera in his camera bag and washed his hands. He stood by the wash basins, leaned his buttocks against them and waited for Rigor and the boy to exit the stall.

Shortly, the boy came out of the stall. Rigor locked the stall door. Spencer activated his microphone, a redesigned Uniball Gel Impact RT pen, by pressing the button twice on the top of the pen that exposed the point. The microphone transmitted any sounds to his laptop computer in his car that was parked near the restroom. Spencer approached the boy and showed him his Washington, D.C., Metropolitan Police Department identification which had been made by one of Jerry's document's techs. He announced himself as a police officer. Rigor was still in the stall. "What is your name, Son?"

"Charlie Newman."

"Let me see your school I.D." The boy removed his wallet and took out his identification. Spencer recorded all of the information on the identification. "I see you've some one-hundred dollar bills in your wallet. Where did you get those?"

"A man gave them to me."

"What man?"

"The man in the stall there." The boy pointed to the stall where Rigor was situated. "Why did he do that?"

"Because he wanted to suck my cock."

"Did he suck it?"

"Yes, but not very well. I've had better."

"How old are you?"

"Thirteen."

"Do you know him?"

"Sure. When we first met, he told me his name was Frank Smith. But I know it's Richard Rigor. I saw his wallet once. I opened it and saw his driver's license. I meet him once or twice a week. Sometimes, I go to his home and sometimes we just do it wherever we are, in his car, in restrooms, in restaurants' restrooms or in the park. He likes to fuck me in the ass, but my ass was sore from his fucking me the day before yesterday, so I didn't want to do it tonight. So, I agreed to just let'm suck my cock."

"How much did he pay you tonight?"

"Two hundred."

"How much does he pay you to engage in sodomy?"

"What's sodomy?"

"Anal intercourse."

"Five hundred."

"Do your parents know you do this for money?"

"No."

Spencer reached into his camera bag and retrieved a clear plastic evidence bag with a swab inside. He opened the bag, removed the swab by the handle and said, "Open your mouth." Newman did and Spencer swabbed the inside of his mouth and placed the swab back into the bag and wrote Charlie's name on it and that of Richard Rigor, the date, time and location. "Go home and stop doing this with anyone. You'll get into serious trouble. Promise me you'll not do this anymore with anyone?"

"Okay, I promise." Charlie left the restroom.

"Come out of the stall, Rigor." Spencer said. The stall door opened. Rigor and Spencer come face to face. "Stand still." He repeated the swabbing procedure with Rigor and said, "Let's go for a ride, Rigor."

"Please don't take me to jail. I'll pay you whatever you want. I'm rich." Spencer and Rigor entered Spencer's car. Spencer's partner started to drive to the White House with Rigor in the back seat.

"How long have you been a pedophile?"

"For as long as I can remember."

"How long have you been engaged in homosexual relations with Charlie Newman?"

"For about six months."

"Do you have sexual relations with adult males?"

"Yes, but I like young boys better."

"Where are we going?"

"To your office. When we get to the gate, tell the guard that we're with you, and we don't need to sign in. Understand."

"Yes, I will." They arrived at the White House and approached the gate. The guard approached Spencer's partner on the driver's side and he put the window down.

"He's with me, Ralph, it'll not be necessary for them to sign in," Rigor said.

"Whatever you say, Mr. Rigor." The gate opened. The partner drove through the gate and parked the car in Rigor's parking place. Rigor and Spencer entered the White House and proceeded past the Secret Service personnel on duty and into Rigor's office that was next to the Oval Office.

"Open your safe, Richard, and give me the president's original copy of the Prague Accord and the 'War Plan' document." Rigor stood there not catatonic but so startled he didn't move.

"How do you know about these things? They're top secret code word?"

"Open it, now." Spencer said. "Not from you. You know McDonald is a sneak drinker and a braggadocio. Ask him if you want to find the leak." *Nothing wrong with sowing a little dissension among traitors.*

"I can't do that, the president will. . . ."

"What's it going to be, Rigor. International disgrace or the documents? Do you really want me to give the audio-video file *Pedophile at Play* and the DNA samples proving you were sucking on Newman's cock to the president, the Washington Post, the New York Times and CNN? Do you really want me to post the video on YouTube? I'm trying to help you, but you don't seem to get it and the gravity of your circumstances. Now, open the safe, I'll retrieve the documents, and we'll leave."

Rigor was devastated. His porcine body perspired. The sweat ran down his face. Rigor opened the safe and stepped back. Spencer put on Latex gloves, approached the safe, saw the envelope he believed held the Accord, opened it, saw the Accord, read it and put it back into the envelope. Then he removed the "War Plan" document, checked to see that it was the original and had both signatures, placed it and the Accord into a plastic evidence bag and placed the bag inside his business suit jacket. He placed his gloves into his right coat pocket.

"Close and lock the safe, Rigor." Rigor closed the safe door, turned the handle, and turned the tumbler. "Now, I'll drive you to your car. Let's go."

"What am I going to tell the president if he asks for the Accord and the Plan?"

"Tell him to get a copy of the Accord from Petrokov and the 'War Plan' from J.P. After all, everyone knows he cannot go to the bathroom without you, that you're his brains. Now that you mention it, I suggest to you most strongly and pronounced that you remember that so far only three people know about your imitation of a Catholic priest abusing a young boy this evening. Let's keep it this way."

"Yes, I agree," Rigor responded. He exhaled with a release of anxiety. They exited the White House without incident. Spencer's partner drove with Rigor in the passenger's seat. Spencer sat in the back. There was no conversation during the ride. The car stopped behind Rigor's car.

"Finally, I want to know how the president's going to go to war and with which country and when?" Spencer asked.

"I don't know."

Spencer's partner removed his right hand from the steering wheel and drove his right elbow into Rigor's solar plexus. Rigor started to gasp for air and made loud desperate sounds. His obesity and the blow caused him to receive air with difficulty." A few minutes passed and the gasping subsided.

"When I ask a question of you, Rigor, I expect a prompt and honest answer. Now, we can do this the easy way or the hard way, your choice. If you wish my hammer to meet your fingernails and have some serious reflective social intercourse it'll not be my pleasure, but for sure it'll not be yours. Your choice."

"I understand. The president asked the DCI, Roger Cliff, to fabricate intelligence so he could invade Iran. But the DCI refused. McDonald and his chief of staff visited the DCI, blackmailed him, with what dirty secret I don't know, and he agreed to do it. What fabrication he's going to come up with I don't know; he hasn't produced it yet. Maybe like the fabrication during W's administration, WMDs, to illegally invade Iraq? As you know, Iran has an active nuclear-enrichment program which they refuse to discontinue so there would be logic there. No one believes it is for peaceful power generation, anyway. Harrison will go to war as soon as McDonald tells him to. Petrokov signed the Prague Accord and will not interfere and gave the president a free hand."

"I'd like to know the 'dirty secret' that swayed an honest man to betray his country, commit treason and attempted murder. I'll be in contact with you, Rigor, for the answer tomorrow. Leave little boys alone." Rigor exited the car, entered his and drove away.

Spencer took the laptop computer off the back seat and placed it on his lap. He executed the necessary key strokes, listened to the quality of the transmission from the Uniball Gel Impact RT microphone on his laptop and was satisfied with the good quality. He then downloaded his camcorder and transmitted all of the evening's surveillance and conversations to MacIntosh's dedicated server for Operation Downfall in California.

# 39

## Day 17   3:00 P.M.   Raymond's Bar

Christopher James, the Los Angeles County Sheriff's homicide detective, met with Mariah in her office.

"So, how long have you been with homicide? Greg speaks very highly of you, says you are honest."

He looked into her eyes and said without an accent, "Sometimes I don't even remember. Ten years plus or minus a month or two or three, and I am."

"Give me a brief rundown on the burial site in the Mojave."

"Two bodies. No ID on either. Randolph Waters and two friends of yours were there. One of your friends gave me his confession. I asked Randolph if it was true, and he said it was. Asked him if he had signed it, and he said yes. One of the bodies he said was Cornell Roberts, former head of security at the Kennington Estate. The other fellow he didn't know. He said Daren Dirk knew him. The two of them buried Roberts and poured sulfuric acid on him. Randolph shot his partner. I don't know who he is yet, and then Randolph poured acid on him. The dummies probably believed that was going to make identification or a DNA match impossible. Not true.

"For investigation purposes I put the two bodies with the coroner under John Does. I'm holding Randolph and the other incompetent that Foster captured in a secure location also under John Does. J.P. Kennington has long arms and has spread more corruption in this city than any other corrupter I know. He's definitely in first position."

"I received an email from Roberts before his death while he was suffocating in J.P.'s vault. I printed a copy for you. Here, take it. Now you can read it on my laptop as I received it for verification as to date, time and authenticity. Also, I can forward it to you if you want."

Christopher read it and said, "I want. Very good. As soon as I get the autopsy report back to make sure Roberts died of suffocation, I'll get a search warrant for the Kennington Estate, the vault and Roberts' safe."

"Speaking of the vault, you may need some assistance if Kennington is not there and/or if his attorney advises him not to open it. I have a lady, Lillian Mc-Graw, you should take with you as back up. She can open it for you if you are obstructed."

"Thank you. I'll call you when I'm ready to go and she can meet me there. I'll try to interview Kennington if he's there, and if his lawyer hasn't gotten to him first. If the recorder is where he says it is, the fecal matter under the table and next to the note matches his DNA, I'll seek an indictment and arrest warrant for the unpleasant Jonathan P. Kennington. I'll be taking forensics with me. Mr. Randolph Waters'll be cooperative. Then I'll see what I can do about seeking the cooperation of one Daren Dirk if he's there. If I have any trouble with Mr. Dirk, will it be alright if I ask you for assistance? Mr. Foster Thompson and his colleagues come to mind?"

"Yes, you may. My pleasure."

# 40

Simon Spencer sat in his car with his partner outside Richard Rigor's apartment. He plugged his digital recorder into his cell and called Rigor. Rigor answered and Simon said, "Do you recognize my voice? So what's the answer to my pending question?"

"Yes. Can you be trusted? I don't even remember your name."

"My name's unimportant. Can I trust *you*, that's the question? The answer's most important. Stop stalling. Give it to me or we'll enjoy one another's company again, and you'll be doing more than gasping this time."

"Alright. It appears Cliff has a mistress. He's married to a wealthy woman who's an international socialite. He has no money of his own and has been embezzling money from the CIA's discretionary fund in order to support his mistress' housing and expensive lifestyle. Or to put it another way, his dick is making all the wrong decisions."

"Speaking of dicks and bad decisions, he reminds me of you, Richard. Is that all?"

"McDonald's chief of staff had ferreted the information from the CIA's inspector general's office. He evidently has a friend there and the friend gave him the information. So far, only the inspector general and his assistant know. Cliff didn't know anyone knew. The chief of staff gave the information to McDonald. McDonald, the sadist, made Cliff come to his office in the Eisenhower Executive Office Building, or EEOB, next to the West Wing of the White House. I understand he turned Cliff into tears, complemented by begging and whining. But in the end after a series of protestations he rolled over, put all four paws in the air and is doing whatever McDonald tells him.

"This makes McDonald at this moment the most powerful man in the world. He has Robert cowered, but then that's easy when you're as dumb as he. Now here's the absurdity. McDonald told Cliff it would be their secret and Cliff believed him if you can believe it. McDonald is evil personified. His only loyalty is to McDonald and his god, Greed. Cliff has become another of McDonald's marionettes manipulated by strings made of extortion. The vice president went into public service as a business. To put it in inside the Washington, D.C., Beltway terms: If you want loyalty, get a dog."

"When we first met you said to me, 'I'll pay you whatever you want. I'm rich.' One of my acquaintances in banking did me a favor and provided me with some financial information on you which leads me to believe you're in debt and having trouble making ends meet. Is this true?"

There was silence. Moments passed and then Richard said, "It's true. In fact, it may be worse than you know."

"You lied to me. To quote the famous Richard Rigor, 'Can *you* be trusted?' "

"The answer is yes, because I have no choice."

"Good reason, just keep it in mind. If you lie to me again, you'll be the lead story internationally. I'd be willing to help you financially if you'd be willing to provide me with accurate information on the VP, especially his shenanigans? Does he keep a diary? Can you turn his chief of staff? Also, you're going to need a job when the president and VP get caught with their pants down holding their dicks in Lafayette Park caused by this war plan of theirs, get impeached by the House and found guilty by the Senate. What do you say, want to put in with the good guys for a change?"

"What's the money?"

"Depends on what you deliver. I know how deep your money hole is. It's major back hoe job. Because McDonald's a draft dodger, and evil as you put it; I suggest we bury him in some out of the way place for federal law violators — the U.S. Penitentiary in Leavenworth, Kansas, comes to mind. What do you say? I'll bail you out for your help with the total downfall of McDonald, the president, their investors, and you'll be clean Gene."

"You have my attention."

"So, rent a back hoe, start digging, be my mole and documents provider. Thank you, Richard. If I have or you have a need, let's be in touch. Don't wait too long or my generosity may wane."

# 41

**Day 18   9:00 A.M.   Walter Rasmussen's Home**

Lillian called and made an appointment with Walter Rasmussen, the director of research and development, at Kennington Chemical and Pharmaceutical.

"Thank you for seeing me. It's been some time," Lillian said.

"Always good to see you, and yes it has."

"You know J.P.'s signature when you see it?"

"Yes. He sends me memos. I know it very well."

"In case you have any doubts, here's a document signed by a handwriting expert, the best in the business, who has verified that this is his signature. This document verifies it was signed by the president of the U.S. I want you to read this, and then I wish to discuss it with you." She handed him the "War Plan" document.

He read it.

"What do you think about that document?"

"I find it incredible. What do you want me to do?"

"What do you want to do?"

"We cannot allow the gas to be used to kill innocent people as a pretext to go to war?"

"Then, why are you making it?"

"We have an order from the DoD. I have developed a bioweapon which has no antidote. The people will die of an apparent heart attack and the residue if any in the body will not be detectable. But, I now see it is just a charade for this plan to go to war illegally. So, what I'm going to do is what the DOD requested. But, with one addition which will be my secret."

"Whose signature is on the order?"

"Samuel Blackwell, undersecretary of defense for intelligence. He's head of the Defense Intelligence Agency."

*Yes of course. He's one of the DIA targets I suckered into a honey trap, a premature ejaculator. I took off my clothes, he got on and got off immediately. Poor soul.* "This is what I would like for you to do for me." She explained her plan.

"Absolutely. Anything else I can do for you?"

"I'm going to give you my cell number. And if anything unusual happens such as production of the gas to use it, please call me. And, anything else if you were in my position you'd want to know if you wanted to stop this insanity. Will you do this for me?"

"Yes, with pleasure."

"The company makes a sleeping gas perfected to prevent airline hijacking. Puts people to sleep almost immediately for about thirty minutes. I'd like for you to make me two small aerosol canisters. Then I'll need a cylinder full. When can I have them?"

"Under the circumstances, in about two days. Call me, and you can pick up the canisters here at the house."

# 42

**Day 18   12:01 P.M.   The Kennington Estate**

J.P. called Robert and said, "I've Sean as my unwilling house guest. Kennington Chemical has developed the gas pursuant to our war plan, but I haven't received my DoD contract for development and no payments. I've tried to get Sam Blackwell on the phone at the DIA to find out why, but he won't take my calls, and he doesn't return my calls. Do you know why? I've other contracts pending with DoD and they've not been approved either."

"I told you, J.P., I'm not going forward with your war plan. I assume the reason Blackwell hasn't approved your contracts or returned your calls is because I've instructed DoD and other governmental agencies not to do business with any of your companies or you unless I personally approve it."

"Well, I've got your son. I'd better get my contracts if you want him to remain safe."

"I want to talk to him now."

"What you want and when you want it are indifferent to me."

"You're such a liar, Kennington. You're bluffing. He called his mother, and said he was alright. If you're telling the truth for a change, you'd better not harm that boy, you evil bastard. You're nothing but the biological father. You're no father to any of your children. It's true, when I first found out you had deceived me I wanted to disown Sean. But he's the good son. I love him, and as far as I'm concerned I'm his father. And I can guarantee you if any harm comes to him or you're holding him against his will, I'll tell you right now I'll use all my power to crush you. You're what you are: a self-centered, egocentric hedonistic pig. You have obsessive greed."

"If you go to war without me, I'm going to expose you for the dumb, corrupt person you are. I'll expose the corrupt McDonald, too. The two of you don't fool me. If you have a plan in which you're going to cut up the benefits and rewards of going to war among the two of you and your friends, you'd better include me, Robert. My companies need the opportunities a war generates before, during and after to grow."

"I'm not going to help you, Kennington."

# 43

**Day 18   3:30 P.M.   The White House, the Oval Office**

Rigor and McDonald stood in front of the Lincoln. Robert sat behind. "Kennington just called. He has my son as a hostage, he says though I doubt it. He wants in on my plan to go to war with Iran. None of his contracts have been approved by the DoD, because I put a hold on them. He's threatening to harm my boy if he isn't included. Anyone care to advise me, assuming the prick is telling the truth for a change?"

"One person's life's not worth abandoning a plan this administration needs desperately," McDonald said. "You need to be re-elected in order for us to increase our net worth. I'm not interested in Kennington having any share of my profits from *my* war. As I see it, there's no contribution he can make which would cause me to believe he would be an asset toward a profitable adventure to benefit me and the investors."

"The problem as I see it, Mr. President," Rigor said, "Kennington has enough information regarding the bribes paid to the two of you to cause you both incalculable damages. Not being re-elected and impeachments comes to mind. The reason I suggested to you going to war in the first place and including Kennington was to get you re-elected, and use Kennington's money and his wealthy Texas connections to do so. Now, it appears according to my sources Kennington's in financial straits and needs the contracts from the DoD and other agencies in your administration."

"I don't care who suggested going to war first," McDonald said. "I've met with my energy people and they are expecting to be able to take over, control, operate and profit from the Iranian oil reserves after we've won the ground war. I've promised all of them they'll have a free hand in Iran. I'll not permit Kennington to include himself in my plans. Our investors will replace the money Kennington was going to contribute to our re-election campaign only if they are convinced war is inevitable."

"The decision is not yours to make, McDonald. I do believe you've forgotten your place. I make the decisions for this country, not you. I know you believe you're the decision-maker, but the people elected me, and I selected you."

"No, Robert, you did what you were told. You even appeared to be religious after Falwell told you about the thirty million evangelicals. You only had two assets. Name value and money from the people I convinced to put up the first fifty million dollars of your campaign, because I promised them I'd guide you and correct any errancy on your part. They demanded before they put up the money that I should be the vice president and you agreed. I'm the guarantor to make sure they get what they paid for after they put up the money. To wit: tax breaks and no immigration reform that would interfere with the hiring of illegals. No one puts up money for good government, Harrison. They all expect a Return on Investment, a ROI. So far, so good. You've a short memory."

"So what am I to do to save my son? If anything happens to him, my mother and my wife will never forgive me."

"Stop being a weakling for a change," McDonald said. "Get some backbone. Get in charge of your family. Money's more important than family."

"But I love my son, and I want him back."

"Then go get him," McDonald said. He and Rigor left.

# 44

"Spencer, I have some information for you. When can I receive some of the money you promised me?"

"What've you got, and then I'll tell you what I've got?"

"The answers to the downfall of McDonald and Robert are with Jonathan Kennington. He lives in Bel Air in California. Evidently, he has bribed the president and vice president into providing him with lucrative no-bid contracts and other nefarious conduct."

"Any details?"

"No, but I know during a conversation this morning when his name was brought up Robert and McDonald were both concerned about revelations he could make if he doesn't get his way. It would cause a scandal that would prevent the president's re-election. They plan on going to war in Iran in order to get Harrison re-elected and profit from it. But if it were revealed they're only going to war to get re-elected, to make profits for themselves and their friends, and the intelligence is fabricated by the DCI, he wouldn't be re-elected. They'd probably be impeached or prosecuted for treason and other crimes. Your path to success is through Kennington."

"You remember the restroom where we first met. I'll see you there at ten and give you twenty-five. Keep up the good work, get details, I need details and documents. Maybe one day you can be a modern-day Deep Throat, a patriot and give up your addiction to absolution."

# 45

## Day 19 10:00 A.M. The Kennington Estate

Christopher James, Los Angeles County Sheriff's homicide detective, and Lillian McGraw, at the suggestion of Mariah, arrived at the front gate. He was in the detectives' uniform of choice, sport coat and slacks on a hefty frame. He pushed the call button and waited for an answer. A man answered. James identified himself, informed the man he had a search warrant for the premises and requested entry. A few minutes passed and the man said, "Mr. Kennington's not here, and I'm not authorized to permit your entry."

"Who's speaking?"

"My name is Oscar Winslow. I'm a member of Mr. Kennington's security, and I'm still not authorized."

Lillian said to him, "Do you still want to get in?"

"Sure."

"Try 1627#."

James put in the numbers, the pound sign, and the gates opened. "That Mariah knows what she's doing. Very smart of her to recommend you for this job. I'm glad now I swore you in as my temporary deputy."

They drove the half-mile to the Tudor house followed by two forensic deputies in their car. James and Lillian exited their car. The forensic deputies stayed in their car and waited. James and Lillian approached the double-front doors and James rang the doorbell. When there was no answer after a minute, he asked her, "Any suggestions?"

"If there's a key out here, is it legal to find it and use it?"

"Yeah."

Lillian stood next to James in her ball cap, sunglasses, shirt and jeans with shined black-dress cowboy boots. Unseen by James, she removed a single key from the shoulder bag which rested against her right hip and palmed it. She walked over to the planter on her right, looked around the base of the plant, put her hand under a branch, dragged the key through the dirt, turned and handed the dirty key to James. He wiped it off, blew on it, put the key into the lock, turned it, opened the front door and handed her the key. She took the key, went to the planter, palmed it and put it back into her bag. She left her hand in there.

A helicopter took off from the two-acre lawn behind the house at that moment.

James and Lillian went in and he closed the door. Two men stood in front of them with revolvers pointed at them. They wore the same obvious security uniforms of the day, dark glasses, white shirts, black ties, black-two piece suits and black rubber-soled shoes.

"I'm authorized to shoot on sight any trespassers," one of the men said. "Put your hands up, James, and remove your weapon from your shoulder holster and put it on the floor. I'm being kind to you. I hope Kennington doesn't fire me for allowing you to enter. How you got through the gate and the front door's a mystery to me, but he won't understand that. Now, get out or I'll be calling the coroner for a pick up. You shouldn't've brought your girlfriend to a gun fight."

James didn't move to leave. But he did do as he was told. In slow motion, he placed his piece on the highly polished marble floor in one of the white three-foot squares of the three-foot squares of black and white marble that covered the foyer floor.

James held up his badge, ID and a copy of the warrant and said, "I'm Detective Christopher James, and I'm serving you with this search warrant." He offered it to the man who spoke. The guard refused it, and James placed it on the floor in front of him.

"I want you two to get out of here. I'm authorized to shoot intruders and call our undertaker for a pick up."

With both of his hands shoulder-high, James said, "I'm placing you two under arrest for interfering with a law enforcement officer in the performance of his duty. I'm going to advise you two of your. . . ."

Both men looked at one another and interrupted James with their disrespectful laughter.

"Which one of you's Winslow?"

The one who had been speaking said, "I'm Winslow. Your boss, the county sheriff, is on J.P.'s pad just like all the other politicians who make decisions in this town. You can't arrest us. If you do, Kennington will have your job at the least and no pension either, Lackey. I suggest you check with your boss for orders." Both men laughed at him again.

"Speaking of undertakers," Lillian said. She fired two rounds into the hearts of each of the men from inside her bag. She removed the 9mm Baretta with a sound suppressor on its nose from her bag, and as they were falling put one round each into their foreheads. Then she moved to them. She placed Winslow's revolver back into his right hand and fired a shot into the back of the front door. Then she did the same with the other man's revolver.

She turned to the startled and speechless James and said, "Looks like a clear case of self-defense if you ask me, a righteous killing. What do you think, Detective James?" Then she handed him her Baretta.

He took the 9mm by the grip and said, "Looks good to me." He picked up his .38 Smith and Wesson from the floor and returned it to his holster. He put her Baretta into his waistband.

J.P.'s employees appeared around the perimeter of the foyer and stood in silence. The two forensic deputies came to the front door and knocked with force. James turned and opened the door.

James picked up the warrant and gave it to the butler and announced to all who he was, displayed his badge and ID. He told them he was going to perform his duty. He called homicide, reported the attempt on his life, the circumstances and requested the coroner to retrieve two dead bad guys.

The four of them passed through the foyer. Lillian nodded recognition to the employees as she passed. Roger Preston, the IT who had been providing her with information, was among them, but Lillian did not stop. The four of them walked down the stairs and to the vault. Lillian put in the code, used the retinal eye scanner, and the green light on the keypad went on. There was no reason for her to bypass the code, scanner and cameras this time. Everything had to be legal.

James and one of the forensic deputies went into the vault. Lillian and the other deputy went to Roberts' office. The deputy opened the safe. He used the combination given to Mariah by Roberts in his e-mail to her. The officer retrieved everything pursuant to the search warrant, including the CDs with the downloaded recordings of J.P.'s orders to Roberts. The CDs were dated and the times of the recordings were on the labels.

Another security man arrived at the vault dressed in the same uniform as the two dead. "Who's in charge here?"

"Detective Christopher James, sheriff's homicide. Who was in the helicopter that left the property?"

"I can't help you. I'm not authorized to provide any information."

"I'm placing you under arrest for impeding the investigation of a law enforcement officer in the performance of his duty. I'm going to cuff you and read you your rights."

"Alright, Tight Ass, I get the picture. Alright, Badge, it was Kennington, Daren Dirk, the head of security, and some guy named Sean Harrison."

"Where were they going?"

"I've no idea."

"What's it going to be? I admire your loyalty, but do you really believe that some scumbag like Kennington's gonna give a shit what happens to you, bail you out or pay your legal fees? So it's arrest, go to your new home in the back seat of my limo while I drive or have some social intercourse with me, your new friend."

"To the Santa Monica Airport."

"Then where?"

"I don't know."

"Why did they leave so suddenly?"

"Kennington got a call from someone downtown and told him you were coming."

"Who?"

"I don't know. Ask Daren Dirk, the head of security, when you see him if you do. He took the call, told Kennington, and he ordered the evacuation. Dirk then organized it."

"Okay, I believe you." James showed him a photograph of Sean Harrison. "Is this the fellow you said was Sean Harrison?"

"Yes, he was a guest, and he was the same fellow who Kennington and Dirk took on the helicopter."

"Thank you, you can go."

The media arrived and set up their television mobile transmission facilities on the street. Their entry to the estate was blocked by the Crime Scene tape and some burlies in sheriff's uniforms.

"James, I found the note and the fecal matter under the table and the recorder on the top shelf behind the chair, just as you told me where they'd be," one of the forensic officers said. "I've bagged it. The note is handwritten and appears to be a dying declaration accusing J.P. Kennington of his murder. I'll get a sample of Roberts' handwriting from the safe and have our handwriting expert verify it is or isn't Roberts'. I've also removed a very small amount of brown material from the floor. Could be fecal matter where Roberts defecated. I'll analyze it, and it'll help prove he was here along with the note, the other fecal material and the recorder."

"The coroner told me just before I got the warrant Roberts died of suffocation. So at this moment if all is true, we've enough to get an indictment and arrest warrant against Mr. Kennington for murder and the kidnapping of Sean Harrison.

Lillian showed up at the vault. James said, "I want you to listen to this recording, and see if you can identify the voices. James played the recorder.

Lillian said, "One is Roberts receiving orders from Jonathan Kennington. J.P.'s ordering Roberts to get his property back, and if he does or doesn't he's to kill Sean, Mariah and me."

"This clinches it. What about the CD backups of Roberts' orders from J.P.?"

"More orders to violate the law, but you'll know best. You'll have to listen to them all. I just heard part of one. But the one I heard is J.P. giving orders to Roberts to kill all three of us. The deputy has bagged the contents of the safe."

Lillian and James went to her former room to search for evidence that Sean was there because Roger Preston, the IT, told her Sean was held hostage in her room. They collected a toothbrush and a bandage with blood on it from a waste basket in the bathroom, but didn't find anything else. James bagged both for evidence. Then he called to have a five-ton truck arrive, empty the vault and catalogue the contents. James and Lillian searched J.P.'s desk in the library and took his daily journal which was in his handwriting according to Lillian.

James wanted to take all of the computers and the server which he had the right to do pursuant to the search warrant. Lillian told him not to and why. He smiled, and she agreed to provide him with anything from them that would aid in sending J.P. to prison.

James, Lillian and the two forensic deputies left the house and got into their cars. James said, "Where did you learn to shoot like that?"

"On a combat range at the Special Forces facility."

"You're really good. Shooting from inside your bag with the suppressor was some life-saver."

"Thank you. It comes in handy now and then."

The media had the driveway blocked at the street. James put down the window on the driver's side and asked the burlies to clear the road so he could pass. Cameras rolled and the still photographers were hard at work. Lillian's ball cap and sunglasses hid her face.

When confronted with questions from the media, James responded, "No comment."

# 46

**Day 19 2:00 P.M. The Kennington Ranch, Near Abiquiu, New Mexico**

J.P.'s Gulf Stream G650 landed on the paved airstrip on his ten-thousand acre ranch. A black Navigator waited to pick up the passengers. The door of the G650 opened and the irascible J.P. went down the stairs and continued his tirade that had begun when he received a call from the Los Angeles County Sheriff George I. Ralston. He informed him a search warrant had been issued by Judge Petersen for the search of his estate in Bel Air. After he cursed Ralston for ten minutes, he realized it was a waste of time though he felt better. He ordered an evacuation and packed for an indefinite stay.

*What did these people think they were being paid for? Nothing but another dishonest politician who didn't honor his promise when the bribe was paid.* The bribe was the usual campaign contribution to the marionette with the puppeteer's strings attached.

J.P.'s entourage arrived at the Santa Fe-style house with its corbels, beams and adobe walls. The house had territorial-style windows with triple panes to help in controlling the hot days and cold nights of the desert. Weathered, thick, wooden-front doors opened to the courtyard with a fifteen foot-diameter water fountain in the middle. The fountain was surrounded by a courtyard covered with terra cotta tiles. Hexagon ceramic tiles throughout the house were partially covered in large Navajo area rugs.

Dirk locked Sean in one of the small bedrooms. He then went to the living room and met with J.P. The servants brought lemonade with ice cubes in a pitcher made of clay adorned with a Southwestern design.

"So, Dirk, what are we doing for security?"

"I've a team of twenty on the way. They'll be here by tomorrow morning."

"Check with your man Winslow and report the status of the search. What did they take, if he knows? See if you can find out what they took and give me a list. In the meantime, I'm going to have something to eat and take a nap. Keep your eye on our guest. I don't want a disappearance."

"Will do."

# 47

James sat in one of the visitors' chairs opposite Eric Rottand, the D.A. Because of the potential political fallout, the D.A. had to approve the presentation of the J.P. Kennington murder and kidnapping case to the Los Angeles County Grand Jury.

James presented a DNA match on the fecal matter found in the vault under the table and on the floor. It belonged to Cornell Roberts. He gave him the note in Roberts' handwriting under the table which accused J.P. of locking him in the vault to kill him by suffocation. It was a dying declaration. The handwriting had been verified by William Morse, the former FBI expert, used by Mariah to verify the signatures of Robert B. Harrison and Jonathan P. Kennington on the "War Plan" document.

The saliva and hair with follicles were found in the vault that belonged to Roberts. He gave Eric a transcription of the recording on Roberts' recorder and CD that had been downloaded that ordered the killing of Sean, Mariah and Lillian. He gave him the coroner's report that stated Roberts died of suffocation.

The statement of Randolph Waters verified he had carried a dead Roberts from the vault of J.P. while J.P. supervised the removal. Randolph had buried him in the Mojave Desert. His statement further verified that he participated with Daren Dirk and others in kidnapping Sean Harrison from Foster Thompson's ranch. Then the email sent from Roberts to Mariah O'Leary: It set forth the facts of his murder by J.P., another dying declaration and the abduction of Sean. The statement of the security guard: Sean Harrison was a prisoner in Kennington's estate and locked in his room. And finally, the DNA evidence from the toothbrush and the bandage with blood taken from the bathroom where Sean was held prisoner matched the DNA of Sean Harrison.

"This looks awfully thin, James. Do you have a confession?"

James came out of his chair faster than a mongoose strike on a cobra, put both hands on the top and front part of Eric's desk, leaned forward within one foot of his face, looked into his eyes and said, "This case is solid. You know it. Your dishonesty is well known.

"I've a dossier on you. It includes every bribe you've taken and every corrupt thing you have done since your election by the dumb voters who were bilked by Kennington's money for campaign ads. The bribes total five million dollars since you've been in office. If you don't go forward with this indictment for murder and kidnapping, this is what I'm going to do: I'll release all of the information to the media and then provide all of it to the California Attorney General and have him indict your crooked ass for more felonies than you can count. You'll die in prison, and I guarantee you I'll make it my life's work. I know Kennington has bought you lock, stock and barrel. I'll make sure every inmate in prison knows you were a D.A. Life span? Very very short. So, what's it going to be Rottand, indictment or seeing your favorite political photograph of yourself on tomorrow's front page of the L.A. Times, on CNN and every TV channel in Los Angeles? Then if you make a plea bargain, don't get a conviction on both counts, and you don't recommend and get a life sentence without the possibility of parole, I'll expose you then too."

"No reason to be unpleasant, James. I just thought it looked a little thin, that's all."

"No, you didn't. This was just another way for you to contact Kennington and shake him down for more money. In addition, you'd better assign your best prosecutor to this case, Robert John Fitzpatrick. His honesty and skills are above reproach. Next, when the grand jury issues a true bill and a warrant's been issued for the arrest of Kennington, I want you to call a press conference. You'll announce the indictment, warrant for his arrest, and the appointment of Fitzpatrick."

"I see you haven't left any stone unturned. Very well." Rottand picked up the telephone and asked his secretary to have Fitzpatrick come to his office immediately. Shortly thereafter, Fitzpatrick arrived.

"Robert, do you know Detective James, sheriff's homicide?"

"Yes, he's the best of the best. Good to see you again, Chris."

"Thank you for the compliment."

"I meant it. What's up?"

"I'm appointing you the prosecutor on the Kennington case to be presented to the grand jury. One count of murder, three counts of attempted murder and one count of kidnapping of Sean Harrison, the son of the president. James is the investigation officer."

"I look forward to working with you again, Chris."

Eric handed the file folder to Fitzpatrick. He and James left Rottand's office.

Rottand looked into his contacts file on his computer, found the number he wanted and called it. "I'd like to speak to Kennington, D.A. Rottand calling."

"Mr. Kennington isn't available. He left two days ago. I've no information as to his whereabouts. I can take a message."

"Tell him D.A. Rottand called and it's urgent." He gave the number to the person who answered and hung up. *Maybe, I can shake him down big time before the media finds out the grand jury has convened regarding him or the announcement of his indictment. There's no doubt he'll be indicted and convicted on the evidence James presented. Sometimes honest cops can be a pain in the ass and an obstruction to enhancing my wealth. So much for J.P.'s above-the-law attitude and his bragging to anyone who would stand still long enough to listen, "I'm untouchable." Now that his pants and underwear are down around his ankles and his ass is exposed, the feds are going to be all over him like white on rice.*

# 48

### Day 23   9:00 A.M. Raymond's Bar

Mariah sat in her office. Jerry sat next to her, and Lillian and Greg sat on the other side of the table. Christopher sat in a chair at the end of the table. The whole world had heard the news and saw the photograph of Jonathan P. Kennington when it was announced by Eric Rottand, the district attorney of Los Angeles County. Jonathan P. Kennington had been indicted for the murder of Cornell Roberts, his former head of security, and for the kidnapping of Sean Harrison, the son of Robert S. Harrison, the president of the United States. He had also been indicted for the attempted murder of Sean Harrison, Mariah O'Leary and Lillian McGraw. A no-bail warrant had been issued for his arrest. He was a fugitive. Mr. Robert John Fitzpatrick was the prosecutor who had presented the evidence to the grand jury, and the investigating officer was Christopher "Chris" James.

The FBI had issued a Most Wanted for the arrest of J.P. Kennington along with his photograph. Anyone having information regarding the whereabouts of Jonathan P. Kennington should call the local number for the FBI. Also, the United States Secret Service had issued a warrant for his arrest and a photograph of J.P. and Sean Harrison. Anyone having information regarding the whereabouts of Jonathan P. Kennington or Sean Harrison should call the number on the screen.

Mariah said, "First things first. A round of applause and a few hear-hears for our champion and hero the incorruptible deputy sheriff, Christopher James. Long may he live with his moral sense of duty." Hear-hears abounded. He rose from his chair with a smile and took a much-deserved bow. Applause rang through the hall of justice, Raymond's Bar.

He remained standing and said, "Having bathed in the glory of the moment I'd like to say thank you." He blushed. "But without Lillian, Mariah, Foster Thompson, a dossier, and all you folks, I'd still be hard slogging it backward up the sand hill of corruption. Thank you all."

"Now, down to business, 'Operation Downfall'. But, with a slight modification. Let us not do the job of the Secret Service or the FBI as we had planned before J.P. shot himself in the pocketbook. Let the two posses do their jobs. Let us have J.P. find us. We know his weaknesses: above-the law-attitude, omnipotent, power hungry, greed without bounds, ego larger than the universe or is it the multiverse. If we strip him of his wealth we will successfully strip him of his power. I asked our champion and hero to be here today, because I trust him. I believe he believes what we believe. This is what I am going to suggest as our plan going forward." She spoke for thirty minutes to a rapt audience of four.

"I am now open to comments, agreements, rejections, suggestions or you name it."

"I always enjoy the comeuppance when it is self-inflicted," James said.

"I call it retribution, or now it's my turn," Lillian said.

Mariah looked at Greg and Jerry and asked, "Gentlemen?"

"I'm in," Greg said.

"Brilliant comes to mind," Jerry said. "I'm in, too."

"Jerry, you will continue with your surveillance teams in D.C. and continue to drain the sewer with your snitch, Rigor. Press him to the limit without his committing suicide until after we are finished with him. If our Deep Throat is caught, our opponents may do it first."

"For sure, Jerry said. "You can count on it, I'll ride him to the wire and for more than eight seconds, too."

"Alright then. This is what each of us will do to bring the plan to fruition." She explained who was going to do what, how and to whom. They all left Mariah's office except Lillian.

"What's on your mind?" Mariah asked.

"I just wanted to thank you in private for all you've done for Sean and me and are going to be doing. He's a good man. And, I wanted to give you this folder you had asked for that I had removed from J.P.'s vault. I got it from our box with a little bit of early morning help from Harry at Chase so I could give it to you now."

"Thank you for the compliment. I do believe this will provide us with the last piece of evidence we will need for 'Operation Downfall'. What we need to do is to stay flexible with our plan. This way when something unexpected happens, and it will, we will be able to handle it and bring the operation to a successful conclusion."

# 49

**Day 23   10:00 A.M.   The Kennington Ranch, Near Abiquiu, New Mexico**

J.P. and Dirk sat in the living room of the sprawling Southwestern-designed home in the desert. A security force of twenty men had been assembled. They wore an eclectic selection and were armed with automatic weapons and Rocket-Propelled Grenade launchers. It was a hodge-podge of bring your own. As each man arrived in Eden, Dirk personally searched each man and his gear and confiscated for the duration of the tour of duty all cell phones and other communication devices.

Canvas tents were set up to provide some relief from the over one hundred-degree daily temperatures and hot winds that swept the desert and blew dirt and dust constantly. The tents, sleeping bags and the clothes on their backs were the only protection from the cold nights. The tent city was near the landing strip and the helo pad. J.P.'s helicopter was on the pad, but under camouflage netting. The G650 was in the hangar next to the strip. The pilot and co-pilot slept in there and used the bathroom facilities.

There were four men to a tent. The sleeping bags rested on the cloth floor. Some brought air mattresses and placed them between the floor and their bags.

Dirk had painted a "big money" verbal picture. But the painting of the environment to be enjoyed and what to bring was brief: your body, weapons and ammunition for an indefinite stay. They came by train, air, pickup and extended thumb along the interstate highways and byways of America constructed during the Eisenhower Administration.

There were no toilet facilities. When one walked about, it was necessary to search the ground constantly unless you didn't care. The combination of heat, fecal matter and urine added to the exotic destination and only offended the olfactory senses of some.

There was a mobile kitchen and one of the mercenaries prepared the gourmet meals, a lot of military Meals Ready to Eat, or MREs, were daily fare twice a day. The men who had been in Iraq and Afghanistan in the field were not pleased to be back with their previous companions, MREs. The beverage du jour was warm water and the same from the portable shower that used gravity feed from the water tower.

The morale was in the sewer. Dirk had promised sign-up bonuses to be paid on arrival in cash. But when asked when, the answer was always, "They're in transit." But there was never an ETA.

"So, Dirk, what did you find out? What did they take from my vault and house?"

"They cleaned out the vault and according to the L.A. Times, they found Roberts' recorder with you giving him orders to get your property back and kill Sean, Mariah O'Leary and Lillian McGraw. Roberts left a note, a dying declaration saying you murdered him. His DNA matched the fecal matter he left in the vault. Randolph Waters, one of my men, took Christopher James, L.A County sheriff's homicide detective, to the burial site in the Mojave Desert. They found Roberts, and the man I sent with Waters to bury him. Randolph admitted killing his partner on my orders. Which were your orders, J.P. If Randolph hadn't been caught, I'd of disposed of him on your orders, too.

"With the coroner's report, only Kennington's fingerprints on the vault and the DNA, the investigating officer James said to the media, 'There's no doubt J.P. Kennington killed Cornell Roberts by locking him in his vault, which caused his death by suffocation. There's no doubt according to the DNA evidence Sean Harrison, the president's son, was kidnapped and held captive by J.P. Kennington at his estate in Bel Air.

"All of this is confirmed by the banner headline in the Albuquerque Journal, New Mexico's largest newspaper, which reads, 'Fugitive Kennington Sought.' Your bribes to the D.A. Rottand didn't pay off. It appears he's running now on your back for re-election. You flushed a lot of money down the toilet for his kind of loyalty. It appears from the media he was the one who announced the indictments and appointed his best prosecutor.

"Then there's an article on the front page with a lead that says, "President offers five million dollars for information for the return of his son and arrest and conviction of the kidnapper, J.P. Kennington."

"Any good news or more bad?"

"The good news is: The men here haven't seen you and don't know who they're guarding. If they did, my problems would be bigger than they are."

"What problems?"

"The only thing that's important in life, money. You told me to hire them, and I gave you the parameters. So far, I've seen no money. I haven't been paid what you promised and neither have they. My problem is: I'm the one who promised them their money, and I've to keep stalling or these people'll be gone, and maybe after they kill us. The word mutiny comes to mind. They're only loyal to money, they're mercenaries. I don't know how much longer I can continue to lie to them. When are *you* going to provide cash?"

"Unfortunately, the bag I gave you and the small amount I almost forgot to take from the vault when I got the call of the impending search is all I had. I called my banker this morning, but he had already seen the news and refused to take my call. 'Turn yourself in,' he told his secretary to tell me. My passport'll be on the watch list worldwide. I do believe I'm in awkward circumstances. I really don't need to be detained in some prison in some other country or prison period. I do believe I've been hung out to dry."

"Well, this charade with my men at best'll only last a day or two more. I hope their mutiny only includes desertion and not assassinations. Then the pilots'll get edgy and just fly out of here, with or without your permission."

"Rather than whining, have you got any constructive suggestions to make before I take four Advil, a Lunesta and a nap?"

"Only this: find a way to get some cash here. I've got twenty men at five hundred a day, plus the twenty-five hundred signing and appearance money. Fifty thousand for the appearance money, plus two days another twenty thousand for a total of seventy. Then there's me and that's a hundred, so you need three hundred because we're almost out of food here. Can't use a credit card or write a check.

"We need a schmuck to ferry some cash in here and be oblivious to the fact he's aiding and abetting a fugitive, a felony and straight to prison. Which reminds me of me. I too am in the same boat. According to CNN, the treasury department has frozen all your bank accounts. You've lost your ability to withdraw any funds."

"All of this because of one greedy entrepreneur and a disloyal employee of yours."

"No, I beg to differ. I'd put it differently: All of this because you believed you were above the law, had bribed all of the necessary people, had all the necessary connections and felt bulletproof. You should've got a dog and trusted it instead of politicians, and you would've been better off." *So, the situation as I see it is pretty simple. Around two this morning, I do believe the moment will present itself to abandon ship because our Dear Leader is in no state to help himself, me or my band of ruffians. I hate to abandon my twenty, but Qué será, será, or Whatever will be, will be. I think that nice new Lincoln Navigator in the garage should be an appropriate getaway ride to the airport and buy a ticket to L.A.*

*Accessory before and after the fact in the burial of Roberts and the other guy whose name I can't remember? Maybe, a little immunity deal with Rottand if I give up J.P.? Besides, I could use the five million Robert Harrison's offering. The question is: How do I get the reward and not go to prison for the kidnapping of Sean, a felony, and conspiracy with J.P., another felony? No immunity there, unless I can talk to the FBI or make a deal with the president and the Secret Service. I may have to stick with this horse. Maybe he'll sleep it off and have an idea in the morning or something wonderful will happen.*

"What're we going to do about Harrison in the other room?" Dirk asked.

"Unfortunately, we've no choice but to keep him with us until I can get the president to do what I want. But having said that, this turn of events is causing me to rethink my decision. For now, we'll keep him with us."

The omnipotent sat on the sofa alone in a state of apparent catatonia. Dirk sat in a chair with a large, oak-burled wood coffee table between them. All rested on a large Navajo area rug.

# 50

## Day 24 1:00 P.M. The Willard Hotel, Washington, D.C.

Mariah and Lillian had checked in to the hotel around ten that morning. The hotel was located in the heart of D.C. They were shown to a two-bedroom suite that was furnished with antiques. The raspberry and green décor was a lovely combination of Federal and American Empire styles.

Edvard Lavananski, president and CEO of International Investment Bank and Trade, aka IIBT, and J.P. Kennington's lender, sat in a comfortable antique chair. Mariah sat and faced him. Lillian sat at a ninety-degree angle to them. The atmosphere was cordial. Lunch had been enjoyed in the suite, and they had moved to the living room.

"Edvard, Lillian and I want to help you extricate yourself from your present untenable circumstances. I have had access to the financial information and the banking activities of the Kennington Holding Company and J.P.'s other companies. I know the lending limits of IIBT and its present financial condition. Neither situation bodes well for you and/or the bank. There is a lack of collateral for the loans that are outstanding and are past due and owing from the Kennington companies. I know why you made illegal loans to J.P."

"I don't know what you mean by illegal."

"Illegal means you have violated the law, the rules and regulations of the Federal Reserve in loaning money without proper collateral under circumstances you knew were an unacceptable risk. Then, you made loans to J.P.'s non-domestic front companies with the same collateral he used for the loans to Kennington Holding Company and his other companies, which you also knew were illegal; it is called cross collateralization. We are not interested in causing you or your bank any difficulty or causing your bank to fail. Not interested in having the U.S. attorney general involved in a criminal investigation either, by the way. What we want is your cooperation, and we will extricate you from this problem. Are you interested in our proposal?"

"Sure. What do you propose?"

"You are aware of J.P.'s present circumstances, his indictment for murder and kidnapping and his status as a fugitive. I know your bank holds all of the voting stock as collateral of the Kennington Holding Company which controls all of J.P.'s companies. The loans are past due. Therefore, for all purposes your bank controls all of the Kennington companies. The reason you have not called the notes is because you know they cannot be paid, your bank will fail and cause a global financial crisis if it does."

Mariah explained to him the real reason he had not called the notes was J.P. had been extorting him with a DVD which had showed him and a young boy having sexual relations at J.P.'s Bel Air Estate in one of the bedrooms. The young boy had been provided by J.P. at Edvard's request. Mariah had the boy's name and address, not a problem. Considering the fact the activity had taken place in California, child abuse, pedophilia, was a felony, and he could go to prison. Also, sodomy was a felony. Mariah told him they saw no reason for him to enjoy his best head shot being prominently displayed on the front pages of the Washington Post, New York and Los Angeles Times. And, they had no interest in giving a private screening for his wife. Mariah asked, "Is this alright with you?"

There was no answer. Time passed and Edvard looked everywhere except at her. He looked at Lillian for help.

"I see the answer is yes. Now let me ease your mind. J.P. no longer has the DVD. Your friend and mentor in this matter is this lady, Lillian McGraw. Two things you should know: Lillian is the daughter of J.P., and she has the DVD. If you wish to see it, we have it with us, and I will be pleased to put it into the Blue Ray."

"Thank you for your consideration. A viewing will not be necessary."

"The proposition is simple. I want you to call a special meeting of the board of directors of the Kennington Holding Company today for the meeting to take place in two days at a time of your choice in one of the conference rooms here at the Willard. You will give Lillian a proxy for this meeting. You will propose to the board and will sell the recalcitrant, if there are any, on voting for Lillian as president and CEO of the Kennington Holding Company. This will put her in control of all of the Kennington companies."

"What qualifications does she have? Yes, it's true I've dealt with her; yes, she knows the business; yes she knows everything about everything, but has no management experience."

"True, and this is where you come in. You are going to be the new chairman. You will retain your job at IIBT and guide her when she needs it. And of course all will be forgiven, and there will be a substantial increase in your net worth.

"Next, today I will receive commitments from the Secretary of Defense and the deputy secretary for contracts for Kennington Industries that will more than repay the loans. Also, the secretary of state will be providing a no-bid contract to

Kennington Industries for security forces to guard our embassies and diplomats around the world. You have my word on it."

"Well, that does change the entire picture. What's not to like? I'll be happy to be of assistance any way I can. I've always admired Lillian's business acumen."

"Good. Having had faith in your good judgment, Edvard, I have invited the media to our suite. They will be here in about ten minutes. More coffee?" She smiled within.

"Yes, thank you."

"One more item: Lillian has in her possession the original wire transfer document from Kennington Oil to IIBT authorizing you to wire five million dollars to a front company for James P. McDonald, the vice president. The vice president extorted J.P. so his oil company could get on the list for oil rights and attendant services in Iran after the U.S. conquered it. This was done about three months after he took office."

"Yes, it's true." He looked at the document and said, "Yes, that's correct."

"Also, you provided at the request of J.P., accommodation banking for McDonald so all of the other wire transfers from the major U.S. oil and energy companies that also were extorted by McDonald could go to the same front company, even though McDonald was not one of your customers. Here is a folder with copies of the transfers." She handed him the folder that Lillian had given her during the previous meeting of the Patriotic Five at Raymond's Bar.

He looked through the folder and at each document. "Yes, this information is accurate."

"Are you aware these bribes paid to McDonald violate the laws of the U.S.? Also, he paid no taxes on the income."

"Yes, I was and am. He told me no one would ever find out. But as you know at that moment in time, J.P. had the DVD of me engaging in a tryst, and I was helpless. I'm glad Lillian has it now. I can sleep at night."

Mariah poured him another cup of coffee from the carafe as the doorbell rang.

The first members of the media arrived and Lillian left for her bedroom to await the end of the festivities. Edvard introduced himself to the members as they arrived. He announced that there was an open bar, and it was self-serve.

The space in the suite was filled to capacity. They were standing in the hall but would be able to hear through the front door which had been propped open.

"Ladies and gentlemen, my name is Edvard Lavananski. I'm the president and CEO of International Investment Bank and Trade. Because of the circumstances you all know surrounding Jonathan P. Kennington, now a fugitive, I will be calling a special meeting of the board of directors of the Kennington Holding Company. The purpose will be to divest Mr. Kennington of all his authority and responsibilities regarding the holding company and any and all other companies that bear his name. The board will elect a new chairman, president and CEO two days from now at ten a.m. in a conference room here at the Willard to be designated. Thank you all for coming. Any questions?"

"How can you do this? Doesn't J.P. Kennington have any say in what you're going to do? After all, the man is innocent until proven guilty, isn't he?"

"The answer to your question is no. Mr. Kennington's stock and all assets are controlled by IIBT. It has nothing to do with the fact he's a fugitive or whether he's guilty or innocent. It's just business. The notes are past due demand notes. I need no one's permission to call them. It isn't personal or related to his indictment and fugitive status. Any other questions?"

"Who are going to be the new officers?"

"It'll be announced after the board votes. Thank you, for coming. Good after-noon, ladies and gentlemen."

The members of the media left. "Well done, Edvard, just the way I like it," Mariah said, "concise, convincing, informative and short. I will see you in two days. If you wish to talk, Lillian and I will be here."

Edvard left the suite.

# 51

**Day 24  8:00 A.M.  The Kennington Ranch, Near Abiquiu, New Mexico**

J.P. watched CNN. He was so troubled, he had not slept all night. Lunesta had not lived up to the advertising claims. He used television as an additional sleeping aid, but it didn't help. He reached for his real sleeping capsules, Nembutal, on the night stand. He opened the bottle, looked in and saw it was full and contemplated. His normal dosage was one capsule. He knew that twenty capsules would be the minimum lethal dose for the average person. He considered his weight and counted out forty and held them in the palm of his left hand. He reached for his carafe of water on the night stand with his right hand. He held both hands in front of him, looked at them, considered his desperate circumstances and lifted his left hand toward his mouth. The travel plans of the Nembutal were interrupted by a breaking news story. He rested his left hand on his left thigh and listened.

The anchor person said, "Edvard Lavananski, the president and CEO of International Investment Bank and Trade, has called a special meeting of the board of directors of the Kennington Holding Company. The company controls all of the Kennington companies. Lavananski said, 'The purpose of the meeting is to relieve J.P. Kennington of any and all authority and responsibilities regarding all of his holdings and interests in the Kennington Holding Company and/or any other of the Kennington companies. Also, the board of directors will elect a new chairman, president and CEO of the Kennington Holding Company which will manage all of the Kennington companies. The meeting will be held in two days at the Willard Hotel in Washington, D.C., at a time to be determined. The FBI, the Secret Service and all law enforcement agencies nationwide are searching for the fugitive, Jonathan P. Kennington, and Sean Harrison, the son of the president. Anyone having information regarding the whereabouts of Kennington and Harrison is asked to call their local law enforcement office." Photographs of both were displayed.

J.P. returned the carafe of water onto the night stand and the Nembutal capsules into the bottle. J.P. went to Dirk's bedroom and awoke him. "Dirk, we need to get out of here as soon as possible. Now, the sooner the better is probably the right time. I must be in Washington, D.C., in two days, or I'll lose control of all of my companies, and that's not going to happen. I've been betrayed. We'll need to drive because flying will be too risky. I need to get there without being discovered or arrested. Because of my temporary inconvenience with money we'll have to sneak out, abandon your security people and drive the Navigator. I can't use my credit cards because that would give me away. So, for the moment we'll use yours until I can get to Washington."

"How do I know everything will be all right when we get to D.C.?"

"You're just going to have to trust me and help me at this time."

"I'll help and trust, but it's going to cost you. I want a substantial bonus, say five million."

"That's some bonus."

"It's some trust and some help."

"Well, alright. But let's get ready to leave. Tell Sean to get ready and pack. I want to leave as soon as possible."

Dirk made a call on his communications radio to his colleague who was in charge of the great unwashed who were on the verge of mutiny in tent city. Daren gave him instructions.

Dirk went to Sean's room, unlocked the door and entered. He awoke him and said, "Get your things together we're going to leave as soon as possible."

"Where are we going? What's going on? When am I no longer going to enjoy the company of you and the other inhospitable? Speaking of which, where's my father?"

"I don't know what you're talking about, but if you're referring to J.P. he's getting ready to leave. So, hurry up. I'll be back for you." He left the room and locked the door after him.

Dirk showered, dressed and ate. He packed his clothes and the necessaries and prepared for the trip. Dirk went to the garage and removed the Navigator and backed it up to the back door of the house so the rear cargo door could open. He propped open the rear door of the house so he could walk to the rear of the Navigator and put all of the bags into the open cargo compartment. He went back into the house, picked up his bags, carried one heavy bag in each hand and walked back to the Navigator. When he reached the rear door, one of his security men moved from behind the outside wall of the back of the house and blocked his path to the cargo compartment.

The man pointed a Smith and Wesson M&P .357 SIG with a four and one quarter-inch barrel at his heart. It was an automatic and held fifteen rounds plus one. "Plannin' a little trip are ya, Daren? Wouldn't be runnin' out on us, would ya? Where's my money, ya lyin' prick."

Daren put the bags down and said, "I've told you, cash is on the way. All I'm doing is putting some bags in the SUV for one of the guests."

"Yeah, well, I see the guest. Yur name's on the bags, you lyin' fuck."

Daren picked up the bags and brushed past the man. The man moved forward and put the muzzle of the .357 into Dirk's torso behind his right bicep and below his arm pit. He set the bags down in the cargo compartment and turned his body to his left so the man's view of the bags and his hands were obstructed. Daren reached up the left sleeve of his sheepskin jacket with his right hand, withdrew his CRT M16-14SF Special Forces Knife from its scabbard which was attached to the inside of his left forearm. He wrapped his hand around the handle with the cutting edge facing away from his body and the tip of the blade pointed to his left. The blade was almost four inches long.

He rotated his body to the right with the skill and speed of a trained killer. He caught the outside of the right forearm of the man with the back of his right bicep which forced the muzzle away from the rear of Daren's body so he was no longer vulnerable. The man was surprised and didn't have time to react. Dirk continued turning his body to the right in a continued movement, elevated his right hand and drew the cutting edge of the blade across the front of the man's neck from Dirk's left to right with such force the knife abraded the man's spine. Blood from the carotid arties spewed in every direction and painted Daren's face and clothes. Daren removed the blood from his knife on the man's clothes.

The man and his .357 fell to the ground. Daren dragged the man around to the back of the garage and left him to dry in the hot sun. He walked back to the SUV, stepped around the blood on the terra cotta tiles, picked up the .357, grabbed a garment bag from the back of the SUV and went back to his room. He showered, scrubbed his knife, the .357 and dried them. He replaced the knife into the scabbard and changed clothes. He reattached the scabbard to the inside of his left arm and put on another jacket. He placed the .357 SIG into his rear waistband. He placed all of his blood-splattered clothes into a thirteen-gallon rubbish bag.

He went into the laundry room and removed a gallon of Clorox. He walked to the rear door and poured all of it onto the blood that adorned the tiles and placed the empty container into a large-rubbish recycling bin. *That should do it.* He carried the plastic bag filled with his blood-stained clothes inside the garage and picked up a five-gallon red can. He carried them both around to the back of the garage where his latest trophy laid. He poured the gasoline all over the body, set it on fire and dropped the bag of clothes onto the burning body. He stood, watched it until he was satisfied the clothes had turned to ash. He left the body burning in its own fat. If he had stayed longer, he could have watched it explode. But then he already knew that. This was not his first gasoline-fueled barbeque.

He returned to the inside of the house, went to J.P.'s bedroom, knocked, entered and asked, "Are you all packed and ready to leave?"

"Yes. You're late."

"I had a temporary inconvenience. But I dispatched it." Dirk picked up J.P.'s bags and placed them in the back of the SUV. J.P. followed behind him and entered the Navigator on the passenger's side.

Dirk went back to Sean's room, unlocked the door and said, "Pick up your bags, and let's go out the back door. Put your bags into the back of the SUV and close the cargo door and get in the car behind J.P." He did, and Dirk bound his right ankle with a shackle to the leg of his seat. Sean sat next to a man who sat behind Dirk, who was going to be the driver. The man wore filthy clothes. The hot sun, perspiration and not bathing since he arrived in this desert paradise produced a fragrance inside the SUV which was a Grasse perfumer's greatest achievement.

"You're going to have some very angry adversaries," J.P. said, as they drove off the property and toward the highway.

"True, very true. But the way I see it, once you get back in the saddle, pay me what I asked, I'm going to retire to a nice, quiet environment somewhere and put it all behind me."

"Yeah, well first things first."

"Sean, I want you to meet your new best friend. His name is Frank, and he's been a long-time friend of mine. Be obedient, Sean, or your companion will be forced to protect you from yourself." Frank smoked dirty, filthy, stinky, carcinogenic, cancer-causing cigarettes. And like all people who use tobacco products, he smelled like a dirty ashtray.

Sean turned to his left and looked at the man who had won an Oscar nomination for the best actor in the remake of "Down and Out in Beverly Hills" as the homeless man.

"Sean here said you were his father. I didn't know that. I thought he was the president's brat."

"Sean has a bad habit of talking too much. Maybe my decision to keep him with us was wrong. What do you think, Sean?"

"You don't want to hear what I think or anything else to do with you. Just drop me off at the White House, or let me make a call. Let me out, and I'll wait to be picked up, Lecher."

# 52

**Day 24   10:00 A.M.   The White House, the Oval Office**

Mariah sat on the sofa to the right of the president. He sat in the right chair at the end of the coffee table looking into the fireplace and close to her.

"Any word from the FBI or Secret Service about the whereabouts of Sean, his condition or J.P.?"

"Nothing, not a word. His mother and I are worried sick about it. I love that boy. I don't care who the biological father is. He's my son. I raised him, loved him, clothed and fed him, nurtured him and educated him. He's my son, and you can bet your ass J.P.'s going to pay the maximum penalty; death comes to mind."

"Sean is a good man, too bad he got mixed up with J.P. My prayers go out to you and Lillian."

"Thank you. I know you mean it."

"I do. I have come to help you, Robert, though you may not believe it when you hear what I have to say. But on contemplation in moments of clear-headedness, and at night when you are alone, you will see the truth and wisdom in what I am going to tell you.

"So you know the information is accurate, let me make one or two perfunctory remarks. Lillian knows all about the Kennington operations. A friend of mine, who will remain nameless and genderless, has the highest of computer skills. This person had ferreted this information. Your puppeteer, J.P., has been selling military secrets to China and illegally selling arms to every place on the globe where there is a war. He has been supplying parts and other equipment to Iran in violation of U.N. sanctions. The money has not entered the U.S., has not gone into any of his companies' bank accounts and he has paid no taxes. All of the money has been handled by IIBT. Or if you wish, laundered by IIBT as an accommodation, because he is or was their best customer."

"I knew he was a rat, but this is treason and other crimes. Do you have proof?"

"Yes, here. Read the material in this folder — they are the originals. Then read the materials in this folder; this is your copy in case you want to show it to McDonald and watch the expression on his face when he finds out he has been caught stealing." She handed him two manila folders filled with a copy and the original of the documentation.

He read, continued to shake his head from side to side in apparent disbelief of what he saw. After fifteen minutes he said, "I believe what I'm reading is true. But I find J.P.'s conduct incredible and treasonous. I can see I completely misjudged him and the other things you showed me on your previous visit." He handed the folder with the originals on J.P. in it to her and kept the other folder with the copies demonstrating the misconduct of McDonald.

"Politicians never judge the giver of bribes, not disguised as a campaign contribution, but judge whether they can take the bribe and not be exposed."

"A little harsh aren't you, Mariah?"

"Quite the opposite. Under the circumstances, it's common knowledge of the relationships between lobbyists, special interests, the wealthy and politicians. I thought bribe was euphemistic and kind.

"You have seen I am sure the announcement by Edvard Lavananski of the removal of J.P. from all of his companies. The bank, in effect, owns all of the stock. Everything he owns of value has been collateralized and loans have been made to him in violation of U.S. banking regulations. Lillian McGraw is going to be the next CEO and president of Kennington Holding Company and will control all of the Kennington companies. Lavananski will be the next chairman. I know you have irreconcilable differences with J.P. I am hoping you will not suffer any disadvantage because of his being a major financial contributor to your re-election campaign. I want you to support Lillian McGraw's ascension to these new positions. Lavananski considers her to be highly qualified. She knows all there is to know about J.P. and the Kennington companies. I want you to assure the secretary of defense and Samuel Blackwell, deputy director of the DIA, to proceed with the granting of all contracts to Kennington and make the necessary payments that are due and owing. Will you do this for her and for you? This will clean up Kennington and stop J.P.'s extortion of the decision-makers in your administration."

"Yes, I will and be thankful to you for it."

"Next, you are aware of the secret McDonald Energy Task Force he set up ten days after he took office in violation of the Federal Advisory Committee Act, also known as the 'open-government' law. It was done under the guise of establishing an energy policy for the U.S. Actually it was a trolling device, known as greed, to increase his wealth. Two months later, he prepared a list of the acceptable U.S. companies that were interested in exploiting Iranian oilfields after the U.S. defeat of Iran. These companies had interests in production, pipelines, refineries and terminals. In order to get on the list to be considered, and there were all the majors and others, they had to pay to play, which they did. He extorted each of them for five million dollars and this included Kennington Oil. Then when the war was over, the companies would have to pay him again, assuming he agreed to let them bid for whatever rights in Iran they wanted. Look at this." She opened the McDonald folder for him that he had placed on the coffee table in front of him.

Robert read the dossier prepared by Geoffrey and Lillian and said, "Unbelievable. Apparently, he got J.P. to let him use the secret accounts of IIBT to hide the payments from all of the companies. I see in this one document he held an auction. He made close to a hundred million dollars. He definitely went into public service as a business. The man's a criminal and betrayed his public trust, treason."

"They all do, and yes he is. Politicians who go into public service as a business, are me first, my constituents second and the American public third. How much of the bribes did you receive?" *Time to sow a little more dissension.*

"None. I didn't know he was doing it. I don't know what to say or do."

"How are you going to get rid of him, Robert?"

"I don't know; I'll have to think about it."

"Well, while you are thinking about it, if you do not give me in writing a statement to the effect you are not going to go to war with Iran, my friends and I may do something you will not like."

"I'll have to work on it. I can't give it to you now."

"May I make a suggestion?"

"Yes, of course."

"I want you to tell McDonald to give the money back to these companies, because you are not going to go to war with Iran. Now if he does not want to and just wishes to keep the money and be accused of taking money under false pretenses, grand theft, other crimes which are felonies, that is alright with me. Let the U.S. Attorney General decide what he wants to do when he finds out about it, and he will. When the stockholders of these companies find out the CEO and/ or president had given a bribe to McDonald contrary to law, the outrage will produce his indictment and conviction. I will see to it, I assure you."

She told him there would be no fabrication of intelligence from the CIA by Cliff instigated by McDonald and his chief of staff, Jacob Goldman. Mariah begged him not go to war illegally like a previous administration did in Iraq.

Robert had not learned anything from that debacle which caused the previous president to be accused of murdering our military personnel and civilians because of his illegal act. The president had committed treason. This way, Robert could get rid of McDonald, not go to war if he was afraid of McDonald and was without courage. The American people were tired of war.

She told Robert he must remember who paid his salary and to whom he owed the responsibility of his office. He owed nothing to McDonald and everything to the American people. If Robert had not made the mistake of selecting him for vice president, he would still be working as just another president and

CEO of an oil services company. He would not be in the process of murdering our military personnel by sending them to war illegally for greed only. She told him to think about it.

He sat quietly for a few moments and then said, "I see your point, and you're right. I'll try, Mariah."

# 53

## Day 24   10:00 A.M.

## U.S. Department of Defense (DoD), Arlington, Virginia

Lillian met with Samuel Blackwell, deputy director of the Defense Intelligence Agency or DIA. He had approved the development of the poisonous gas for the "War Plan" proposed by J.P.

"Thank you for seeing me; I know you're busy."

"How can I help you, Lillian? It's been awhile."

"Yes, it has. You're aware of the present circumstance surrounding J.P. Kennington, are you not?"

"Yes, tragic. I called the investigator, Christopher James, sheriff's homicide, in Los Angeles. He provided me with the details. Most disturbing. A man of J.P.'s stature engaged in such criminal activity causes me many problems. I don't believe the DoD can go forward with Kennington Industries."

"The purpose of this meeting is to inform you of two things. First, I have a present for you." She reached into her bag and handed him a DVD in a jewel case. "This is the DVD, and there are no copies, that J.P. used to extort you. In two days, I'll be the next CEO and president of the Kennington Holding Company which controls all of the Kennington companies. J.P. will be removed from all the Kennington companies and from the board of directors. He'll be powerless and destitute. I want you to pay to Kennington the money that's due and owing. Next, I'd like you to consider awarding contracts to Kennington Industries now that it'll be under new management. Will you do this for us?"

"Yes. Kennington has always produced high-quality products for the DoD. It was just the unpleasantness of having to deal with J.P. and his henchmen and lobbyists. Also, the president ordered us not to do any business with J.P. Kennington or pay him any monies due."

"Thank you. You won't regret it. I'll give you an honest first count, not pad the bill as before and will handle the relations of Kennington with you personally.

There'll be no 'henchmen' again. If you have any doubt about the veracity of what I'm telling you, you have my permission to call President Harrison. I believe he'll now favor DoD awarding contracts to Kennington Industries."

"Thank you. I'll call the president. And, Lillian, thank you for the present. It's a good way to start a relationship. A little honesty goes a long way with me. Actually, now that I think about it, your present to me is a sufficient show of integrity that I'll not need to call the president. I'll arrange it all with the Secretary of Defense or SecDef.

"Thank you, and good day to you, Mr. Blackwell."

# 54

## Day 24  11:00 A.M.  The White House, the Oval Office

Robert asked McDonald to come to his office. He came in and sat in one of the visitor's chairs in front of the Lincoln. "I didn't ask you to sit, McDonald, stand with respect until I ask you to sit, which I'm not going to do."

McDonald was so surprised by this change of attitude in his marionette, he rose quickly and stared at Robert. Robert enjoyed these rare moments of superiority.

"I was dumb enough to believe you wanted to determine an energy policy for this country when you set up the McDonald Energy Task Force. Some very disturbing news has come to my attention with supporting documentation. But all you really wanted to do was to defraud and extort the big-oil companies, utilities and other energy companies of monies to enhance your wealth. You've been receiving bribes in substantial amounts from the participants in your secret energy task force. You've gone into business for yourself, you dishonorable prick. You've been hustling the suckers into believing you had the ability to grant contracts and licenses to produce oil from the Iranian oil fields in the future and supporting infrastructure. You've tried to commit my administration without my knowledge, permission or ability to award contracts. Well, you'll not get away with it.

"This is a violation of the law. You're a criminal. I want your resignation effective immediately. I want you to return all of the monies collected and send each sucker a letter informing them you acted outside of your authority and without my knowledge. And if you don't, I will. If the media were to find out, it would cause me to lose my re-election campaign. And to top it off you cheap bastard, you didn't offer to share any of the ill-gotten gains with me. Remember, I'm the president. The people elected me, not you, so don't forget it. Here, read the materials in this folder while you're standing."

McDonald rested the folder on the front of the Lincoln, opened it and turned the pages. Recognized them all and said, "Who gave you some spine, O'Leary? I understand she visited you this morning. Have you been drinking again? Who's filling your head with these forgeries?"

"They aren't forgeries, I saw the originals. I've already called the secretary of the treasury to prepare a dossier for you. He has already verbally verified the information. You will not be receiving any salary or benefits as vice president from now on. In addition, he's frozen your bank account that holds the bribes and all your other accounts, including your wife's. Your investment account at Goldman Sachs and all credit cards are also frozen.

"So, what's it going to be, McDonald, resignation 'due to health' because all the world knows you've a bad heart, or 'I want to spend more time with my family', the other excuse no one ever believes when a politician gets caught dirty? And you've been caught dirty. And no one I know would want to spend any time with your aggressive and unpleasant wife, which could be called torturous. It's common knowledge you hate her. And, so does everyone else that knows her."

"I'm not going to resign, send the letter or give the money back. If I go down, you'll go down." He threw the folder onto the Lincoln and left without any parting amenities.

# 55

**Day 24   11:30 A.M.**

**McDonalds Office in the Eisenhower Executive Office Building (EEOB)**

James McDonald, the vice president, Jacob "Jake" Goldman, the vice president's chief of staff, and Richard Rigor sat in the vice president's office.

The bald, obese and bespectacled McDonald wore his two-piece suit like a large, heavy-duty burlap bag filled with Idaho Russet #1 potatoes; ill-fitting came to mind. Rigor was portly, almost bald with his porcine face. Jake was slender and in good physical condition, attractive but not handsome, always well-dressed.

"Gentlemen, I've some distressing news. The president has discovered our scheme from my energy task force. I don't know who informed him, but I've a feeling it was his lawyer, Mariah O'Leary. He asked me to resign, give back the money and write letters to the contributors, telling them I acted without his permission or knowledge. He said if I didn't do as he asked, he was going to expose me. I told him if I go down, he'll go down. The problem with my marionette is he may be dumb enough to do it. The problem with dumb people, you never know what they're going to do. Maybe the pressure of his missing son and not knowing his condition has affected his judgment. Or his lawyer's responsible for the probable reversal of our potential fortunes. I do believe we're in awkward circumstances. Do either of you wish to give back the money you received?" *No reason to tell them I'm broke. What I need is a friend with lots of money who believes I'm rich and hasn't heard about my inconvenience.*

There was silence. The vice president looked at the two of them and said, "I didn't think so. So, what do we do about it? Any suggestions? You're two smart political operatives? I welcome your suggestions, no matter the method of overcoming."

"As a part of his re-election campaign, we could set up a parade in Dallas and have him pay homage to Jack Kennedy and while he's passing the grassy knoll we could have a reenactment." Only Goldman and McDonald laughed.

"Damn good suggestion, I'd like to be president and not have to put up with this buffoon any longer. Not original but a good suggestion; nothing wrong with being a hero by coup d'état. Then we could add the Robert S. Harrison Memorial Plaza to the existing John F. Kennedy Memorial Plaza. The problem with it is too many participants to get it done and have to get rid of everyone with knowledge afterward — messy, tedious and too risky."

"As an alternative to my previous suggestion, how about having lunch with him again and just put some maculotoxin and tetrodotoxin in white powder form into his food which will cause respiratory arrest? There's no antidote. We can blame the White House steward who served the food, a fall guy? We'll tell anybody who asked he ate the wrong seafood. We can arrange so there'll be no autopsy. And even if there is one, we can get a 'Death by Natural Causes' and cremate him immediately pursuant to his wishes. You know, do a little modern imitation of Lucrezia Borgia, the daughter of Pope Alexander VI. Supposedly she used catarella, her deadly slow poison of choice. We'll get to wear black armbands for ten seconds and pretend we're grief stricken. We'll have a parade with a horse and empty boots facing backward in the stirrups in the lead, the symbol of the fallen soldier."

"How do you know so much about poison, Jake?" Richard asked.

"I did the research. We started planning his assassination right after the inauguration. The head of the investor group suggested the use of the neurotoxin. McDonald reminded me of it some time ago. In fact, during a recess in one of the first meetings of his energy task force. We talked about it, and he told me to look into it and make some decisions. So, I made a call to the head of our investors' group and arranged it when needed.

"As soon as Robert stopped taking orders, became unpleasant or obstreperous we'd institute the plan. And he's getting worse. One of these days he's going to start believing he's running this country, and we can't allow that.

"The people who put up the first fifty million dollars, our investors, are the ones who are calling the shots in this administration. They decided to back Robert if McDonald was on the ticket. Harrison had name value and money, so he was electable. It was the investors' plan from the beginning the president would die in office, and their man McDonald would be president.

"J.P. Kennington had called McDonald and told him the president was no longer cooperating with him. This isn't good. J.P. was one of the contributors who had paid McDonald to have auction rights in Iran. He's one of the investors.

"According to McDonald the right moment evidently came today. Robert is an alcoholic, was the king of Ds, Fs and Incompletes in college. He only graduated because his rich father bribed the president of his college. All he knows about running the country you could put on the sharp end of a pin and have room for Tolstoy's *War and Peace,* the twenty volumes of the *Oxford English Dictionary* and the *Encyclopedia Britannica."*

"You're awfully quiet, Richard, any suggestion?"

"Not really, I'm afraid I'm not up on ways to kill people. You're right about one thing though. For some reason, he has developed a mind of his own, and it appears the marionette has cut his slave strings from you, McDonald."

"True, but what now? Our war plan appears to be in jeopardy. If we don't go into Iran, there'll be a lot of angry energy executives wanting their money back. Good luck to them. So, the only way I see for us to keep what we have, make more and not provoke our contributors or investors is to go forward with Jake's plan. Jake, can you get us some white powder?"

"Sure, the only things money can't buy are love, immortality and poverty. So, I'll take care of it."

"There's no doubt we can make more money when I'm president than as vice president. No reason to go into public service if you don't get really rich and not get caught. Unfortunately, caught is the operative word here."

"Richard, because you made no suggestion, made as much money as Jake, you're the designated assassin. Jake'll give you the neurotoxin, we'll have lunch with Robert, I'll distract, and you'll insert."

"Are you kidding me!? I don't want to do this."

"You'll do as you're told."

"I don't work for you, I work for the president."

"You've been working for my government within his government from the day you started here. Who do you think runs this country — me. Not him, for sure.

"You wanted money to solve your financial problems. I offered a solution, you got your money, and you're in to the end of my administration. I told you this from the beginning, 'Once you're in, you're in for life.' I'll be running for re-election as president when my term expires. So plan on giving me your undying loyalty for as long as I'm president.

"If we don't do him now, we'll have a worse problem later. After the invasion of Iran, when I tell him to invade Syria, then Lebanon and depose of Hezbollah as a force there, he may balk."

"Congress and the American people are not going to sit still for this new world order of yours, McDonald," Rigor said. "It'll be murdering more people including our military personnel, enemy combatants and noncombatants. Besides, we won't be in office long enough for you to accomplish your goal assuming you could."

"Maybe yes, maybe no. But it has to be done."

"There'll be outrage," Rigor said. "How many times do you believe you can deceive the media and the people into believing Iran, Syria and Hezbollah are an imminent threat to the U.S.? How many times can you get a DCI to use forged documents like a previous administration did, marketing to the world an imminent danger so they could illegally invade Iraq? Your desire to be the first unitary president and shift this democracy toward fascism is frightening.

"You're already rewriting the legislation that has been passed by Congress for the benefit of an unitary presidency. You're benefitting yourself, big business, your investors and wealthy contributors by having your legislative assistant make the necessary changes. Then you have the president sign the legislation by using presidential signing statements, and the legislation is modified to your personal satisfaction, the American public be damned."

Jake and McDonald stared at Richard. McDonald saw something he didn't like; Richard was thinking and wavering. *I do believe the golden rule of assassination will need to be implemented. What's needed is an assassin to kill the assassin after the assassin kills Robert. I'll have to discuss this with Jake.*

Richard sat with consternation, never a good companion. *What do I do now? Do I tell Spencer about the plot and my involvement? What about the unitary presidency? Do I tell him about this and McDonald's desire to shift toward a dictatorship? Can he stop it, can I? Can I give up the money I've made with more to come, if nothing unusual happens? Not hardly. Trusting these two is right up there with gross stupidity, another bad companion. After I kill Robert, how long will it be before they invite me to lunch with Jake's two companions, Mssrs.* Maculotoxin and Tetrodotoxin, *or bless me with some other lethal misadventure?*

Richard left the office. He reached into his coat pocket and turned off his digital recorder.

# 56

**Day 25   9:00 A.M.**

## The Central Intelligence Agency Headquarters, Langley, Virginia

Mariah and Jerry Spencer sat in the two visitor's chairs in front of Director Roger Cliff's desk. Jerry activated his digital recorder.

"The president said you had something important to ask me," Cliff said.

"Yes, we do. I know the president asked you to fabricate intelligence so he could order the invasion of Iran. He has changed his mind about invading Iran. I know the vice president and Jake Goldman are pressuring your Middle East analysts to fabricate intelligence. I know there is no intelligence that would lead a reasonable person to believe that Iran has any intention or capability of an imminent attack on the U.S. They may dream about invading or attacking Israel, but it's just propaganda for worldwide-jihadist consumption, pandering to the populace sometimes known as bullshit. So, we are in no danger of being attacked, unless of course, someone in the administration stages a massacre of American citizens, and you blame the vice president's country of choice, Iran. May I be assured by you that you have no intention of fabricating intelligence or using forged documents so the vice president and his energy-producing friends can use Iran as their own personal goldmine with the U.S. as their security detail?"

"You have me baffled, Ms. O'Leary. Where did you come by this information?"

"From the president. Please, pick up the phone and call him. Do not stall me. I want an answer."

"I don't believe you're in a position to give me orders. I have no need to call the president. He gave me orders previously, and I'm following them."

"Let me show you something. Will you recognize the signature of the president?"

"Sure."

She removed from her briefcase the "War Plan" document and William Morse's report that the signature was that of the president. "Here, please read these and hand them back to me." She handed them to him, he read them and handed them back.

"Why did he do this? I find this incredible, murdering our citizens for greed."

"Without giving you all of the details, J.P. Kennington forced him to sign it or he and his investor group would not arrange for the necessary money for his re-election campaign. J.P. needed the president re-elected so he could get more DoD contracts and other government benefits to save his companies."

"Incredible."

"Next, are you aware of a document called the Prague Accord?"

"No."

"Read this and return it to me. Will you recognize the signature of Petrokov?"

"Absolutely." He read the document and returned it. "I was never told about this. They've already decided to go to war with Iran and disguise it as a war against terrorism. It's so transparent, it'd be laughable if it wasn't so horrible. It's just money and McDonald's desire to have a new world order designed by him, fascism."

"Yes, it is," Mariah said. "And what is more incredible is a supposed honorable man like you embezzling millions and willing to commit treason so you could continue to chase your penis."

" 'Embezzling millions,' I don't know what you mean."

"How unfortunate. Here all the while I was naive enough to believe you were smart and a patriot and would not engage in treason and the attempted murder of our military personnel. For you surely will be guilty of both, and then murder if they die if you provide fabricated intelligence or use forged documents as a pretense.

"Logic does not seem to be working with you, so how about this? Mr. Spencer will enlighten you. As you know, he is one of the agency's most decorated field agents and operatives. Jerry, see if the information you have might change the mind of the DCI."

"I've a friend of mine, who'll be nameless. My friend's an expert with computers and investigations. He has, and I've the documents with me, and a copy for you if you wish to see them, that leads me to believe you've embezzled . . ." He paused, looked into the folder and said, "Let me see here. To be exact, four million two hundred and sixty-three thousand dollars from the CIA discretionary fund as of this morning.

"You're married and have not placed any of the money into your bank account. According to the IRS, you haven't paid taxes on any of it. But what you have done is spent all of the money on one Russian actress by the name of Olga Kurakova. Bought her a beautiful home in Georgetown, and it's held in the name of a front company which you set up and own. I'm sure the Russia desk here would be most interested in this information. They'd love to roast you on the front page of the Post. In addition to the monies you've lavished on her and yourself, I've an interesting DVD I'd like to show you. May I use your Blu-ray DVD player? The quality of the audio and the visual are remarkable. There's no doubt as to the players."

"No, you may not. What is it you two want?"

"You are starting to remind me of Robert Harrison," Mariah said. "The only difference I see between the two of you is: you are thinner. What we want is what I asked for, short memory? Do not, I repeat, do not fabricate or use any forged documents as intelligence so this administration can invade Iran or any other nation in the Middle East with a pre-emptive strike and stop stalling me. If you do, I will show all to your wife. Then to the media worldwide. And considering you are a poor civil servant and she is really rich, I foresee a reversal of fortunes on your part, capisce? Also, you are conspiring with McDonald and Harrison to commit treason." They looked into Cliff's eyes with disrespect.

"I see." He sat, looked at the two and contemplated his next action. *I do believe it may be time to retire or something more drastic.*

"Do you want to be remembered as a patriot, one who cares about people? Military personnel and noncombatants come to mind. I will be pleased to give you these two suggestions." She gave him the two suggestions, looked at him, did not blink and waited for an answer.

Cliff sat, looked at her and said, "I'll take the two under consideration."

"If you do either, Ms. O'Leary and I'll forget this meeting, shred the documents and the DVD, and you'll hear no more from us. You'll only have to worry about McDonald and the CIA's inspector general. If you do the right thing, I can give you information on McDonald which'll checkmate his mouth and his ability to write. And if you want to make it public, it'll drive him from office. Maybe between the three of us we can cut off the head of this man who worships the money god, Greed, and wants to be a dictator, not euphemistically called an unitary president. So, this'll leave the inspector general, and with him I can't help you. Is this alright with you?"

"Yes, more than fair under the circumstances."

# 57

**Day 26   10:00 A.M.**

**The Willard Hotel Conference Room, Washington, D.C.**

Edvard Lavananski, president and CEO of IIBT, had spoken to all fifteen members of the board of directors of the Kennington Holding Company after his meeting with Lillian and Mariah. He had informed them that the bank controlled all of the stock, and the holding company controlled all the Kennington companies. The board agreed to his plan so Kennington Holding would not have to file for bankruptcy and to avoid the collapsing of his bank and the global fallout. He left out the part about he had violated banking laws to make the loans to the Kennington companies, had taken bribes from J.P., laundered money and was being extorted by J.P. Kennington.

Lillian, Mariah, Jerry Spencer and five of his operatives sat in the chairs around the wall. Jerry and one of his operatives sat in chairs on either side of the entrance into the room. The board sat in tufted chairs around a rectangular table that was adorned with a table cloth and pleated skirt of red and gold. Each member had a pad and glass of water in front of them.

After the reading of the minutes by the secretary, Jonathan P. Kennington was voted out as chairman, CEO and president by unanimous vote. Next, the meeting was open to nominations for his replacement. Edvard nominated Lillian McGraw, another member seconded it. No other nominations were made. Edvard called for a vote and it was unanimous. Edvard adjourned the meeting by unanimous vote. That was the fastest one hundred thousand dollars each board member had made to attend a board of directors meeting, plus all expenses.

The door to the conference room opened and J.P. and Dirk walked in and approached the table. J.P. was dressed in a two-piece suit and tie. Dirk was disguised as a bodyguard in a black two-piece suit, white shirt, black tie, black rubber-soled shoes and Oakleys.

"What's going on here, Lavananski? I heard about this bloodless coup. You're not going to steal my company."

At this moment, Jerry and one of his operatives came from behind J.P. and Dirk and tried to apprehend them without a struggle. The other operatives moved from their chairs and joined them. Dirk turned to his right, J.P. turned to his left and they faced one another. They looked at Jerry, who was only two feet away. Dirk drew his weapon with his right hand from under his coat and behind his left bicep. It was a Walther .380 PPK, and he aimed it at Jerry.

All eyes in the room stared at J.P., Dirk, Spencer and the operatives. Spencer struck Dirk on the outside of his right forearm near his wrist with the outside middle of his right forearm. The blow forced the muzzle away from Jerry's torso when the shot was fired. Jerry drove his right fist into Dirk's solar plexus. Dirk bent from the waist, dropped the Walther and gasped for air. Jerry grabbed him by the hair with his left hand and pulled his head backward and down. His neck was vulnerable. Dirk looked into Jerry's eyes. Jerry maintained eye contact and drove the second knuckles of his right hand into his Adam's apple, crushed his windpipe, and the knuckles' forward motion did not stop until they reached Dirk's spine. Dirk gasped again, fell to the red and gold patterned carpet and was still. He was dying of suffocation. Another good deed done by those who care. Jerry put a ball-point pen into the muzzle of the Walther and placed it on the conference table. He instructed the people in the room not to touch it.

J.P. lay on the carpet with a bullet hole in his torso. Jerry said, "Call the police and an ambulance."

The members of the board left the conference room to attend to other pressing business. They didn't want to enjoy the publicity to follow with their attendant photographs on the evening-news programs and leading print publications.

The police and ambulance arrived. Jerry turned over the Walther to the police and an officer bagged it for evidence. Dirk was dead. J.P. was taken into custody and placed into the George Washington University Hospital. He would now have new watch dogs who would attend him from the Washington, D.C., Metropolitan Police Department, or MPD. When he recovered from surgery and was conscious his seeker, Christopher James, would be looking into his eyes and would be his first visitor. The honest James had won. James pinned the warrant for his arrest on the front of J.P.'s hospital gown. He had already shown it to the chief of MPD.

After recovery and discharge, J.P. would not be flying to Los Angeles in his G650 or enjoying the facilities at his former estate. His new home would be the Los Angeles County Jail in a high-profile prison cell alone. He would find it difficult to find an attorney with skills who would represent a homeless and penniless pauper.

# 58

**Day 26 10:11 A.M. The Willard Hotel, Washington, D.C.**

Jerry's operatives' mission was the rescue of Sean Harrison. They had the Willard surrounded. They looked for the arrival of J.P. They spotted a black Navigator. Dirk parked it on the street. J.P. was in the passenger seat. Frank and Sean were in the back seat behind them. Dirk and J.P exited and walked briskly to the front entrance of the hotel.

While Dirk was not enjoying his misevaluated skills with Jerry during their confrontation in the conference room, the operatives used their binoculars to evaluate their plan for the rescue of Sean and the takedown of the bodyguard. On the communications receiver-transmitters in their ears, they heard from the team leader, "Two and Three approach the vehicle. Two, take Sean's door and Three take the door of the body guard. Disable the bodyguard by any means necessary under the circumstances. Don't expose yourself or Sean to great bodily harm. Remove Sean and proceed to the conference room as planned. Four and I'll be in support. I'll take the bodyguard down if he poses a threat. The operatives approached the vehicle. Two grabbed the door handle of the door next to Sean with his latex-covered left hand, but it was locked. Frank drew his weapon and aimed his piece at Two. One, the team leader, stood next to Three by Frank's door where he sat. One shot him twice in the heart and once in the middle of his forehead with his suppressed .45 Glock 21 through the glass in the door. Sean unlocked the doors. He was shackled to the seat leg. One opened the door, went through Frank's pockets with his latex-covered left hand and found the keys to the lock on the shackle. Frank was left in the SUV as artwork titled: "Dead on Arrival, Artist Anonymous."

The operatives took Sean and his luggage into the conference room. J.P. lay on the carpet unattended.

Lillian saw Sean and walked to him and said, "I missed you so."

"Me, too. What're we going to do now?" Sean looked down at J.P. "Is he dead?"

"Unfortunately, no. His punishment will be worse than death, the rest of his life in prison. What do you want to do now?"

"Shower, throw all these clothes away, get some new ones and spend the next few days with you, just the two of us."

"Sounds good to me. We'll talk and decide."

The police and the ambulance arrived.

# 59

**Day 26   2:00 P.M.   The Willard Hotel, Washington, D.C.**

Mariah, Lillian and Jerry met in Mariah's suite. "One-third of "Operation Downfall" is now completed with the arrest and imminent prosecution of J.P.," Mariah said. "He is now homeless and soon to be penniless. Thanks to Geoffrey, the money he made from the sale of illegal arms was located. That was J.P.'s last hurrah.

"I spoke with Edvard about the money, and he agreed to accept it as a good-faith payment against the debt of the Kennington Holding Company. In exchange, he will now transfer title to the Bel Air estate, cars, homes and the G650 to Lillian and any other personal or real property owned by J.P. She is now in control of Kennington Holding and will operate all of the Kennington companies. This way, she can honor her promises to the DoD and other commitments of the Kennington companies. As part of the deal I made with Edvard, he will have access to the G650 if he is acting as chairman of Kennington Holding.

"Thank you, Mariah, for all you've done for me. Thank you, Jerry for rescuing Sean. I'm overwhelmed with gratitude to Geoffrey, Greg and you two. And of course, to the honest cop, James. I understand what he had to overcome. There appeared to be a D.A. on J.P.'s pad."

"My operatives are still here in D.C.," Jerry said. "It appears Rigor is cooperating, but who knows for sure? Mariah, I've given you all the latest intel from Rigor. What's next?"

"Part two and now three of "Downfall", Mariah said. "As you know, it was originally to remove Harrison from office if he pursued his war plan. Well, I see we need to include the vice president. According to Jerry's information from Rigor, McDonald wants to remake the world as he sees it. He wants an unitary presidency. That's a euphemism for dictator.

"He wants to invade Iran, Syria, remove Hezbollah's stranglehold on Lebanon and any other country he sees as an impediment to his new world building. The way the world should be according to McDonald, a real hardliner and traitor. He does not realize or does not want to accept the only way to kill fundamentalist-Islamic jihadists is with a better idea. Instead he should use the overwhelming majority of moderate Muslims to do it for him. They need more motivation.

"Or maybe it is just power-hungry jihadist Muslims using the illiterates as pawns and disguising their lust by appearing to be religious and teaching hate for the West and moderate Muslims. There is no doubt Saudi Arabia is in the lead when it comes to teaching hate in the madrassas they fund around the world. They want to live in the seventh century and continue to oppress women. Lillian, now that Sean is back, what are your plans?"

"I planned on spending a few days with him. We agreed to discuss our future together. If you need me, I'd like to be a part of finishing "Operation Downfall", before returning to California and operating Kennington."

"Good. Stay here for a few days with Sean or wherever. Just be able and available to Jerry and me by cell.

"Jerry, this is what I want you to do before we set the plan to dethrone McDonald and remove the president by resignation or impeachment." She explained her plan to him.

# 60

**Day 28  8:00 P.M.  Rigor's Residence, Georgetown, Washington, D.C.**

Jerry and his partner watched Richard Rigor drive into the garage of his apartment. They waited for ten minutes and then Jerry got out of his car and went to Rigor's apartment. His partner booted the laptop, opened the recording software and prepared to record the audio-video activity within. Jerry knocked on the door. Rigor inquired and Jerry identified himself. Rigor let him in.

"I haven't heard from you, so I thought I'd stop by and see how you are, and what's new that I'd be interested in."

"As I told you previously, McDonald wants to invade Iran, Syria and Lebanon and rid the Middle East of Hezbollah. He's a real hardliner. That's about it."

"No, there's something else. You're not giving me all of it. What's the matter, Richard? What happened? You're nervous and preoccupied. You don't look at me when you talk. What's up?"

"Nothing. Overworked, I guess. Another hard day in the White House."

"I don't believe you. You're used to stress and 'Another hard day in the White House'. There's more. Please, don't make me become unpleasant. Give it to me, or I'll give it to you, your choice. I've kept my word to you so far, you've given me some good intel, but now I want the answer to my question."

"I haven't slept for four days."

"Why? Give it to me, and let me help you. I'm a good problem-solver."

"I'm afraid the problem's beyond your control and generosity." Rigor sat on the sofa with his suit coat off. He loosened his tie, removed it and unbuttoned the two top buttons of his shirt. He leaned his head back and rested it on the top of the back of the sofa. He stared at the ceiling and then closed his eyes.

Jerry sat in his two-piece dark suit, white shirt and no tie in an over-stuffed chair and watched him. He sat back in the chair with his black shoes flat on the area rug. He decided to let the circumstances dictate and not press Rigor. His thought was that Rigor may be on the verge of a nervous breakdown or, worse, suicide.

Jerry looked at his Breitling Super Avenger BlackSteel Limited Edition watch, saw the time, the second hand rotated, he sat in silence and watched Rigor. It was obvious the man was agonizing over what to do. Thirty-two minutes had passed.

Richard rose from the sofa and walked to his desk. He picked up his digital recorder and set it on the coffee table in front of the sofa. He turned it on, leaned back and rested his head again on the top of the back of the sofa. They sat quietly and listened to the recording.

Richard leaned forward, put his forearms on the tops of his thighs behind his kneecaps, looked past the coffee table and at the area rug in the living room and said, "What you just heard is James P. McDonald, the vice president, Jacob Goldman, his chief of staff, and me in the vice president's office four mornings ago.

"The president is just a politician no better or worse than the rest of them. He'll say anything whether it's true or not, if he believes he won't get caught. Or, he'll do anything whether it's legal or not, if he believes he won't get caught. And here we have it. He sold his soul to be president. Robert had to agree to have a watchdog selected by special interests-investors as a vice president. They chose McDonald. Harrison didn't choose him. He's just a pawn of McDonald, who represents the investors who paid to get Harrison elected so McDonald could run the country. And of course, McDonald is the pawn of the investors. He takes orders, but he believes erroneously he's in charge. Or as McDonald so graphically puts it: 'Harrison's as useless as tits on a bull.' That's one of those Texas cattle baron investors' expressions. McDonald has always been amoral and classless."

Richard told him the plan from the beginning was for Robert to get elected, resign and McDonald would be president. Robert would be president in label only. McDonald would be the man behind the president, the dictator or unitary president, whichever label you wish to use. He had been doing this from the very beginning by having Robert issue executive orders and presidential signing statements. He has rendered the Congress impotent in any area the investors don't like.

"Well, as fate would have it, much like turning a child loose in a candy store, once elected Robert reneged on his promise to retire due to ill health, the rigors of the office or to spend more time with his family. Probably reveled in duping the suckers who put up the money and who trusted a politician to keep his promise. He probably planned it all along. Even smart guys get duped now and then, particularly if the stakes were high enough. And being the most powerful man in the world was a real adrenalin high and an aphrodisiac.

"So now, money had a problem. They were not getting what they had paid for and wanted McDonald as president. Oh, they got the tax cuts they wanted, and they got no immigration reform so they could keep getting cheap labor from Mexico so they could try to bust the unions and increase their profits.

"It was the same old story. The German industrialists backed Hitler in the 1930s so he would get rid of the Communists and the unions because they believed erroneously they could control him. Well, they misjudged him, too.

"So what do grumpy children do when they don't get their way, other than throw a tantrum and blame someone else for their problems? In this case, they were blaming McDonald for not controlling the marionette. The marionette had bolted, had the bit in his mouth and was doing what real presidents do, make their own decisions. Not good for McDonald and the investors.

"McDonald saw his dictatorship slipping away. The investors were pressuring him, because he assured them he could control Harrison. He had defrauded energy companies of enormous amounts of money, can't deliver on his promises to give them oil rights and infrastructure support contracts in Iran. The president had threatened to expose him if he didn't resign. Also, he wanted McDonald to return all of the money he had taken and write a letter telling the executives he defrauded them and acted without the knowledge or authority of the president. He refused. But the president may do it anyway and go down with McDonald. You never can tell what a dumb person will do."

Jerry sat and watched Rigor use him as a psychiatrist and priest. His catharsis was evident. But absolution would not be available this night.

Rigor leaned back and rested the back of his head on the top of the sofa and stared at the ceiling again. "I've a quandary. People who are desperate use poor judgment. And I, too, am a member of the club. After the inauguration, McDonald met with the investors. He again assured them that all was well and Harrison would take orders. And all was well until McDonald believes his attorney, Mariah O'Leary, started stirring the pot. Then J.P. Kennington tried to kill and then kidnapped Robert's son, Sean Harrington, to get some documents and other personal belongings back. Then the information came to Robert about McDonald defrauding the energy companies and McDonald not sharing the spoils with him. And that was the moment he stopped taking orders and asked the vice president to resign. The president tried to pressure DCI Cliff to fabricate intel so he could go to war in Iran. McDonald and Goldman had extorted DCI Cliff into agreeing to fabricate intel. Another act of treason."

Rigor told him, "At the investors' meeting with McDonald after the inauguration they wanted insurance, a back-up plan, in case Robert decided not to be a good doggy. If you can believe it, the plan was assassination. If you hear McDonald tell it, he resisted. But then the investors appealed to his greed, told him how many hundreds of millions of dollars he would make, and he succumbed to the temptation and agreed."

"Are you telling me these insane people are actually going to kill the president while he's in office so McDonald can take over? I heard it on the tape, but they're actually going to do it?"

"Yes, but worse. As you heard one of the plans was to send him to Dallas for a parade as a part of his re-election campaign and kill him as he passed the grassy knoll, if you can believe it. They all laughed when one of the wealthiest Texas investors suggested it. Isn't that what sycophants do? Laugh at rich people's jokes.

Instead the richest investor of them all made a decision and decided on using poison, and McDonald appointed me as the assassin. Goldman's going to provide the poison to me, and I'm to put it into Robert's food at a lunch meeting."

"What hold does the vice president have on you, that you would even consider such a thing?"

"When McDonald defrauded the energy companies, he gave some of the money to me and some to Jacob Goldman, his chief of staff. He knew I was in desperate financial straits. I succumbed to the temptation and believed erroneously that he was helping me out of generosity. I thought it would be the end of my financial problems. Little did I realize it was only the beginning of my real problems.

"He forced me to inform him of everything the president did. I had become amoral like him. I was nothing more than a low-life snitch. I was tethered to him like every other dog he has in this administration.

"People ratting out co-workers to receive his blessings and nothing other than that. So you see, there's really nothing you can do for me."

"You disappoint me. You have no faith. This is what I suggest if you're willing." Jerry explained his plan to him.

"Yes, I'll do that and gladly."

"I'll be back tomorrow night about the same time. Is that alright with you?"

"Yes."

Jerry took the recorder with him.

# 61

**Day 29  11:00 A.M.  The Willard Hotel, Washington, D.C.**

Mariah and Jerry met in her suite. He had given Rigor's recorder to her. She listened to it, went to the concierge and put it in her safe deposit box.

"There's a bloodless coup d' état afoot to take some phrasing from my favorite detective, Sherlock Holmes," Jerry said. "It appears the greatest American traitor since Benedict Arnold, one James P. McDonald, has decided if you can believe it, to assassinate the sitting president of the United States and become an unitary president. This with the blessing and cajoling of the corrupters, McDonald's and Kennington's colleagues, whom funded the presidential campaign for Harrison. Richard Rigor cleansed his soul with Clorox in my presence after McDonald had appointed him the modern day John Wilkes Booth. Because of the recording, he'll be a co-conspirator and have no deniability."

"Yes, I know, what do you want to do about it?"

"This is my thought, but like most things in life we're going to need a little help from a friend."

"And who might that be?"

"One Geoffrey MacIntosh. The question is: can he do it from California, or does he believe it will be necessary to be here? Maybe, set him up here at the Willard?"

"What did you have in mind?"

Jerry explained his plan.

"I will call him and let him decide. That's one helluva plan, Mr. Spencer. Audacious does not even describe it."

"Isn't it, though? But fitting, don't you think?"

"Oh, yes it is fitting. But you realize if everything does not go as planned, we could all go to prison? Leavenworth in Kansas comes to mind."

"Yes, but it reminds me of revolutions, and I feel like a revolutionary," Jerry said. "If the revolutionaries win, they're heroes. If they lose, they get executed for treason. But you must admit it's worth the try. Nothing wrong with worldwide humiliation, some much-deserved comeuppance for the man who would be king. And with a little bit of luck, he'll be sent directly to Leavenworth for the rest of his life after his conviction for treason, attempted murder and other crimes and not hanged. Because king he'll be under his plan."

"Too bad we cannot inform the Secret Service. The White House is a sieve, no secrets there. I am sure McDonald has informants in the president's detail. So, we are going to have to do this on our own. Cannot even use the MPD.

"I'm going to meet Rigor tonight around eight at his place. I'll explain it all to him. I'll call Geoffrey, discuss the plan with him, and I'll arrange for everything I need in D.C."

"From what you tell me, is Rigor going to hold up and be able to handle this pressure without giving himself away?"

"Good question, I don't know. It's one of the risks of being a revolutionary hero or being hanged. While he was talking to me, I actually thought he was going to have a nervous breakdown or commit suicide."

# 62

## Day 30   10:00 A.M.

## The Eisenhower Executive Office Building, McDonald's Office

After speaking with Geoffrey MacIntosh yesterday, Jerry went about designing and constructing the inside of a briefcase. He met with Rigor last evening at his apartment. He showed him the contents and how to operate it. Inside was a super-high gain inline microphone attached to a digital camcorder. The briefcase's devices had the ability to record and transmit the audio and video to Jerry's laptop as he sat on a bench in Lafayette Park across from the White House. He waited for Rigor to turn on the audio-video recorder.

Rigor walked into McDonald's office, placed the brief case on a twenty-five inch high side table between two chairs near McDonald's desk and pushed the start button on the handle.

Jerry could see McDonald and Rigor with good quality. He waited for the audio.

Rigor sat in the visitor's chair closest to his brief case in front of McDonald's desk in a position so McDonald would have to look at him to talk to him. "Pardon me, Mr. Vice President, my shoelace is untied. Just a moment." He bent over, removed an audio transmitter pack from inside his suit coat and placed it on the carpet underneath the bottom left-hand drawer in McDonald's desk and activated it.

"Thank you, for seeing me, Mr. Vice President. I haven't slept for five nights since you ordered me to poison the president. I've never killed anyone before. Even though he isn't very smart and just another politician I still like him. You must admit after all he's charming and the president."

Jerry smiled. The audio was excellent and video was high-definition. "Another good day for the good guys."

"I wanted to discuss it with you. You said Jake was going to supply the poison, the maculotoxin and tetrodotoxin, and would have it in a few days. Is it ready yet, and when do you plan on having the lunch so you can have me assassinate him pursuant to your orders? When will I get it?"

"Jake told me it should be here today or tomorrow. When I told my investors about Harrison's misconduct, they became concerned. This made my investors most anxious to get this done so I can be sworn in by the chief justice of the United States as soon as possible. I'll be sworn in right after the doctor pronounces him dead. My investors have already booked hotel reservations for the occasion.

"I'd imagine I can schedule the lunch in two days. Jake'll give you the white powder when we arrive in the Oval Office for lunch.

"When he's dead *my* people will enter, take charge and get the death certificate signed by the doctor. It'll be 'Death by Natural Causes', have him cremated, and it'll all be over. There'll be, of course, the wearing of the obligatory black arm bands. I see you've had a change of heart. You realize my world view is good for me, my investors and good for America."

"Yes."

At this moment, Goldman walked in and said to Rigor, "Why are you perspiring so much? Are you sick?"

"No, I just haven't been sleeping. I told McDonald I'd cooperate."

Goldman stared at him and said, "Stand up." Goldman went to him and frisked him. He opened his shirt, felt around it, around his suit but found nothing.

"What are you doing, Jake?" McDonald asked unpleasantly.

"Checking for a wire."

"Damn embarrassing, he's one of us."

"Maybe yes, maybe no." Jake searched him and said, "Sorry, Richard, I just wanted to be sure. Maybe I'm the one who's a little nervous about the coup."

"I believe an apology is in order, Jake," McDonald ordered.

"Yes, I apologize to you, Richard. I know you're loyal to McDonald. My mistake."

"When will you have Mssrs. Maculotoxin and Tetrodotoxin in white powder form for the president's entree?"

"Today, I think. We'll be using thirty milligrams of Tetrodotoxin and/or Saxitoxin; they're neurotoxins. For his weight, it should be sufficient. It's one thousand times more deadly than cyanide. He'll be dead shortly after enjoying a special lunch ordered by the VP. There's no antidote. It reminds me of the death-row inmate's last food request before execution. He'll be joining the Last Lunch Club." Jake and McDonald laughed, Rigor smiled but was embarrassed.

"Thank you, for the appointment, Mr. Vice President. And to you, Jake, for the massage." They all laughed.

He walked to the side table, picked up his briefcase, left the office and pushed the stop button on the handle. *So, Jerry was right. He foresaw the frisk, and that's why he used the briefcase. Smart man. I made the right choice.*

# 63

Jake stood in front of McDonald's desk. "You know we're going to have to kill him as soon as the president's dead."

"What about at the same time?" They laughed.

Jerry watched his screen and listened through his ear buds as the transmission of the conversation between McDonald and Goldman was recorded on his laptop.

"Let's think about it and come up with a solution," McDonald said. "I've an idea. Let's send someone into his apartment and kill him while he sleeps. Make it look like a burglary gone awry in the crime capital of America, Washington, D.C."

"Good plan, let's do it. I'll call a man who has a man who's just right for the job. I'll take care of it."

# 64

**Day 30  11:14 A.M.  The Willard Hotel, Mariah's Suite**

Mariah sat on the sofa in her suite and Jerry opposite her in an over-stuffed chair with the coffee table between them. Jerry had made a copy on a DVD of the meeting that took place between McDonald, Rigor and Goldman in McDonald's office earlier in the morning. They had two cappuccinos from room service and had watched and listened to the DVD. They listened to the CD of the conversation between McDonald and Goldman as they conspired to murder Rigor after the death of the president and after he had left the vice president's office.

"If I did not know better I would swear we listened to plans to change regimes in a third world country and/or a banana republic. It is obvious McDonald and Goldman are without moral sense and believe they are omnipotent and above the law."

"What do you want to do about it?" Jerry asked.

"Same as you. Save the president and give the two conspirators a one-way ticket to Cocytus with Virgil. When that is in the mill, then remove the president from office by his resignation or impeachment; that is what I want to do about it. What about you?"

"Sounds good to me. Which way do you want to do it? I see some obstacles. Who do you trust in the Secret Service — no one. So it has to be done without their aid. I have this question for you, counselor. Do you believe right now we have enough evidence to present to the U.S. attorney general?"

"Enough, yes. Enough legal evidence to get an indictment for a conspiracy to commit two murders; ah, there is the sticky wicket. We have the recordings and the testimony of Rigor. We cannot count on Goldman testifying against McDonald for immunity. Therefore, it appears to me we must prove McDonald and Goldman guilty beyond any doubt. There is the possibility McDonald has the AG in his pocket. And of course, it could be argued that our recordings are illegal and not admissible.

"I want you to call Geoffrey. Have him go into Goldman's emails, and see if we can find his connection for the neurotoxins. If so, let us brace the supplier, have you interrogate him and have a little corroboration. If not as a backup plan, you will need to have a session with Rigor. Also, see if Geoffrey can determine who McDonald's investors are? We will want to expose them as plotters in the assassination of the president. This is what I have in mind." She explained her thoughts to him and her plan.

"It appears lunch is going to be served tomorrow or the next day. Time is tight, so we need to be prepared. If our plan fails as is, I may have to step in, we will see. Make copies of the DVD and CD, give them to me and then leave the originals with me, too. I'll put the originals in my safe deposit box downstairs. I may need them. Stick with Rigor. Keep him together. Prop him up. Be his best friend. He is essential to Plan A. Good work, Jerry."

# 65

Jerry and Rigor sat in his living room. Rigor on the sofa and Jerry in the same over-stuffed chair.

"How are things going?" Jerry asked.

"Worried, no sleep, no appetite."

"It appears to me you could lose some weight. It'll make you feel better." They laughed.

"You're right about that."

"I came to tell you not to worry. I'll need to know the day, time and place of the luncheon McDonald, Goldman, Harrison and you are going to attend."

"McDonald set the lunch for day after tomorrow. It's to be in the oval office at noon. He has ordered lunch for the four of us. Goldman told me today he has the neurotoxin and will give it to me when he walks into the oval office. I told him, based on your advice, that I was ready. He was pleased, and he said McDonald'll be pleased to hear that I'm on board. Here's a recording of it. I made a copy from my laptop with the program you gave me." He handed the CD to Jerry.

"Good, well done, my friend, well done. Shall we watch some television, talk and I'll tell you how we're going to win this battle against the traitors?"

"I've always loved multiple-choice questions. So, I'm going for 'D': 'All of the above'."

" 'D' it is. Does the president have a plan to get McDonald's signature? Is he going to expose him? Or as they say today, 'out him'? Whatever happened to expose him?"

"He's afraid to do it. If he did, the VP would shower Robert with all of his misdeeds. Not good for getting re-elected. He's afraid he's not going to be re-elected as it is. This is the reason he and J.P. Kennington signed the 'War Plan' document I gave you, and the Prague Accord he signed with the president of Russia. It's easier to lie to the public about going to war against terrorism than it is to tell them the truth. The truth is: we're going to war to enhance the financial portfolios of the president, vice president, their families, friends and investors. And, oh, by the way, we'll kill your son and daughter as I get richer. What's your thought?"

"The only thing a first-term president wants is a second term, no matter how he gets it done."

# 66

**Day 32   11:45 A.M.   The White House, the Oval Office**

Rigor arrived in the oval office with his briefcase that had been prepared by Jerry with the help of Geoffrey MacIntosh. He greeted the president and placed his briefcase on a table and in a position to digitally record and transmit simultaneously activities in the office. He pushed the button on the handle and activated the equipment inside.

Jerry sat across from the White House in Lafayette Park. He looked at the screen on his laptop, and when the audio-visual signal from the Oval Office displayed on his screen, he smiled. His computer started recording the transmission and he listened to it with his ear buds.

Moments later the vice president arrived. Harrison, McDonald, and Rigor sat in front of the fireplace. Harrison sat in the right chair at the end of the coffee table and next to Rigor on the sofa on his right and opposite the fireplace. McDonald sat on the sofa to the left of the president.

"McDonald, are you going to resign effective immediately?"

"No, I've already told you this. And, I'm not returning any money or writing any letters either by the way."

"Then I've no choice. I'm going to end your political career. And the career of anybody else I know who's like you. I'm going to remove the vice president's government and expose you for what you are. This country only needs one government. Not a government within a government, and that's what you've been running. Your unitary president euphemism you keep spouting to anyone who'll listen except to the American people is just another name for a dictatorship. You want to remodel the world and remove democracy in the process. You can return to your investors and your god, Greed."

At this moment, Jacob Goldman entered the Oval Office and interrupted the conversation to the delight of the vice president. "Good day, Mr. President." He walked toward where they were seated. He walked between the coffee table and the sofa where Rigor sat in the middle. He sat on Rigor's left side, looked at the vice president and acknowledged him with a smile, a nod and placed his right hand into the left-suit coat pocket of Rigor and deposited a small glass container with a rubber stopper.

"You're not above the law, McDonald," Harrison said. "I'm going to do everything in my power while I'm still in office to have you impeached and found guilty by the Senate. I'm going to ask the attorney general to start an investigation into your energy task force. Investigate the people who bribed you and send some CEOs and you to prison. I find your brand of corruption appalling.

"Yes, it's true the campaign contributions and off-the-books payments to members of Congress are bribes. They deliver to special interests right after the payments are made by their lobbyist or representative. It's always palms-up and extended outward with them, the corrupticians in Congress.

"But you took bribes, not even disguised as campaign contributions. And worse, bribes to a government official and in my administration. It led your bribers to believe that I've sanctioned this illegal conduct on your part and I haven't. It makes me look as corrupt and dishonest as you. And bribers have no respect for dishonest politicians, but they're pleased to own them."

"You've been talking to O'Leary again," McDonald said.

"Yes, I have, and I'm proud of it. She advised me to scrap our war plan. But I didn't listen, but I wish I had. Let me tell you about her. She's the only person I know who's got a strong moral sense. She's a lady who cares and she helps people. And as far as I'm concerned, this country can use more O'Learys, and no people like you or me. She helps the poor and gives to charities in her neighborhood. Fortunately, she's too smart to run for public office."

The steward brought in the lunch table and set it up. The president asked, "So, what's for lunch today?"

"The vice president ordered a Japanese delicacy. Because, as I understand it, the prime minister is going to be here next week for a state dinner. And he thought it would be a nice talking point to tell him how much you liked Fugu. Lunch is ready, Mr. President."

"Thank you. Shall we?" The president rose from his chair and gestured to his guests to join him at the table. The president sat, then Rigor sat on his left, McDonald on his right and Goldman across from him. Goldman placed his cell phone on the seat between his thighs. The steward served the food.

When all were served, the steward said, "Enjoy your lunches, gentlemen." He left the Oval Office.

Goldman looked into his lap and pushed 666 on his cell, smiled and listened to the president's private line ring.

"Excuse me, I must answer this." The president rose from his chair and walked to the Lincoln.

At this moment, Rigor moved his right fist from his right coat pocket which was closed around a vial of white powder over the president's Fugu and sprinkled a white powder on it. The vial was not seen by the vice president or Jake. He put the vial back into his right pocket and smiled at them and nodded. They acknowledged him. He began to eat his lunch.

Goldman disconnected a second before the president picked up the handset.

The president picked up the handset and said, "Hello," waited, said it again and again. "I guess it was a wrong number or we were disconnected." He returned to the table and started to eat the Fugu and said, "This is delicious. I must thank you, McDonald. It was a good suggestion. I'm going to mention it to the prime minister. Fugu, I need to remember this."

"Please do, Mr. President, I'm sure he'll be impressed."

They talked about the upcoming re-election campaign, world affairs and which member of Congress had been caught lately engaged in another scandal. Twenty minutes later, lunch was over and the vice president and Goldman excused themselves. Rigor sat at the table with the president for about fifteen minutes while the president assigned him tasks for the afternoon.

Jerry watched Rigor move toward his briefcase and then the signal was disconnected. Jerry waited in the park.

Ten minutes later, Rigor arrived in the park and sat next to Jerry and said, "The vial Goldman gave me is in my left coat pocket, and I've not touched it so his fingerprints should still be on it."

Jerry removed the vial with a pair of metal tongs and placed it into an evidence bag and said, "Good work, Richard. I'll take this to the lab now. I'll have the fingerprint expert and the toxicologist examine the vial and the contents and give me a report. I should have the results soon. I'll call you at home and give you the results. You're a good man, Mr. Rigor."

"Thank you, Jerry. I feel redeemed."

"You should. Be careful. Your two best friends Mssrs. McDonald and Goldman are lethal. Killing people creates fear, and fear keeps people in line."

Rigor left. Jerry remained and waited for McDonald and Goldman to return to the vice president's office so he could hear and record their reactions. He did not have to wait long.

# 67

### McDonald's Office in the Eisenhower Executive Office Building.

McDonald and Goldman argued about why the president didn't die. "When is he going to die?" McDonald asked. "I saw Rigor put the poison on Harrison's fish. Are you sure it was a neurotoxin?"

"Yes, I'm sure."

"Did you have it tested before you gave it to Rigor?"

"No. I assumed the delivery was the genuine article, the neurotoxin. It came from an unimpeachable source, Abel Live (pronounced Leave)."

"Live wants him dead more than I do as do his friends in the Petroleum Club of Houston. I think we've been taken advantage of. Are you sure somebody didn't just give you powdered sugar? So you don't know whether we got poison or not."

Jerry sat in Lafayette Park and smiled. He recorded the conversation and downloaded it to a CD for Mariah.

# 68

**Day 32   5:02 P.M.   The White House, the Oval Office**

Mariah met with the president. Harrison watched the DVD from McDonald's office when he met with Rigor and Goldman, discussed his assassination and told Rigor about the delivery of the neurotoxin.

Then they listened to the CD Jerry recorded after Rigor left. It was the conversation between McDonald and Goldman about the murder of Rigor in his apartment.

They watched the DVD of the lunch which showed Rigor sprinkling the white powder on his Fugu. She stopped the DVD and said, "The material he put on your fish was powdered sugar. It looked like the neurotoxin. Goldman and McDonald didn't know the difference. They didn't know or see that the vial in Rigor's hand was not the same vial that Goldman had given him."

They listened to the CD of the conversation in the vice president's office after the lunch.

"I have affidavits from Rigor, Jerry Spencer, the head of my special-ops team, the lab's toxicology report and the fingerprint expert. Goldman's prints were on the vial he gave to Rigor. The content of the vial was a lethal dose of neurotoxin, and it would have killed you if we had not intervened. There is no antidote."

They had a discussion about what he should do. He listened to what she had to say and said, "I'll take your advice."

She gave copies of the DVDs, CDs and affidavits to him. The original DVDs, CDs and affidavits resided in her safe deposit box at the Willard. She was not going to take any chances a politician or anyone else would lie to her. The originals could just disappear. Not unusual when one is involved with the worst scum society has to offer, traitors.

She said to him as she parted, "McDonald's arrogance has led him to believe he is omnipotent. This belief will be his downfall."

# 69

**Day 32   9:00 P.M.   The White House, the Oval Office**

The president had been given free air time on all of the networks, CNN and cable stations in the U.S. His speech would be viewed worldwide.

"Good evening, my fellow Americans. I'm speaking to you from the Oval Office. I've recently discovered some unsettling information which I wish to share with you.

"James P. McDonald, the vice president, has been operating a government separate and apart from my administration to the detriment of you and me but for the benefit of himself, people he calls his investors and his rich colleagues. He asked me if he could produce an energy plan for the U.S. to wean this country from the dependency on oil. I agreed and thought it was then and still do believe it's a good idea to remove our dependency. So, with my permission — not knowing the true nature of the reason — he set up the McDonald Energy Task Force. He held secret meetings with executives of the major oil companies, utilities and other energy companies. He refused to provide any information regarding these meetings to the Congress or other government agencies when requested. His excuse was: he wasn't a member of the executive branch. This preposterous statement was but one example of his arrogant misconduct.

"The people who put up the first fifty million dollars for my campaign for president did so on the condition that I have McDonald on the ticket. These people who McDonald calls his 'investors' have been running his government in my administration without my knowledge or consent. He's the investors' pawn, and he does what they tell him to do.

"Instead of using the task force for the benefit of the United States, that's the American people, he used the energy task force to extort almost two hundred million dollars from the major oil companies, oil service companies, utility companies, natural gas companies and other energy-related companies. These payments to him were bribes.

"He has been begging me to invade Iran. The bribes paid to him were in exchange for the right to bid on Iranian oil production leases, supporting infra-structure and other energy and non-energy contracts after the U.S. defeated Iran. The companies would make billions of dollars and the millions paid in bribes would be one of the expenses of doing business.

"There was no consideration given to the loss of lives to our military person-nel, Iran's military personnel and the lives of noncombatants on both sides of the conflict. The only consideration was greed.

"He advised me I couldn't be re-elected without a war like a previous president did illegally to get re-elected. Pursuant to his plan, he got a major contributor, Jonathan P. Kennington, who's in the oil business and a major U.S. defense con-tractor, to sign a 'War Plan' agreement with me. This called for the murdering of many poor Americans with poison gas, which would be produced by the Kenning-ton Chemical Company. The vice president ordered the Department of Defense to issue a contract to the chemical company to produce the gas and the DoD did. The murders would be labeled a terrorist attack which McDonald would blame on Iran with the help of the CIA. McDonald would then give speeches providing misinformation — lying.

"Then he asked me to ask an honorable man, Roger Cliff, the director of the Central Intelligence Agency, the DCI, to fabricate the necessary intelligence or use forged documents to prove Iran was responsible for the murder of our poor citizens and Iran was planning a nuclear attack on the United States. Mr. Cliff refused my request.

"I told the vice president Cliff had refused. He was furious and wanted him fired immediately. He told me, 'I want a dishonest person appointed in his place immediately who'll take orders.' I refused.

"A previous administration had gone to war illegally based on fabricated and forged intelligence for profit. The administration suffered well-deserved disgrace and infamy. And I refused to allow greed to interfere with my responsibility to Americans.

"I discovered recently McDonald and his investors had a plan to assassinate me at the time I didn't take orders from him. I refused to take these orders when I found out within the last ten days that he had taken bribes from the energy com-panies and other companies. I asked him to resign and he refused. I asked him to return the bribes, he refused. Then I asked him to send a letter to each company's executive who was involved in the conspiracy to bribe a government official, stat-ing he had acted without my permission or authority and had defrauded them. And again he refused. He had committed high crimes, felonies. Each bribe is a felony punishable by a long term in prison. Planning to murder Americans by going to war illegally, civilian or military, is treason and he's a traitor.

"I have a DVD which I'm now going to play for you which will show McDonald, Jacob Goldman, his chief of staff, and Richard Rigor, my political advisor, conspiring to assassinate me by poisoning me with a neurotoxin at lunch with them today. The vice president ordered Rigor to put the neurotoxin on my food, or he'd expose him for having received money from McDonald as a result of the vice president's extortion of the energy companies. Rigor did put a substance on my fish at lunch. It was not a neurotoxin, but it was powdered sugar. He saved the life of the president.

"McDonald ordered Rigor to assassinate me, and he agreed to do it. But, when he left the vice president's office he sought advice and help from my attorney, Ms. Mariah O'Leary of Los Angeles. Ms. O'Leary, Mr. Rigor and her special-operations people produced the evidence I've just told you.

"I'm going to take a short break and show you the DVD of the conspiracy to assassinate me. When the DVD stops, I'll continue my address." The DVD of the meeting in McDonald's office was shown.

At the conclusion of the DVD viewing, the White House Press Corp in the press room was in a state of pandemonium. They were on their cell phones. The president continued.

"When Mr. Rigor went to the meeting you have just seen, you saw him plant an audio transmitter under the vice president's desk. He activated it at that time. I'm now going to play a CD recording for you of the conversation between McDonald and Goldman after Rigor left." The CD started to play. Again, the press corp was agitated. The president continued.

"Not only did your servant, James McDonald, the man whose salary you pay, want to assassinate me, but wanted to minimize the witnesses involved and con-spired with Jake Goldman to kill Richard Rigor and blame it on a burglar.

"Tomorrow morning, I'm going to request the House Judiciary Task Force to investigate James P. McDonald, vice president of the United States, for the purpose of determining if impeachment proceedings in the House are appropriate. And if so, to issue a Bill of Impeachment and send it to the Senate for his trial.

"Further, I'm going to ask the attorney general to investigate Jacob Goldman, Jonathan P. Kennington and any persons who conspired to defraud the American people as a result of the vice president's pseudo government, including energy com-pany executives who paid bribes to the vice president. And, any and all officials of this administration who are or were engaged in corruption.

"Also, the attorney general will investigate McDonald's investors and others who conspired to assassinate the president of the United States.

"I believe James P. McDonald and those people involved in defrauding the American people and who tried to assassinate the president are traitors and should be treated and prosecuted as such.

"As president of the United States, I'm responsible for the misconduct of these people in my administration. I didn't do my job. I didn't serve the American peo-ple correctly. I allowed James P. McDonald, the traitor, and the J.P. Kennington's among us to fail you good people. And therefore, I'm responsible for the illegal conduct of the vice president even though I didn't know what he was doing.

"I had Congress give tax breaks to the rich, the top two percent of income earners so they would be encouraged to give me campaign contributions. I forgot my responsibility to the people who made and make this nation great, our middle class. Tomorrow I'm going to ask Congress to rescind those tax breaks. If anyone deserves tax breaks, it is those people who have spent their lives building this great country. One percent of the richest Americans account for twenty-four percent of the nation's income. I'm going to ask Congress to raise taxes on those folks to help others whom are less fortunate. Why is it that the richest country in the world will not care for our seniors whom are in need? I'm going to try to change this.

"Nothing trickles down from the rich to the middle class and the poor; except, maybe tax-deductible contributions to charities in order to assuage their guilt and their beliefs that they can buy their way into their non-existent afterlives.

"I have defiled my fiduciary responsibility. My shame's so great, I want you the American people to be the first to know. I haven't even told my wife. I've decided not to run for re-election, and I'll not be drafted by my party to run.

"What this country needs is to elect an honest statesman or stateswoman as the next president. I realize this is going to be hard to find, but this is what you Americans need to do. If you can sift through the misleading marketing of candidates on television, maybe in there you'll find the right person. You must stop electing politicians whose souls and votes have been bought by special interests through lobbyists, for they belong to them, and you'll have no chance to get an honest first count. No one gives substantial campaign contributions to politicians for good government. They want quid pro quo, something in return. The politician who has been bought goes into politics as a business and to make money. His interests come first, his corrupters second and the people he represents last. This is a person who has betrayed the American people and is a traitor to his country.

"Thank you, ladies and gentlemen, for allowing me into your homes this evening. God bless you and God bless the United States of America."

# 70

**Day 32   10:00 P.M.   The Willard Hotel, Washington, D.C.**

Jacob Goldman had had a busy evening after the surprise address of the president the night before. When the address concluded, he had made some calls and found Mariah O'Leary was staying at the Willard. He arranged to see her. She called Jerry Spencer and asked him to come to the hotel. The three met in her suite.

Jake asked her to arrange immunity for him if he would provide the information as to the conspirators-investors whom were involved in the plot to assassinate the president.

She agreed that she would represent him and would try. In exchange, she asked him to provide all of the information he had. For four hours, he provided the information to them. They sat at a small table with a digital recording machine between them. He had brought his Blackberry and gave the names, addresses, email addresses and telephone numbers of all of the investors' homes and offices. He told her that Abel Live of Live Industries in Houston, Texas, was the decision-maker of the group, and the one who made the decision as to the time, place and how to assassinate the president. He also provided the neurotoxin.

He told her Live was displeased when J.P. Kennington had told him Harrison refused to go forward with the war plan that he had signed with J.P. Next, the VP had told Live Harrison had asked McDonald for his resignation, had told him to return the money to the energy companies and to write a letter telling them he acted without the authority of the president. Live then had decided this was the moment to assassinate the president, because he was no longer following orders from the VP. McDonald took orders from Live.

She told him to go to the office and get more admissions and information from McDonald, and that one of her sp-ops people would be recording the conversation. She told him not to remove the transmitter from McDonald's office in the EEOB. He agreed not to. If the conversations were not recorded, she would know he had betrayed her. He agreed to the arrangement but was desperate for the immunity. He did not want to lose his license to practice law and go to prison. The rule for getting immunity was a simple one. The co-conspirator's lawyer who got to the prosecutor first got the immunity most of the time, if the co-conspirator could deliver the necessary evidence to convict the decision-maker or makers.

When the session ended, she connected her recorder to her laptop, download-ed the file into a Word document and produced an affidavit. She printed it out. She asked him to read it for accuracy. He did and said it was accurate. She called down to the concierge and asked for a notary to attend the signing of a document. A notary arrived. The notary watched Jacob Goldman sign the document, Mariah O'Leary signed as a witness and Jerry Spencer signed as a witness. The signatures were notarized. The notary had Mariah, Goldman and Jerry sign his notary's book, and he left the suite. He also signed her fee agreement. She received a check for two hundred and fifty-seven thousand as a retainer fee and a week's expenses in advance. He gave her two thousand in cash for the four hours of work.

*If you want loyalty inside the Beltway or in politics, get a pet.*

# 71

**Day 33  9:00 A.M.**

**McDonald's Office in the Eisenhower Executive Office Building**

Jerry sat across from the White House in Lafayette Park awaiting the meeting between Goldman and McDonald. He did not have to wait long.

Goldman arrived at his office and went in to see McDonald. Jerry had loaned him the special briefcase he had designed for Rigor. Jake walked into McDonald's office and set the briefcase on the same table Rigor had used. He pushed the Start button.

He walked to McDonald's desk and sat in the visitor's chair he always used. The vice president asked, "So, what are we going to do now? Punt, pass, kick or run? For the good of the country I think you should accept the responsibility for the plot to assassinate the president and tell the world I knew nothing about it. Then I'll arrange for a pardon, and you won't go to prison or lose your license to practice law."

"Who's going to pay my millions in legal fees?"

"I'll get Abel to do it."

"I'd like to get a cash advance from Abel, say five hundred, right after the attorney of my choice gives me a number. Which president did you have in mind? Harrison or the next one? You've embarrassed yourself. Live gave you the orders to kill the president after you told Abel he refused to take orders. I called Abel at your direction to get the time, place and method of the assassination. It was Live who gave me the neurotoxin and told me to serve the president Japanese Pufferfish, Fugu. I then told you what he said, and you agreed that it was a good idea.

"Then we had the meeting with Rigor and you ordered him to put the neurotoxin on the president's fish at lunch. The only reason Rigor and I got involved was because of the money you gave us after you defrauded the energy execs to keep our mouths shut. We got crumbs. Nobody's going to believe I was anything but your bagman. You dealt with the execs directly and extorted them yourself. I wasn't present, nor did I speak with them or solicit any of the bribes. Then J.P. Kennington took your bribes and ran them through IIBT to launder them for you. I don't see how any prosecutor's going to believe I was the front man and responsible for your crimes."

"Yeah, sure what you say's true. But our investors, Live and all the others, decided after inauguration to kill him if he didn't resign so I could be president. Or if he got out of line, didn't take orders from me and started thinking for himself, to assassinate him then. Those were Abel's orders."

"I received a call from Abel. He believes Rigor switched the neurotoxin for a placebo powder. He has arranged for Richard's termination at his apartment in the early-morning hours two days from now. He agreed with your plan to kill him in his apartment and make it look like a burglary gone awry.

"All is well that ends well. Good, no witnesses."

"Right you are, Mr. Vice President." *Except me, of course.*

Jerry waited in Lafayette Park to see if any additional incriminating information was going to be forthcoming. He waited for two more hours, and he thought nothing would improve. He believed he had an iron-clad case against the two conspirators. He checked the transmission reproduction and was satisfied it was of good quality. He left the park, went to the Willard and met with Mariah. He waited for Goldman to bring back the briefcase.

# 72

## Central Intelligence Headquarters, Langley, Virginia

Roger Cliff, the DCI, called a press conference in the press room. After considering the information provided by Jerry, the options proposed by Mariah, and the accusations of the president against McDonald, he had decided his course of action.

"Good morning, ladies and gentlemen and thank you for coming. Consistent with the address of the president last evening, I've an announcement to make. When I'm finished, there'll be no questions, thank you.

"The vice president, James P. McDonald, and Jacob Goldman, his chief of staff, had made frequent visits to this agency on a weekly basis in the past months. Their goal was to pressure my analysts and me to provide fabricated intelligence or use forged intelligence regarding Iran. Forged intelligence had been provided by Iranian nationals regarding Iran's nuclear weapons program and its weapons of mass destruction. The nationals wanted to be paid substantial sums for these forgeries. But McDonald, Goldman and their cabal had already decided to go to war with Iran. They were looking for a fall guy, me, to take the blame for using the fabricated or forged intelligence.

"As you know from the president's address to the nation, he and J.P. Kennington signed an agreement to go to war against a Middle East country of the vice president's choosing. This country was to be Iran. This would take place after Kennington Chemical developed a poisonous gas and used it on thousands of poor American citizens. These murders would be blamed on Iran. An attack against the United States for which they could retaliate illegally. They wanted to go to war illegally for profit only, and control the oil production of Iran and the distribution of oil from the gulf. Recently, this agency had been forced by the previous administration to used forged intelligence which the agency had known at the time was forged so the president could be re-elected and for profit.

"As a result of what I have said, I've decided to resign from the agency effective immediately so no one could possibly believe I'd conspire to commit treason against my country. I can't say the same for the vice president or his chief of staff or their cabal. For I truly believe these two people have betrayed the trust the American people have put in them, and therefore, they're traitors and should be tried for their high crimes.

"In closing, I'll tell you there's no credible intelligence that leads this agency to believe this nation is in imminent danger of an attack from Iran. These are just dreams of the greedy among us whom want to profit from war.

"Thank you, ladies and gentlemen, for coming. God bless you all, and God bless the United States of America." *Boy, does it feel good to shave, take a shower and wash the corruption of this administration from my hair.*

Cliff walked from the podium, but was pummeled with loud questions from the members of the media. He ignored them and left the press room.

# 73

## Day 34  Time 1:00 P.M.  The Home of Abel Live, Houston, Texas

James P. McDonald had a sporadic night and morning of sleep in his Washington, D.C., residence. He arose in his bedroom, showered and dressed in jeans, dress cowboy boots, Wrangler-blue shirt, dark aviator glasses and ball cap without a logo. He drank a cup of coffee in the kitchen, took his vitamins and heart medication with cranberry juice and went to the garage.

He eluded his Secret Service detail and drove to the Ronald Reagan Washington National Airport and parked near Signature Flight Support, the company that handled General Aviation services. He saw and recognized the Gulfstream G650 which had been adorned at the owner's request with Abel Live Industries, the name of his company. He walked directly to the plane, up the stairs and into the cabin. He was the only passenger. The door closed behind him, and he sat in one of the luxurious leather chairs. An attractive slim-of-hip statuesque blonde approached him and said, "May I get you anything?"

He said yes, and she complied.

The pilot started the engines and moved to the airstrip for takeoff. He would fly at Mach .09 or 956km/h and cruise at 41,000 feet.

McDonald landed at the William P. Hobby Airport about seven miles south of downtown Houston. He deplaned and entered the back seat of a Lincoln Town Car without the aid of the driver who remained seated in the driver's seat and left the airport. The driver did not speak to him. Thirty minutes later, the driver turned right off the highway, stopped at the gate, put in the code and the gate opened and closed behind them. He drove under the wooden arch over the gate which read Abel Live Ranch. It had been burned into it. They drove along the private road for two miles to the main house. The owner did not know for sure how many thousands of acres he owned or how many head of cattle he had.

A man answered the door in Western attire, dark sunglasses and had a companion under his left bicep held in place by a shoulder holster. Never can tell when you might meet a snake while wandering through this barren land and need to defend yourself. Some of the snakes had two legs.

Abel Live, the owner, waited for his guest in the sun room where lunch was in the process of being served. He was seated and already had started to engage in fine dining. He was a healthy-looking sixty plus years of age on what one would call a medium frame. He was tanned and had a full head of attractive salt and pepper hair.

McDonald walked into the sun room and Abel said, "Sit down, McDonald." Abel did not stand, did not offer his right hand for the customary perfunctory handshake nor did he even look at him. He was preoccupied with the more important things in life, self-gratification, food and fine wine.

McDonald sat opposite him at the round table covered with a linen table cloth and a napkin surrounded by an 18-kt gold ring that was three inches wide. Live had branded the ring with his initials like everything else he owned or with his name, another eponymist. The Georgian flatware was sterling.

McDonald sat and watched Live eat his entrée, drink his wine and eat his dessert for twenty minutes. Live had not spoken a word or given a glance to him. The servant took away Abel's dessert plate, but left the wine glass and the bottle with the remainder of the 2000 Chateau Lafite Rothschild Pauillac (750ml) at around twelve thousand dollars a bottle. He pushed his chair away from the table just far enough so he stayed within reach of his crystal wine glass which held part of his twelve thousand dollars.

"Are you hungry after your flight?" He asked with a Texas drawl.

"Yes, I didn't have time to keep the schedule you set up, have breakfast and still make the flight."

Abel signaled his servant. A few moments, later the man brought a salad of sliced tomatoes with a three peppers and pepper-corn seasoning on top and a New York steak medium-rare.

The servant asked, "What would you like to drink?"

"I'll have whatever Mr. Live is having."

The servant looked at Live. Abel gave him the no sign, so McDonald could not see it. The servant left the room. Shortly a glass of wine appeared and was put in front of his luncheon plate. Then a bottle with a label that read 2000 Chateau Lafite Rothschild Pauillac (750ml) was placed next to his wine glass. The servant had taken an empty bottle of 2000 Chateau Lafite Rothschild Pauillac (750ml) which Live had consumed the night before and filled it with VEO Cabarnet Sauvignon from Chile at nine dollars a bottle on the high side. Deep discounts were available if bought by the case. Live kept VEO on hand to serve to members of the lower classes, particularly to politicians.

McDonald ate his meal. He did not savor his food.

"J.P. called me right after Harrison told him he wasn't going to go forward with the "War Plan" document they signed. At that point, I knew I had a problem.

That's when I decided to get rid of him. The information you provided me afterward only confirmed a decision I'd already made.

"So, what have you and the other fuck-up, Goldman, decided to do with the rest of your lives? May I assume you didn't tell anyone you were coming as I instructed?"

"Yes."

"Look at me when you speak. Say it again."

"I didn't tell anyone I was coming to see you, not even my wife."

"Speaking of your wife, how is the most unpleasant person I've ever met?"

"She's fine."

"How unfortunate for us all. You must be some masochist to put up with her. I hired a posse to see if I could find anyone inside the Beltway that liked her, but John Wayne came back empty." He laughed out loud and asked, "How's your heart?"

"I'm going to need some additional heart surgery."

"That's good," he said with a smirk. "Maybe you'll die on the table during the operation. But I don't want you to disappoint me again, so I'm not going to rely on the malpractice of your surgeon. So, I'm going to perform some public service. So, what's the answer to my question?"

"Jake and I discussed it the following morning after the president's address. I was going to hire a lawyer. But all of my bank accounts have been impounded by the secretary of the treasury. This includes the accounts that IIBT handled for me. I had almost two hundred million in there. Now it's frozen. My portfolio of stocks and investments are also frozen. I thought the reason for this visit was you were going to offer me assistance if I needed any help from you, and I do. I need the best lawyers possible to defend me.

"I called two or three oil men and others in the energy business I know, but no one is accepting my calls. It appears I've a highly contagious political disease, scandal. And my wife's not talking to me, either."

"Better not get rid of her. Good wives like that are hard to find." He laughed out loud at him again.

"Well, Dumb Fuck, as a result of your stupidity I've already received a call to my office from an assistant U.S. attorney in D.C. wanting to talk to me about our plan to assassinate the president. I called my attorney, and he said he's handling it, whatever that means. I'm speaking on behalf of all of your investors. When we got involved with you, I advised my colleagues not to. But they went ahead anyway and dragged me along. Do you know how the U.S. attorney got my name so fast?"

"I guess when Harrison received the first fifty million from your group, his campaign listed the contributors."

"We told the two of you not to do that. When you get involved with dumb people, you never know what they're going to do. John Wayne told me once, 'Life's tough. It's even tougher if you're stupid'. You'll see how true this is shortly.

"So what are you and Goldman going to do now that you and Goldman revealed that we wanted to get rid of Harrison and make you president for our all of our financial benefits? How are you and the Jew you decided to hire, against my orders, going to clean up this shit storm you two big-mouths have created? Speaking of dumb fucks.

"Then your greed got you involved defrauding the energy companies, according to the media accounts. You were dumb enough to believe you were above-the-law. Only I and my friends are above the law. We pull the strings on you, Marionette.

"To say we're all displeased with you two doesn't even begin to describe it. Are the two of you going to stand up, take the blame or roll over on your investors and give us up so you can receive immunity, maybe? Are you going to become dirty rat finks, the scum of the earth?"

"No, of course not," he said. He did not look at Abel.

"Look at me when you speak, Dumb Fuck."

McDonald looked at him and said, "No, absolutely not. Jake and I'll not provide any information to law enforcement that you personally made the decision, with the backing of your group, to assassinate the president. I'm trying to get Jake to take the fall, so I can still be president and do what you ask."

"I don't believe you. You had put forth the persona of the arrogant asshole who's tough, but I believe you're a wimp. Because you lack intellect, you make up for it by bullying people. You're just a bald, bespectacled, obese bully. I see your weakness in your eyes. You lied to me like every other politician I've had the misfortune of getting involved with. You corrupt assholes remind me of women. Can't live with 'em and can't live without 'em."

McDonald looked away and did not respond. He perspired and waited for the next assault. "I feel tingling in my lips and mouth, and I'm starting to get dizzy."

"I do hope so. I was starting to wonder if my neurotoxin was ineffective. The media said you ordered the president Fugu, Japanese Pufferfish, for lunch. In Japan you need a qualified chef who's licensed in order to prepare it. So, your sidekick got the Fugu neurotoxin I had delivered. You thought Rigor put it on the president's food, and the president didn't die. You three dumb assholes can't even conclude a simple plan. I believe Rigor took the toxin from Jake and then used a white powder placebo.

"To add comfort to your departure, you'll be pleased to know an attorney friend of mine called Goldman, offered his services and my financial aid during these trying times, and they agreed to meet at one of my homes in Georgetown." Abel looked at his watch. "About this time, the attorney and Goldman are having a breakfast meeting. The same material I had put into your entrée today will be placed into Goldman's breakfast this morning by my chef, after the meeting and just before he leaves my house, unbeknownst to the attorney. Fitting, don't you think, that you should both die the same way and about the same time? Good enough for a president, good enough for two incompetents.

"After Goldman leaves, he'll die someplace else. Maybe he'll get dizzy, be involved in a traffic accident, die, and they'll never do a toxicology report. He should be feeling the tingling in his lips and mouth about this time, too. The difference is: he'll be driving.

"Tomorrow morning around two or three Eastern Time, Mr. Rigor will be receiving a visitor. When the visitor leaves, he'll be dead. The detectives are going to call it a burglary gone awry. You may thank Jake for calling me, so I could make these arrangements before he went to breakfast. The three of you'll not be spending any time with one another in the nonexistent hereafter, be it heaven or hell, depending on your delusional religious beliefs.

"The two gentlemen standing behind you will escort you to your guest quarters. There's no antidote for the neurotoxin. But there's a treatment which could save your life. It consists of taking you to the very good hospital nearby, telling them you believe you have eaten Japanese Pufferfish that was not properly cooked. If they know what to do, they can support your circulatory and respiratory systems for twenty-four hours until the poison dissipates. And I'm willing to do this to save your life, but alas, I have no car or driver to take you. Besides, you should be dead within the hour anyway."

"But if I'm president, I'll do what you say, I'll be loyal."

"You may count on one sure thing in this life which is this: I don't give a rat's ass who's president. He'll do as I ask, loyal or not. Only nations and religions generate loyalty. Everyone else is a mercenary.

"What I should do to you is take you to my thoroughbred horse pavilion, bend you over a barrel, secure you to it and have one of my stallions with the biggest dick fuck you in the ass until you die of heart failure. Then you'd know how it felt when you fucked all those people in your political life, me included. You fucked me with your big mouth by mentioning your investors and contributors. But I'm not going to do it because my stallion wouldn't like me when he found out what a bad fuck you were. You lied to me when you said you could handle the alcoholic-brainless twit Harrison. I'll tell you this: I'm the last person you're going to fuck. How I ever allowed myself to get involved with a piece of two-legged garbage like you, I'll never understand. I must be dumber than you.

"Back to my two gentlemen and your guest quarters. Today is garbage collection day. Gentlemen, you may collect it."

The two-waste disposal cowboys wore shoulder holsters filled with .45 calibers Colts. They approached the obese McDonald from the rear and assisted him out of his chair. They walked him to the front door, through it and into the Lincoln.

"Where are you taking me? What's going on? I'm the vice president of the United States. You can't do this to me."

There was no response from either one; both were heeled. They rode for about thirty minutes to a funeral home and parked behind the facility. McDonald was assisted from the car, supported under his arms and dragged through the back door.

McDonald's protestations were not heeded when he said again, "I don't think you realize that I'm the vice president of the United States. You can't do this to me." The mortician did not blink or care what the soon to be forgotten said. He waited until the two cowboys got him into the cremation container. McDonald was still alive.

The two cowboys put the coffin on the rollers in front of the furnace and pushed it in. The furnace door closed. The furnace was activated and burned between sixteen hundred and eighteen hundred degrees Fahrenheit. The body would be cremated in about two to two and one-half hours. Considering the weight of the obese vice president, probably two and a half hours.

When all was done, the mortician removed the residue, the cremated remains of the bone fragments. Then he used a magnet to remove any metals from the remains. Then they were processed into fine particles and placed into an urn. The mortician handed the urn to one of the cowboys three hours after they had arrived, and they left.

The cowboys drove back to Live's ranch and handed him the urn and left the house. Abel went into his bathroom and flushed the ashes down the toilet and threw the urn into the trash.

*So much for the power of being the vice president. I'm always amazed how these asshole politicians can continuously believe they're in charge. Each one of them is owned by someone. Not even the president is out of reach. The only decision to be made is: is it worth it? Using money is so much easier than disposing of a marionette.*

# 74

**Day 35  8:00 P.M.  Rigor's Residence, Georgetown, Washington, D.C.**

Richard arrived at his residence around eight in the evening, his usual time. He parked his car in the garage. He walked from the garage to the rear exit of his apartment building and then walked to the street behind the building. Two of Jerry's operatives waited in a car for him. They drove him to the Willard, went into the adjoining rooms arranged by Mariah, and they prepared to spend the evening.

When they left, Jerry entered through the back entrance to the building and let himself into Rigor's apartment with the spare key Rigor had given him. He turned on the lights so the watchers would believe Rigor was home. He sat in the same overstuffed chair he had used on previous occasions.

He opened his Thermos, drank some coffee and watched television. His partner and another operative sat in Jerry's car and listened. Around eleven thirty, Jerry turned out all the lights and sat in the dark.

He had prepared the bed with pillows to make it appear Rigor was in bed and sleeping. The only feasible way for entry was through the front door. The bedroom and living room had sliding doors that opened to the same balcony. Jerry placed metal rods into the tracks so the doors could not be opened from the outside. Rigor had placed a round table with an umbrella through the hole in the middle of it and four director's chairs around the table on the balcony. A good setting for enjoying the outdoors.

He sat in the dark, waited for the uninvited and said, "Are you receiving?"

His partner answered, "Yes."

Jerry's .45-caliber Glock 21 with a nose job, was on top of the right arm rest. It was the weapon of last resort. He wanted to enjoy the company of the uninvited so they would have a nice chat about the intruder's employer. Whether it was to be pleasant or unpleasant for his guest would be the decision made by the guest.

Rigor's apartment was the only one on this floor. When the elevator stopped on Rigor's floor, the intruder would be in the elevator foyer with only one door available for entry into the apartment. There was a stairwell that was available for emergencies to the right of the elevator as one exited. Jerry did not envision a mountain climber or a former special-ops trained visitor repelling from the roof to the balcony. But he closed the curtains in the bedroom and the living room in case he was mistaken.

The coffee's acidity finely got to him. The heartburn forced him to take one of those patent medicines the snake oil salesman used to sell out of a covered wagon drawn by a horse during the nineteenth century, West of the Mississippi. Now the generations to follow were in the pharmaceutical business. They were still peddling products that were not good for your stomach, sometimes called antacids, basic salt with flavor. The user did not know you could get the same relief from your salt shaker in the kitchen. It was a matter of Ph.

Around three thirty, his two operatives in the car on the street with a view of the building said, "I believe you're about to have a visitor. He appears to be alone."

A few moments passed, and Jerry heard movement outside the front door. He rose from his chair and moved into the bedroom and behind the door. Someone was having trouble picking the lock. Jerry thought maybe he should have left it unlocked, but that may have aroused suspicion. *I hope this guy's better at killing people than he is at picking locks. I wonder if I should open the door and help him? Seems overpaid already.*

When the door opened, there was no light coming from the elevator foyer. The intruder had spent some time taping it with duct tape. The visitor walked in and closed the door without a sound. Jerry put in his ear plugs and waited. The intruder walked into the bedroom and fired five rounds of 9mm ammunitions into the head area and the torso of Jerry's sculpture. It was now ready for display with the other modern art at the Hirshhorn Museum and Sculpture on Independence Avenue SW in D.C. The question to be determined was the attribution. Jerry was a man with moral sense and would not plagiarize. So he considered two artists should be credited. The work was titled "Death by Holes Disease" by Jerry Spencer and Anonymous.

When he finished firing, Jerry stepped from behind the bedroom door. Jerry struck him with the sharp edge of his right hand, a karate chop, to the base of his skull. The intruder dropped the gun and fell to the floor. Jerry turned on the lights, removed his ear plugs and put them into his right-jacket pocket. He put a pen into the barrel of the 9mm SIG Sauer P226 and placed it into a plastic bag and marked it. He took plastic zip ties from his pocket. He bound the wrists of the sculptor behind his back. He bound his ankles with another tie. He dragged the man to a metal chair he had set up in the middle of the living room and sat him in it. He placed his arms and wrists behind the back of the chair. He ran a web belt from his ankles, under the chair to his wrists and pulled the belt until it was taut. Then he took another web belt, ran it around his hips to the back of the chair and pulled it until it was taut. He placed gauze over each eye and wrapped duct tape around his head and over the gauze. He then placed a black bag over his head and pulled the drawstring so it was taut.

Jerry spoke and the transmitter receiver in his ear broadcast to his two operatives on the street, "Alright, you can come in now. Bring the equipment. The door's open." He walked to the front door and opened it. Two minutes later, two operatives arrived.

The two operatives set up the camcorder so it would record just a head shot. When the sculptor awoke, they would turn on the two lights and shine them directly into his face at an angle that gave the camera an unobstructed frontal view that would not record the lights. Then they would take off the hood, duct tape and gauze and Jerry would go to work.

Jerry moved a small rectangular table to within four feet of the man. He placed the microphone, a speaker and his laptop with the voice-morphing software loaded onto the table. He activated his stress analysis software so he could determine the truth or falsity, with some degree of accuracy, along with his evaluation of the statements made by the intruder by watching his eyes, throat and body language. He attached a microphone on the front of the guest's shirt and plugged the microphone cable into his laptop and waited for the awakening. He pulled up a chair and placed it in front of the table.

One of the operatives set up Rigor's printer and connected it to Jerry's laptop. All was ready.

One of the operatives noticed some movement and turned on the light. He removed the hood, gave the man a facial massage with the back of his right hand, and the man became aware. The operative removed the duct tape and gauze while the man complained.

"What's your name?" Jerry asked, with his voice morphed by the software.

The man was dressed in jeans, a Wrangler blue shirt, a Levi jacket and cowboy work boots. The man did not answer.

"Your ID says you're from Houston, Texas. Driver's license says you're Raymond Weatherman. Is that right?"

"Yeah," he said with a heavy drawl.

"You've got a business card in your wallet from a long-time friend of mine, Abel Live. I haven't seen him for a while, how is he? Still has the Gulf G650? Did he let you come in on it, or did the cheap bastard make you go coach to Ronald Reagan?"

"Coach, the cheap bastard. Never let me ride the Gulf," he said. "He's okay." He spoke the dialect of the class of people in Texas with a limited education or none at all.

"I didn't realize Abel was using cowboys to do his dirty work, his wet work. He must think you're worthless and doesn't give a shit about you. Have you ever done this before for him?"

"Naw, I ain't never been trained for no killin'. I've done other jobs for 'im. On the job trainin' ya know."

"I see. How did you get the SIG onto the plane?"

"I didn't. One of Mr. Live's men met me at the airport and gave it ta me. I took a cab."

"Well what did Abel tell you to do? Oh, by the way, when you get back home tell him hello for me, will you?"

"Shor will. Yur a real gentleman, I can tell. He tol' me ta come ta the address and kill the sleeper. He said his name was Richard Rigor and then come home."

"Did Abel personally order you to do this?"

"Shor, he always do."

"Anyone else present when he gave you the orders?"

"Naw."

"Good, so this is what you're going to do for me and especially for you. I want you to call him at home and tell him you did what he ordered you to do and Rigor's dead. Will you do this for you and me? Were you supposed to call him when the job was done."

"Shor."

"I'm going to give you your cell phone. I'm going to attach a device to it so I can record the conversation, and then I want you to call him. Is this okay with you?"

"Shor."

One of the operatives cut the tie on his wrists and the web belt fell to the floor. The operative handed him his cell phone with a latex-covered hand. Jerry connected his recording device to the cell and plugged the listening device into his ear.

Raymond selected Abel's number and pushed Send. The phone rang about seven times. Abel answered and said, "Yeah."

"Mr. Live, it's Raymond. I did whut ya asked. Rigor's dead."

"How many times did you shoot the scoundrel?"

"He was sleepin' just like you said, and I hit 'im five times with my Sig from close range just like ya tol' me ta do. One in the head and four in the body."

"You're a good boy, Raymond, come on home, and I'll give you a bonus for a job well done."

"Thank ya, Mr. Live." He disconnected and the operative took the cell and placed it an evidence bag and marked it with name of the caller, time and place of the call.

"How many people have you killed for Abel, Raymond," Jerry asked.

"'bout eight or nine, I guess."

"Do you work on the ranch?"

"Shor do. Ten years now."

"In the last few days did you happened to see an obese guy, about sixty, bald, wearing eyeglasses, jeans, blue Wrangler shirt and cowboy boots? Do you know what the vice president, James McDonald, looks like?"

"Yeah, shor. He comes ta the ranch frequently. He hunts there. He's dangerous. He's shot a fellow hunter. No body'd hunt with 'im if he weren't the vice president."

"Did you see him lately?"

"Did I see 'im? Another hand and I picked 'im up at Hobby when he flew in on Mr. Live's jet the other day. He had lunch with Mr. Live two days ago."

"Where did McDonald go after lunch?"

"Well, Mister, McDonald got sick. I'ma thinkin' Mr. Live put somethin' in 'is food. I don't know what it was, but he called it a neuro somethin'. He tol' the vice president that another guy by the name of Goldman was gonna die the same way and at the same time at one of 'is homes in Georgetown. Mr. Live said his chef was gonna put the neuro somethin' inta his breakfast. Then my friend Roy Keyes, another hand at the ranch, and I were ordered ta take 'im ta 'is guest quarters. Roy and I laughed to ourselves, winked at one another and escorted 'im ta the car. We drove 'im ta 'is guest quarters, a funeral home. He was still livin' but ailin', and we put 'im in a cremation container and cremated him. The mortician give me 'is ashes in an urn. Roy and I drove back ta the ranch and gave the urn ta Mr. Live. He thanked us and gave us five hundred each for the job."

"Would you like to tell me about all the murders you did for Abele Live? I'm fascinated."

"Shor." For two hours, Raymond related the details of the killings, and the digital camcorder recorded the information.

"Thank you, Raymond. That'll be all."

"Cuz I've been a good guy and tol' ya all this, Mister, am I gonna get immunity?"

"That'll be up to the prosecutor. But if you cooperate and testify against Live, there's a good chance you'll do short time if they don't prosecute you for all the murders you've committed. Are you going to testify against Live?"

"Ya can bet yur bottom dollar and yur sweet ass I'ma gonna. Thank ya, Mister, yur a real gentleman."

Jerry went into the kitchen and called Mariah at the Willard. They had a discussion for a moment and she said, "I have it arranged. I'll call Lt. Whitmore at MPD Homicide and have him and his team arrive and take over now."

Jerry and his operatives removed all of the audio-video surveillance and recording devices from the apartment which had been installed when Jerry was first assigned by Mariah to watch Rigor. Then one of the operatives removed all of the surveillance equipment from Rigor's car.

Twenty minutes passed, Lt Whitmore arrived with his forensics team. Jerry turned over Raymond, the Sig in a plastic bag, the camcorder and Raymond's cell phone. He gave him the digital recorder that had recorded the conversation between Abel and Raymond.

"You're as good as Ms. O'Leary said you were. After all, if the chief of staff for the president of the United States calls you on the telephone and asks you politely to cooperate with a lady, what choice does a gentleman have?"

"None, in my experience, Lieutenant."

"May I assume Mr. Rigor is well?"

"He is, in fact. He's presently enjoying the company of two armed companions of mine whom are critiquing his sleeping habits." They smiled. "Say hello to Mr. Live for me when you arrest him for the murder of James P. McDonald, Jacob Goldman and conspiring to commit the murder of Mr. Rigor and the president of the United States."

The operatives packed up the lights, Jerry's laptop and left Rigor's apartment to the professionals. The serious question which confronted Richard Rigor was: where was he going to buy new linen, a pillow and a mattress?

# 75

**Day 36   10:06 A.M.   The White House, the Oval Office**

The president sat in the right chair at the end of the coffee table opposite the fireplace. Mariah sat on the sofa to his right.

"I see the overnight polls after you addressed the nation were favorable. A little humility admitting poor judge of character and blaming others for your incompetence is always a good idea as long as the voters do not realize what you have just done to them."

"Not very kind, Mariah."

"May I be assured by you that you will not run for re-election under any circumstances? I know you will appoint a new vice president now that McDonald is dead. Better this way. Avoids the impeachment and being found guilty in the Senate, prosecuted by the attorney general and going to prison for the rest of his life."

"Yes, I'll be out of here when the new president's sworn in next year in January."

"I hope so. Because if you do not, I am going to give you up and reveal all your illegal activities from head to toe. Well, you did admit you were part of the cabal.

"Thank you, for the help with Lt. Whitmore. It would appear Abel Live is in serious trouble. A little bit of conspiracy to commit murder of Richard Rigor and the murder of McDonald and Goldman and conspiring to assassinate you. If the U.S. attorney general needs any help from me or my operatives, let me know, and we will help all we can.

"The question I have for you, Robert is: what am I going to do about you and your wayward ways? Jones gave you up. I recorded it. He signed an affidavit telling all. You ordered him to retrieve documents from your son, or Lillian McGraw and/ or me. And it was alright to kill us in the process.

"Jones came to my office with two tree trunks. He threatened me and was going to engage in violence. My bartender and I had to disarm him and his goons. We captured them. They have been the guests of a friend of mine awaiting the outcome of the deadly coup attempt by McDonald, Live and his group. I am turning them over to the police for prosecution. I am sure you will be receiving an invitation, sometimes called a subpoena, to join the fray. And knowing Jones for what he is, he will rat you out. This is another problem for you to consider."

"I did not tell him to kill anyone. I just wanted the documents and my DVD with Lillian back and any other incriminating information." He did not look at her during his denial.

"Robert, you have not changed. You have been caught lying so many times, I cannot count them and neither can the media. Jones recorded the conversation he had with you in this Oval Office. I have the recorder, Jones and his two goons. What am I to do about this? You have committed felonies sometimes called high crimes. If I do not report them, I will be guilty of compounding a felony and lose my license to practice law. If I lose my license, I will not be able to help all those poor people in my neighborhood who are far more deserving and important than a dishonest president like you."

"What do you want me to do?"

"I also have the original of the Prague Accord, the 'War Plan' document and J.P. Kennington's diary. It's prison time and throw away the key. You will die there."

"Why should I resign? Bill Clinton didn't when he got caught in a sex scandal and committed perjury."

"The difference here, Robert, is: This is not a sex scandal. This is a conspiracy to commit murders of three people and you are a conspirator. Not only a conspirator but the originator and the one who gave the order to murder three people. Also, you conspired with J.P. to murder thousands of Americans just for greed. To quote Teddy Roosevelt, another Republican, 'No man is above or below the law'. And, that includes you and the other criminal, Richard Nixon. Do not start acting like Richard Nixon, who believed erroneously he was above-the-law when he said, 'When the president does it, that means that it's not illegal.'

"You two remind me a lot of one another. Nixon's political life started with dishonesty and continued throughout his career in politics until he was forced to resign. Unfortunately, for the American public, it is not often you criminals get caught red-handed, speaking of Richard M. Nixon, William Jefferson Clinton and Robert B. Harrison."

Mariah asked the president to have Rigor come in. He came in and Mariah said, "Good day to you, Mr. Rigor, have a seat." She indicated the sofa opposite her and to the left of the president.

Marian explained to Harrison in detail how Rigor had saved his life. Then she said, "I want you to give him the Presidential Medal of Freedom at a photo-op session covered live by the media. Is this satisfactory, Mr. Rigor?"

"Yes, thank you."

"I'll take care of it, Mariah."

"Thank you, Mr. President, I will be leaving. They shook hands and she said, "Mr. Rigor, will you walk me out please?"

Mariah spoke with Rigor privately while they walked. "Stay away from little boys or. . . . Do you understand me?"

"Yes."

"You do have some moral sense. You saved the life of the president of the United States, not the corrupt life of Robert B. Harrison. There is a difference. Do you understand the difference? Good choice."

"Yes, I do," he said.

Mariah reached into her bag and turned off the recorder. Then she smiled. *Now that I have it, what am I going to do with it? I do believe I have a thought.*

# 76

**Day 38  12:00 P.M.  The Willard Hotel, Mariah O'Leary's Suite**

Mariah had called Foster Thompson at his ranch and had him turn over Jones and his two goons to Christopher James. Then she called a number in New York and made an appointment for a visitor to be here at two this afternoon.

Sean and Lillian McGraw arrived and sat in the living room. "What have you two good people decided to do with the rest of your lives?"

"Sean has decided to move to Los Angeles, move in with me at the house in Bel Air and learn about the Kennington businesses. It was my suggestion and at my urging. He has a degree in business administration and can do graduate work for his MBA at USC or UCLA."

"Good news, today. Getting away from Washington, Sean, will be good for you. Your father, and as a result, your mother have rough times coming. When are you two leaving?"

"We are flying out when we leave you."

"Sean, have you seen your mother and father since you have been here?"

"Yes, Lillian and I went to the White House. I introduced her to her grandmother, Lillian McGraw Harrison, my mother, and father. It was wonderful. We had dinner with them."

"That's wonderful." *So it appears Sean still does not know Lillian knew the president and was pregnant by him. No reason to tell him. And of course, Harrison is not going to say, "I believe we've met. But, I didn't recognize you at first with your clothes on." If Sean finds out, it would always be a phantom that never went away. It is like a floater in your eye, you always see it. It could never be erased from his memory.* Mariah hugged them both and they left.

Jerry walked in and sat down in a chair opposite Mariah who sat on the sofa. "I wanted to thank you and your operatives for a job well done. Have they all been paid?"

"Yes."

"I want you to think about bonuses for them, Greg and you. Please, decide what would be appropriate and acceptable to all concerned, you all surely deserve them. I will provide the cash when I get home and you will be the paymaster. When are you leaving?"

"This afternoon."

She rose from the sofa, gave him a kiss on the cheek and a hug. She looked into his eyes and said, "I could not have done this without you and your friends."

"Thank you. It was our pleasures." He left.

Frank Merriam arrived on time for his two o'clock appointment. He walked in and sat in a chair near her. She sat on the sofa.

"Mariah, you're as beautiful as ever," he said with a Boston accent.

"I am doing the best I can for a lady my age."

"When I saw you last year, you looked dynamite to me."

"Have you had lunch?"

"Yes, before I went to the airport in New York. Thank you. Just a glass of water, thank you."

She brought him a bottle of water and a glass.

"Are you still enjoying being the best investigative reporter for the New York Times? I read about you all the time."

"Yes, I find it challenging. There's so much corruption to uncover in the present administration, it's a full-time job."

"Did you watch or read the president's address to the nation?"

"Yes. I was in the press room. My cellular Bluetooth device was growing out of my right ear."

"What was your thought?"

"The assassination attempt was a surprise, but the bribes to McDonald were old news in informed circles. I've been writing about the bribes and corruption of the administration on a daily basis for a book, but not published yet. There was never anything but rumors and the media with few exceptions, no modesty intended, had rolled over, didn't report the misconduct out of fear. The fourth estate abandoned their responsibilities. The administration was governing by fear. Evidently the president must have had some documentation, or he wouldn't have said it.

"So, when you called I heard the word Pulitzer. I would've come to see you without the word. So why don't you tell me what you want to tell me, and then if you're not busy, dinner."

"I'm not busy. Start here." She handed him the documentation on the bribes McDonald took from the energy companies. She played for him all of the DVDs and let him listen to all of the CDs that Jerry Spencer and the operatives had produced regarding the attempted assassination. Then she played for him a copy of the DVD that showed Raymond Weatherman's confession and his implicating Abel Live in the assassination attempt of the president and the assassination of

McDonald and Goldman. She gave him the name of Lt. Whitmore of MPD in Washington, D.C.

Then she provided him with a CD of the president and Jones talking in the oval office and the president's order to kill Sean, Lillian McGraw and her if necessary to get the documents and a DVD back, which was incriminating to the president and J.P. Kennington. She gave him copies of the "War Plan" document and the Prague Accord.

After he had seen and heard it all, she told him about J.P. Kennington and gave him copies of those recordings she had made.

When he had finished with all of the materials, he sat and was exhausted.

"I want to tell you why I am doing this," she said. "Someone must take a stand. I cannot stand by and wait for someone else to do something about the corruption of the United States Congress and the present administration. The culture inside the beltway is corrupt. So how does a freshman congressman or senator save his moral sense from this culture? If we make an example of those whom are corrupt, maybe, just maybe things will change. I am not a dreamer, but I am a hoper. When Abel Live, his cronies in the Petroleum Club in Houston, the CEOs of the energy companies who bribed McDonald, J.P. Kennington and the president are sent to prison, maybe executed, for their illegal activities regarding this administration, it will put members of Congress, the lobbyists and other corrupticians on notice that they could be next.

"Will human nature change? No of course not. Will this stop the bribery? No, of course not. But maybe, just maybe, the Congress might change the rules regarding the taking of bribes by their members and start working for their employers for a change, the American people, instead of themselves and the people who bribe them.

"Here's the focus of the story. Abel Live and his rich friends ran the United States government for their own personal financial gain. How far back I do not know for sure, but they did run this present administration. Abel Live and his group must be exposed. Those good ol' boys are really going to be grumpy when you expose them for what they are, traitors.

"And we might as well start at the top with the downfall of Abel Live. Now here is the topper. No one has seen or heard from McDonald or Goldman for four days. Why? You saw the Weatherman interrogation. So it is fair to believe that they are dead. Let me tell you what I think? Abel sent Weatherman to kill Rigor, who was going to be a witness against him. Weatherman is going to be a part of the downfall of Live.

"When this all started as a result of our surveillance of Rigor, we then started watching and listening to McDonald and Goldman. We had operatives working around the clock monitoring their conversations and activities.

"My operatives had Rigor under surveillance since I arrived here in Washington, D.C. Then an incident took place which is of no moment, and Rigor started to provide information.

"At my direction Jerry Spencer, a former field officer for the CIA, has been running the operations. As a result of that information, he and his operatives retrieved audio and video surveillance of McDonald and Goldman plotting to assassinate the president.

"The operatives tailed McDonald to Reagan airport and to General Aviation. He got on a Gulf G650 wearing his cowboy outfit. The jet belonged to Abel Live. Jerry checked the flight plan. It went to Hobby Airport in Houston. No one has seen the vice president since. Abel lives in Houston.

"Next, about the same time McDonald would have arrived at the Abel Ranch, Goldman was having a meeting in Georgetown with an attorney who works for Live. Jake went into the house, but he never came out. The attorney did, but Goldman did not. I am sure at some point unbeknownst to my operatives, Abel's cleaners came to the house, extracted him and sent him on his way to wherever traitors go when they die. Guess what? The house is owned by Abel Live. No one has seen or talked to him since. This information corroborates the information received by Jerry Spencer from Raymond Weatherman, the killer who worked for Live.

"And, as I have said and you knew, Live and his group were the people who put up the first fifty million for the Harrison campaign on the condition he accept McDonald as the vice presidential candidate. So, what do you think, Frank?"

"I think what you already know. Abel Live, not a nice human being ever, has been eliminating witnesses to try and prevent his group of traitors from being indicted and prosecuted for conspiring to assassinate the president of the United States, conspiring to go to war illegally in Iran, attempted murder of Rigor, the murder of McDonald and Goldman and other crimes. That's what I think. What do you think?" He laughed.

"I think . . ." She stopped, and they both started laughing.

She gave him J.P.'s diary. It had all of the bribes paid to whom and the activities in it that were connected to the present administration. All who took and were on J.P.'s pad were in there.

"I don't know what to say, Mariah. I'm overwhelmed. No one has ever given me a chocolate cake this size. I can't even see over the top of it, it's so big. I guess it's possible, if I played my cards right I could get more than one Pulitzer. The book alone would be close to a thousand pages."

"Happy birthday, Frank. It is your birthday, is it not?"

"Yes, it is. I'm going to leave you now, go to the Concierge get a safe deposit box, deposit my gifts, take a shower, change into a suit, take you to the best restaurant in town, with the best food and wine and hope I can get lucky afterward."

"As you would say, '. . . if I played my cards right . . .' I might just get lucky afterward too." She smiled at her brilliant and handsome friend.

All politicians should attach their corporate-sponsors' logo's patches to their business suits so the public would know who owned them, a form of modern-day liberal slavery. Or, what about a "For Sale" sign hung around their necks? The scarlet letter "A" would not be appropriate for them, even though they may be eligible for other reasons depending on their sexual orientations and lack of moral sense. But appositeness it would be to make them wear a mandatory scarlet "C" or "T" — corruptician or traitor.

If you believe you are doing the right thing, be tenacious.

Getting caught and found guilty of everlasting infamy is worse than death.

In death there is resolution.

In infamy there is no resolution.

# Acknowledgments

To those among us whom care, are making a difference and contributing to the betterment of our society have inspired my writing.

I want to thank Jim Luksic, my editor, for his advice, skill and support.

I am grateful to Elaine Revelle for the dedication and compassion she showed during her proofreading for detail and the suggestions.

The technical information came from research and conversations with the knowledgeable.

Finally, I want to thank the corrupt culture of politics which supplies a cornucopia of misconduct by politicians whom confirm my belief in the never-ending and ongoing corruption.

# About the Author

Daniel McNeet retired from the business world, uses his experiences and what he knows to expose what he considers to be the important things in life — a lack of moral sense, corruption in politics, injustice and the intolerance in our society. He definitely does not stand by waiting for someone else to make a difference.

www.ingramcontent.com/pod-product-compliance
Lightning Source LLC
Chambersburg PA
CBHW060801120626
46557CB00001B/53